Maybe I wasn't the best PI around, but none of my cases had been likely to get me killed—until now…

Lane grabbed my arm, pulled me in front of her, and shoved me toward the hallway.

"I can walk on my own." I shrugged her hand off my shoulder. Everything my eyes landed on I measured for use as a weapon.

"Go sit."

I walked to the lanai and flipped the light on. She flipped the light off and grabbed my hair to steer me toward the chair. The moon was huge, white, and in position with the tops of the palm trees. I blinked and slid my eyes toward the closed and barred sliding doors.

"How'd you get in?" I asked.

"Jimmied your side garage door. You really need a deadbolt on that if you're not going to lock the inside door."

"Well, shit." I couldn't believe I'd been so concerned with the sliding doors and not the side door. After all, it's how I got in to her house.

"I'm sorry to have to do this," she said and gave my hair an extra twist. "I just couldn't think of a cleaner plan."

"I could help. There are nicer plans. Maybe you didn't give it enough thought?"

"You're so weird all the time," she said.

Moonlight radiated from the barrel of the revolver, a Ruger Single Six. I hid my panic while Lane backed in to the chair next to mine. She still had my hair in her hand, pulling out hair and stretching my scalp with each inch she moved. Tears came to my eyes, and then she let go of my hair.

"Do you think anyone would be surprised if you're found floating in the pool?" Lane asked, once she situated in the chair and had the revolver aimed at me just so.

Cassie Cruise wants her life back as a kick-ass PI. Trouble is, she has zero credibility since bungling a case on reality TV. After a public tantrum, she slinks off to bury her head in the sandy beaches of Southwest Florida. Just as she starts over as the owner of The Big Prick Tattoo Shop, a body is discovered in the trunk of her burning car. Cassie's aware there are those who'd get in line for their turn to torch her car. But murder? You don't have to like her, but you damn well better respect her. And get out of her way—this is one case she intends to solve, with or without an audience.

KUDOS for *Lane Changes*

In addition to having a female private eye, Ellis shows further creative flare in making the main protagonist's sidekick an artistic, ethnic, active, septuagenarian, who will hopefully be taking a larger role in the next book. A captivating introduction to a cozy female PI series with potential for wide appeal. ~ *Kirkus Reviews*

In *Lane Changes* by S. L. Ellis, Cassie Curse is a PI who also owns a tattoo parlor. One night her car is torched and a body is discovered inside the trunk. While the police don't really suspect Cassie, they don't seem all that capable of finding the killer, either. So naturally, Cassie is determined to solve the case, even though the cops tell her to stay out of it. The book is a fun read, with entertaining characters and a complicated plot. As cozy mysteries go, this one is a winner. ~ *Taylor Jones, Reviewer*

Lane Changes by S. L. Ellis is a murder mystery with a light side. True, the murder is pretty gruesome, a body in the trunk of a burning car, but it's told with a sardonic sense of the macabre that's very refreshing. The characters are enchanting. Cassie is very sympathetic, even when she shoots herself in the foot, so to speak. At least she acknowledges it. The plot is strong and kept me guessing as to what hair-brained scheme, our beleaguered heroine would try next. A great book for a cup of hot tea and a rainy afternoon. ~ *Regan Murphy, Reviewer*

ACKNOWLEDGEMENTS

I would like to express my gratitude to Barry for always listening, encouraging, and believing in me. Jim, Jamie, and Jake, thanks for the many ways you showed your support. Thanks also to Uli. That first synopsis taught me more about writing than any class or workshop, and that's just a smidgen of your generosity.

Lauri and Faith at Black Opal Books, I appreciate your guidance and patience.

LANE CHANGES

S. L. ELLIS

A Black Opal Books Publication

GENRE: MYSTERY-DETECTIVE/SUSPENSE

LANE CHANGES
Copyright © 2014 by S. L. Ellis
Cover Design by Dustin Tuliao
All cover art copyright © 2014
All Rights Reserved
Print ISBN: 978-1-626942-14-1

First Publication: DECEMBER 2014

Published by Black Opal Books **http://www.blackopalbooks.com**

DEDICATION

To my mom, Nancy Lee Sholl, for passing on her love for good books, black coffee, and cozy afghans.

To Dad, Sheryl, Susan, Daniel, and Shelly for sparking the stories.

CHAPTER 1

Bad things happened in threes. That was the thought that ran through my mind—right after *holy shit*.

This was number three.

A scorched breeze moved through the trio of Queen Palms situated in the side yard. I watched their fronds whisper and nod as if remarking on the scene in the street beneath them. An intermittent glow from the fire truck's lights and the clunk and clang of firefighters putting away equipment underlined the quietness.

Just a few people continued to hang around and gawk. I searched the gawkers for familiar faces, wanting Vince, my fiancé, to appear, or if not him, then Janice, my friend and neighbor, would do.

No such luck. Instead, the only recognizable face was a neighbor, Sammy Porter and, when he walked up, he aimed a flashlight over and around the car. I watched with an anger I thought I had left back on the decaying streets of Detroit.

I'd moved here because I thought I could safely hide in this neighborhood of retirees, trimmed palm trees, screened-in swimming pools, and manicured St. Augustine grass. I'd done my homework, but it seemed pointless now. People were supposed to be safe here of all places. Wrong and wrong again. Apparently, it didn't matter how aware you were, or where you lived, violence could creep up on you anytime and anywhere.

Sammy bent down near the trunk. "Hey, it's still on fire back here, still got a fire here." With the help of his flashlight, I saw a meandering spiral of black smoke escaping between the cracks of the trunk lid.

A sudden anxiety raced through my veins and, as if dipped in cement, heaviness weighed down my legs and arms. I wanted Sammy to go home and mind his own business. In fact, everyone should leave. It was my car someone had torched, my business, my loss.

"Get away from my car!" I yelled.

Sammy ignored me, but my yelling did get a firefighter's attention. He grabbed a pry bar, elbowed Sammy aside, and popped open the trunk.

Sammy swallowed and then looked over at me. "Oh, my."

The firefighters bent to get a closer look and, lured by the looks of horror on their faces, I went to the car.

Bile rose in my throat. Inside the trunk was a charred and still-smoldering body.

Oh my God.

The nose was completely gone and overall there wasn't much flesh remaining on the face.

Oh. God.

Sucking in my breath, I turned away from the face, only to catch a view of the relatively undamaged organs behind the ribs and the incinerated flesh of the chest. Dizziness hit and I grabbed the outside edge of the blackened trunk to keep from falling face first into the charred body.

"Back away from the car."

Turning toward the voice, I felt vindicated, thinking

he was speaking to nosy Sammy, but no one else was near the car. Just me, bending over the trunk of a car—my car, as I had so recently and loudly reminded all—ogling, with no outward signs of repulsion at a barbequed human corpse. I shoved down the trunk hood, straightened up, and took a step back.

✑✑✑

It began as a typical interrogation.

"Your full name, please?"

"Cassandra Leah Cruise. You can call me Cassie."

"Would you go over what happened tonight, Ms. Cruise?"

I knew this was the part where they were supposed to get a feel for whether I was guilty or innocent based on my behavior during questioning. Also, they would be aware of where I looked as they question me. My sister, Rachel—Sergeant Rachel Cruise—had told me all about interrogations before she was killed in the line of duty eighteen months ago.

"I don't know what happened," I said.

Looking at the paint-covered cement block walls of the interview room, I thought they were probably cool to the touch, and I wondered how odd it would seem if I stood and laid my forehead against the wall to soothe the ache radiating from behind my eyes. I decided on somewhere between odd and *extremely* odd. Looking away from the block wall, I gave my attention to the detectives in the room.

They both wore button-down shirts and khaki slacks, but that's where the likeness ended. I zeroed in on the older detective. He was close to my forty-nine years and handsome in a rough kind of way. The tiredness of his eyes, the wrinkles in his shirt, and his old-style slicked back hair reminded me of the Detroit Homicide Bureau detectives I knew from a previous career. He caught me looking and returned my stare. Suddenly, I felt both homesick and needy and I shivered with another emotion I didn't want to put a name to.

Running my hand through my purposely-shaggy auburn hair, I looked at the younger of the two. He appeared to be in his late twenties or early thirties. His slacks had a nice crease. He was well groomed, clean-shaven. He even had a style to his military-short hair.

"What's your name?" I asked the young detective.

He scrunched his face and cleared his throat before answering. "Stephan. It's Detective Lieutenant Craig Stephan," he said.

I shot him a smile. "I'm Cassie."

Stephan ignored the smile. "You have a charred body in the trunk of your car, and you don't know what happened?"

"I don't know how a body ended up in the trunk of my car." I looked to the right. Per Rachel, when a person is remembering, they tend to look to the right. That's because the right side of the brain is the memory area. If they look to the left, they're lying. *Or did I have it backward?*

"It's your car, isn't it?" Detective Stephan asked, interrupting my thoughts.

"It is my car, but it's not my body. I mean, I don't know who the body is or how it got in the trunk."

"We think you know," Stephen insisted.

"I've told you I don't know," I said, again looking to the right.

The older detective put out his hand. "Detective Brick Winslow, County Sheriff's Office."

He shook my hand as a man should shake a woman's hand. Warm and firm.

"For real? Your name is Brick?" I asked.

"You have to know my parents to understand," he said.

I nodded. "I only know what I saw."

"Okay. Tell us what you saw," Detective Winslow said after releasing my hand.

"I was outside watching the firefighters with a few of the neighbors who were still hanging around."

North Harbor's Detective Stephan grimaced and rubbed his hand over the short, bristly hair on his head. "What's that got to do with the body?"

Winslow held his hand up in Detective Stephan's direction. "Just let her talk," he said and then turned to me.

I again saw a tired, work worn, big city detective. Someone who seemed as out of place as I felt in this small Florida town. And I also saw a person who would likely understand parts of me that not many others could.

"Go ahead, Ms. Cruise."

I nodded my appreciation to Detective Winslow before continuing, "So I decided I'd had enough and yelled, 'Get away from my car!'"

"Having someone near your car bothered you?" Stephan asked.

"Yes."

"And?" he said.

"One of the firefighters popped open the trunk." I folded my hands on the table in front of me and tried to find a way to describe a horribly burned body without having actually to see it in my mind's eye.

Detective Stephan slumped down in his chair, letting his arms hang slackly alongside. "Ms. Cruise, come on, just tell us what happened."

What a freaking whiner, I thought before responding. "Look, I'm trying, but I want you to understand this first because I think I know how it looked to others. It took me a few seconds to catch on to what I was seeing, and when it registered, I instinctively slammed the trunk. I wasn't trying to hide anything."

"The body..."

I took a deep gulp of air and looked longingly at the cement wall. "That body, what I saw, I'm not so sure I'll ever stop seeing it." Keeping my eyes fixed on the wall, I described in detail the charred corpse.

They were both quiet for a few seconds, but eventually they worked into the confrontation part of the interrogation. That was where they made accusatory statements regarding the suspect's involvement and tried to raise the stress level.

"Come on. You know more than you're saying. In fact, I personally think you skipped an important piece of the story," Detective Stephan said.

"What piece? I didn't skip anything," I said.

"What about how and why you killed the person found in your trunk? How about that part of the story?" he asked.

"I'd like you to think about that. Why would anyone kill a person, put the body into the trunk of their car, and then light it on fire on their own street, in their own neighborhood? Bring all that attention to the body they're supposedly trying to hide? Does that really make sense to you?" I asked.

"It'd make sense to a certain washed-up PI who made a fool of themselves on TV. I mean maybe that washed up PI wanted to bring some attention back to themselves and—"

I cut him off with a sugary voice and fake smile. "You've just made it abundantly clear you're a fucking moron." The last thing I wanted to think about or hear about was the television show debacle.

"Why did you park the car on the street?" Detective

Winslow asked, diverting the moron from saying anything in return.

"I fell asleep watching a movie and didn't move it into my garage," I said. This question raised my stress level, and I couldn't stop myself from looking to the right three or four times in a row.

"Are you feeling okay?" Detective Winslow asked.

I nodded, filled my lungs with stale air, and let it out while trying to rid my mind of illogical feelings of guilt. So much for Rachel's stupid interrogation tidbits.

Detective Winslow stared at me for a few seconds. "Okay, so normally you park in the garage? This time, just by coincidence you left it on the street."

"Yes, that's what happened."

Winslow looked down at his pad of paper. "Tell me about the vehicle."

"Like I said, it was my sister's. It's a 1997 Mercedes Benz 500SL Roadster, in great condition. I mean it was in great condition. I don't know what else to tell you."

"Okay. Go over again why you parked your car on the street and not in your garage."

"Again?"

He nodded.

"Laziness, I guess."

"That it?" he asked.

"Okay. No, that's not it. Not all anyway. I mean, I had to pee." I was suddenly embarrassed over the fact that I was embarrassed to talk about a normal body function.

"What the hell?" Detective Stephan said.

Turning toward Detective Winslow, I explained. "I gulped down a huge amount of iced tea while working at the shop and left in a cranky hurry. I ran some errands, and once I turned onto my street, I felt an overwhelming urgency. So I parked the car on the street, hopped around

while trying to concentrate enough to get the bags of
landscape rock I'd bought at Home Depot out of the trunk.
I gave up halfway through and ran inside, barely making
it to the bathroom in time. As I said earlier, I then
grabbed an old movie from my collection and popped it
in the player. *Dead Ringer* starring Bette Davis."

"Who?" Detective Stephen asked.

Ignoring him, I said to Detective Winslow, "It's what
I do to relax. Anyway, about half way through I fell
asleep on the couch. Not the fault of the movie, mind you.
I was exhausted from the day. I never went out to move
the car into the garage. I forgot about moving the car."

Rachel would understand, wouldn't she?

"No idea why someone would do this to your vehicle?"

"Nope, can't think of one."

Big. Fat. Lie. Probably many people would have
stood in line for their turn to torch my car. I was not the
world's most careful driver, but more to the point I was
not what you'd call a people person. I couldn't play the
games required to enjoy popularity. I didn't like fluff. I
didn't like false emotions. I didn't know how to change
my so-called snotty, sarcastic ways. Therefore, people
didn't really like me. Most times I was okay with it.

"No idea who the dead person is?"

"No idea."

Rachel's description of the next step in an interrogation didn't hold up either. Supposedly, it was something
called theme development. They made up a story about
why the suspect did the crime, hoping he would start filling in the missing spots, give reasons of his own, or
blame the victim. Instead, it seemed both of the Detectives floundered and became stuck. They never got to the
point where they were supposed to speak in soothing
voices in hopes of lulling the suspect into a sense of false

security, thus allowing them to confess. Eventually, I tired and asked to leave and, surprisingly, they let me go.

Detective Winslow asked if I wanted to call someone for a ride home. I said no, I could get myself home, even though I desperately wanted to call Vince. It was called biting off your nose to spite your face. I walked the mile home in the dark and the ninety-four degree heat and humidity as a personalized form of self-flagellation.

Inside the house, I tripped over my purse and key ring lying in the entryway, picked them up, tossed them on the dining table, and then phoned Vince. After allowing him the privilege of soothing me, I gained his promise to come over and comfort me.

I looked out my window at the now quiet neighborhood and felt a tenseness building between my shoulder blades. Turning away from the window, I picked up a magazine from a nearby pile and flung it across the room. And another. And another. Not stopping until I hit a framed painting on the far wall, knocking it to the floor with a crash.

Why? Who was the poor victim? Who did this? Why my car?

Rubbing the tears off my face, I returned to the window and watched as a dark sedan, lights off, crawled towards my house, almost coming to a stop in front of the new neighbor Lane's house. The driver—from my window just a dark faceless shape—turned in my direction and then sped up, popped on the lights, and went on down the street out of the neighborhood.

Could be nothing, just a forgetful driver. The streetlights were in good repair and spaced evenly enough along the street. But now, everyone and everything came under suspicion. It was weird how something was inconsequential one day and then important and suspicious the next.

Damn, I'll never have a car like that again.

As on almost any other day, I then heard the voice of my long-dead sister. "Uh-huh, tell me about it," she said.

My failure to protect her now crispy and blackened Mercedes-Benz convertible overcame me. Another failure. Another public failure. I grabbed the partial pack of cigarettes I'd thrown in the trashcan under the kitchen sink earlier and lit one up with shaking hands.

This was a murder. Someone placed a body in my trunk, torched my car, and walked away as if the body was never a person, as if they hadn't ever meant anything to anyone.

No one should walk away without paying for this.

One, two, three. Bad things always happened in threes.

CHAPTER 2

Most mornings were beautiful in Florida, and as much as I appreciated them, my born-and-bred four-season sensibilities never got used to them. It was always a surprise to me—blue skies, ocean breezes, warm ocean water, and tropical palms. What more could a woman ask for in life—other than respect and a new Mercedes-Benz.

The morning after the car fire, I thought of the gray weather in Michigan, and a tiny part of me wished I could go back. It seemed so much easier to wallow in self-pity when the weather was nasty. Instead, I walked around my yard in North Harbor, grumbling at the black spots on the rose bushes and cursing the baby's breath for having the nerve to shrivel under the hot sun.

North Harbor was a village on the sunset side of Florida, located north of Charlotte Harbor and about fifteen or so miles from the Gulf of Mexico. My home was in a rather exclusive neighborhood with a gated entrance and formal landscaping. Simply put, it looked stuffy and mostly it was. It was also a haven for retirees.

Just to stir things up, I occasionally tried to encourage the Neighborhood Association to incorporate tacky garage sales and block parties. Since I really hated the idea of neighborhood garage sales or block parties, and in fact, I would fight the idea if anyone else brought it up, I guess you could call my behavior perverse.

I liked to think my goal was to make sure the Association didn't start feeling blasé about their environment. I didn't want people here to be complacent, so that meant I tried to make sure they couldn't have their peace and quiet without working for it. I liked to think stirring the pot made them appreciate what they had.

That was what I'd like to think, but really, if forced to be truthful, I would have to admit it really was downright perverse behavior. I didn't want to return to my noisy, troublesome old neighborhood, but I didn't want to be content and forget where I came from either.

As I pulled weeds from the flowerbed near the empty garage, I thought of the car and the body again, and then my thoughts turned to my sister. She died from a bullet to the head by putting herself in the middle of an attempted robbery. As told to me in bits and pieces by her fellow officers, it happened in a matter of minutes. No one in the store knew there was anything going down until Rachel tried to diffuse the situation on her own.

At some point Rachel must have recognized Terrence, a kid from my old neighborhood. I couldn't help feeling that if she hadn't known him through me, she would've handled the situation differently. She would've seen him as a potential killer and not as a neighborhood kid.

They said Terrence, at one point, looked her in the eyes and said something no one else could hear. She shook her head, and then he reached under his shirt, pulled a gun from his waistband, and blew her away.

Just like that, she was gone. I couldn't forgive her for not following her own advice. Really, I just couldn't forgive her for being dead.

Did the body in the car have a sister? Surely, there was family worrying and wondering. Maybe they had identified it by now and an officer was knocking at the family door as they had knocked on our door to tell us about Rachel.

God. The whole thing seems surreal. A body in my car.

Stuffing the weeds I had mindlessly pulled from the flowerbed into a bag, I then plopped down in the grass and closed my eyes against the brightness of the sun. Unwillingly, I was back in time and looking at blackened arms wrapped around upraised knees and a charred and faceless skull. I realized then and there the body would most likely haunt me forever.

Horrid.

I was damned sure going to find out who did it. No one should get away with this type of thing, and if I had my way, no one would.

"Oh, there you are."

Shaking off my thoughts, I looked up to see Janice strolling through the yard. I stood and watched as she, an itty-bitty thing with smooth toffee-colored skin, high elegant cheekbones, and snow-white teeth, held out her arms to hug me. The sunlight seemed to shine directly on her elaborate hairdo—an arrangement of braids, rolled curls, and Marcel waves. If at some point a person took in all of that, they could then notice the tribal-Celtic mix of tattoos covering her upper and lower extremities.

Seeing the tattoos made me grouchy, reminded me about the albatross hanging around my neck—otherwise known as The Big Prick Tattoo Shop—and since it was her fault I now owned it, I shook my head no to her hug. I didn't want comfort. I wanted answers. I wanted to…

Damn. It. All.

I went to her for the hug.

"Hey," I said.

"Why didn't you come down this morning for coffee?" she asked.

"I didn't feel very social. Sorry."

"I had coffee all by myself."

"Sorry."

"Did the, um, 'barbeque' keep you up last night?" she said.

"You heard, huh?"

"Yeah. Everyone's talking about it." Janice looked over my mud-spattered shoes and worn blue-jeans shorts. "Why aren't you ready?"

"Ready for what?"

"Golf, Cassie."

"Oh, crap. I forgot."

"Tee time is at eleven. You've got twenty minutes."

"Janice, I can't. Really," I said.

"An appointment is an appointment, just like a promise is a promise," Janice said.

Her annoyance was obvious and I guessed I didn't really blame her. I tended to forget about golf dates on the day after my car burns to a crisp and the police questions me about having a dead person in the trunk.

I gave in. "Come on in. I made coffee." Arguing with her took too much energy and I didn't have any to spare. Besides that, an argument with Janice usually lasted longer than the time it took to play nine holes.

Janice smiled because she knew I had cigarettes inside. She didn't buy cigarettes; she'd bum them off anyone in sight. She'd steal them, too, if it was easier than asking.

"Tell me what you heard about last night," I yelled from my bedroom closet.

Janice's house was three lots down, on the same side of the street as mine.

Janice sat on the couch in the lanai near the sliding doors that lead to the bedroom with her coffee and cigarette. "I went outside to smoke. I had just lit the damn thing when I heard scuffling sounds, sort of like a bar fight, only quieter. You know, it brought back some memories, made me want a gin and tonic and a good comfy bar stool."

She laughed in her signature hooting style, and the sound of it made me smile.

"Anyways, I walked toward the front when I heard glass shattering, and that's when I saw the smoke and flames. I headed down here, but some fireman stopped me from getting too close."

I finished dressing, grabbed my shoes, and sat next to Janice to put them on.

She looked me over. "Ready?"

"Yep."

We hopped in Janice's golf cart to go the three blocks to the course. As we left my driveway, we watched as a blond-haired, tan-skinned, work-out-seven-times-a-week type of guy walked from my neighbor's home to an expensive looking sports car parked at the curb across the street. My neighbor, Lane, walked out the side door of the garage and waved as he drove by.

He raised his arm out the window and smiled. I guessed it was Lane's boyfriend, Del.

I watched as Lane looked toward the back of her lot and began walking to the pool house. She stopped, looked at Janice and me, then turned around and walked back into the garage. The garage door came down behind her.

"Did you see that, Janice?"

"What?"

"That car. The one that just drove past us."

"So?" Janice said.

"Nice car."

"Yeah, uh-huh. So?"

"Maybe someone was mistaken. Maybe they meant to put the body in that car instead of mine." Turning in the cart, I looked at the area where I had left my car the night before.

"Why would you think that?"

"They sort of look alike, for one. Same size, similar color, both sporty. And I don't normally park my car on the street. Seems like it would be easy to mistake mine for another on a dark night."

"I think you're fishing without a worm, dear," Janice said.

"Well there's no reason for a body in my car. I mean, I guess if it was just that someone torched my car, I could believe it was an attack against me. But not a murder. Just doesn't make sense to me," I said.

"Who do you think would cram a body in the trunk and blow up a car like that?" Janice asked.

"Someone with a serious problem."

"Jeez, Cassie. Is that a confession? Did you need a new car that bad?" She looked at me with big round eyes. I crinkled my face at her and she laughed. "Isn't it covered by insurance?"

"Yeah, the Benz is pretty old, so now because I bought the tattoo parlor and have no savings, I guess I'll get to choose between some granny-type sedan and an old man-style truck as a replacement. What a deal," I said. Then I told her, "They didn't blow it up anyway. Whoever did it used gasoline and rags, not a bomb-type device. So it was a fire, not an explosion."

"Thanks for the clarification. Now let me clarify. No one forced you to buy the shop. Stop whining about it and get busy making it a good thing," Janice said.

She was right about the whining, but I didn't want to admit it.

"Most likely they didn't cram the body either. They arranged it. My bet is the person was either drugged or dead before going into the trunk. Also, because the majority of the damage was on the face, common sense tells me that's where the perpetrator started the fire. Very calculating and personal." I shook my head as I pictured someone going through the act of neatly arranging and torching a body.

"How do you know all this? Did the detectives give you the information?" she questioned.

I shrugged. "Good old investigation."

"That so?" she said, not looking at me, but rather looking at the green. We were near the first tee when Janice jumped out of the cart.

I knew she was no longer listening to me.

"No," I said. "I asked a purple penguin, and he said he'd tell me but I had to swear on my grandmother's grave that I would never speak of it to the big-haired tattooed lady."

She stuck a bright pink tee into the ground and adjusted it to the perfect height. I waited patiently for my turn and tried convincing myself I enjoyed sweating profusely while hitting a little ball around a mile of well-tended grass.

"Did you hear me, Janice?"

Janice nodded as she pulled out her driver and handed me a five wood from her set of clubs.

I rubbed my eyes and put my hand over a yawn as she addressed the ball.

େ∕ଅେ∕ଅ

"I'll have a gin and tonic and she'll have iced tea,"

Janice said as we were bellying up to the bar in the club-house after our nine holes. The bartender set the drinks on the bar and returned through the swinging doors into the kitchen area.

Janice was quiet and held her drink, staring at nothing, so I thought she was mulling over my golf score and wondering how she could help me better it, but she surprised me by bringing up the fire.

"It could have been a random thing. You know, any old car will do. I mean obviously someone wanted to cover up the fact that they killed a person," Janice said.

"I don't know, but not much else makes sense, does it?" I said.

"What about that new girl? The one across the street from you. You pissed her off, didn't you?" Janice asked.

"I didn't piss her off. Not like that anyway, nothing she would want to get revenge for by killing someone and putting the body into my car. Remember?" I had already explained the discussion to Janice the day after it had happened. "Lane's boyfriend has an ex-girlfriend who, according to Lane, isn't quite right in the head, and she's been bothering them. Knowing that, she still asked the guy to move in with her."

"But wasn't that girl mad at you? Miss Maybe You Should Do This and Maybe You Should Do That."

"Huh?"

"Wasn't she?"

"Who?"

"That Lane girl," Janice said.

"I sort of told her it wasn't a very smart thing to do," I said, bored with the subject already.

"Oh. Just the usual butting in where you don't be-long stuff," Janice said.

"Right."

"Couldn't have been her then. People sure don't get

mad about that." Janice slapped her thigh and whooped out a laugh. She took a sip and then, looking at the glass, said, "Still, there has to be a reason. Even if it was a mistake and they thought your car belonged to someone else." Ice cubes clinked and echoed off the walls of the empty clubhouse as she raised the glass to her mouth for another sip. "Wait. Does this have anything to do with the television show, um, issue?" Janice asked.

"No. Damn you."

She took a quick look around and scratched a match to light a cigarette, ignoring the no smoking signs plastered on the walls.

"I don't need to ask you where you got that cigarette, do I, Janice?"

"Anyways…" she said in a dismissive manner.

I leaned toward the bar and looked over Janice's shoulder in the direction of the entrance. "Oh, there's the owner of the club! Yoo-hoo, over here!"

Janice quickly dipped the lit end of the cigarette into her drink. She then wrapped it in the paper napkin she took from under her glass and gulped down the remainder of her cocktail before looking around. When she saw no one, she slid off the bar stool and slammed down her empty glass.

"I think I'm starting to understand that revenge thing now," she said.

℘℘℘

Janice let me off at my house. I stood outside and watched her until she disappeared inside her garage. I then walked over to Sammy Porter's house. He opened the door an inch and mushed his face into the opening. I could only see one of his eyes and half of his lips as he spoke. "I'm not sure you should be here, Miss Cassie."

"Huh?"

"Well, I'm probably considered a witness. You know, because of last night, an' all," he said.

I forced myself to look away from his moving lips. Watching half of a mouth speak through a crack felt freakishly hypnotic. "That's what I'm here to talk about, Sammy. The fire and the body. Can I come in so we can talk?"

"Oh, no. Talking to you would most likely taint my testimony, an' all," he said.

"Testimony? Are you kidding me?" I asked.

"Discovering a dead body is no joking matter, Ms. Cruise," Sammy said.

And then I understood. I was making light of his five minutes of glory.

"Sammy, testimony can't be tainted if there's no apprehended perpetrator. If there's no perpetrator, there's no case, thus, no testimony is tainted." I deliberately combined nonsense and pseudo cop-speak in hopes it would either reassure or confuse him and get him talking to me. "I'm a PI, anyway, so it's okay. Please open your door," I turned away again from the door crack before he answered.

"Ever heard of fruit of the poisonous tree?" he asked.

"Of course. I told you I'm a licensed private investigator." I sort of knew what he was talking about. Regardless, it would take two minutes to look it up.

"I'm not so easily fooled. I know what you really do to earn a living these days," Sammy said.

"Um, yes. Because I just told you," I said, looking at the eye and lips in confusion.

"No. I'm talking about that immoral tattoo parlor, an' all. Now, you need to go on home." The lips had begun to take on their own personality.

"But, Sammy, I'm just trying to find out who put a body in my car and set it on fire."

The lips disappeared and the door smacked shut.

As I turned to step down from his porch, I heard the door creak and before I could look back, I heard Sammy's lips whisper, "Hussy."

The remaining nearby neighbors who answered my knock and allowed me to question them knew nothing more than I did. In other words, not one of the neighbors had an intelligent thing to say about the fire.

The next day, after a restless and nerve-racking night, I went across the street and knocked on my new neighbor's door. She was the last on the street I needed to question. But just as the day before, there wasn't a response to my knock. Stepping off the porch, I decided to walk to the tattoo parlor.

Once there, I put in a few hours of employee bashing and weirdo watching. When I tired of that, I sat near Janice and watched as she finished an intricate henna-style tattoo on a young woman's foot.

"You're a real artist," I said after she'd finished. For the first time ever, I considered getting a tattoo.

"Of course I am. Although, I never thought I'd hear you admit it. Now what is it you want?" she said.

"I need a distraction." I didn't want to go home and mull over the car fire. I didn't have any idea where to begin getting answers and every time I closed my eyes or had time to sit and think, I saw the body. But it was more the huge ball of anger stuck in my craw that kept me from relaxing or sleeping.

As I spoke, I caught my reflection in the mirror and froze in place. *What the hell*? There was a psycho looking back at me. With amazement and a new lucidity, I saw what Janice, Vince, the people at The Big Prick, and possibly my neighbors had been seeing for who knew how long. The "young for her age" woman seemed to have disappeared, and in her place was this crazed-looking stranger.

I remembered reading somewhere that stress could cause all types of unusual behavior. It'd been almost a year, but I still couldn't stop thinking about being the laughing stock of the PI industry, and a loser on national television. Being a public loser was stressful enough, and then add in the tattoo shop, and now the body in the trunk of my car. Stress was doing a number on me. That would be the reason for the smudged and panicky eyes and the red splotches on my cheeks and forehead.

Janice drove us to the mall. Once inside my favorite department store with the lenient credit card approval methods, I had a facial, manicure, and pedicure. Afterward, I shopped with a mellow feeling and, by the time I found a great looking golfing outfit in Janice's size, I felt well enough to check out and go back home.

When I headed toward the cashier, I noticed a large woman with burgundy hair standing at the back wall of the lingerie department. My mouth dropped open as she stuffed a handful of plus-sized lacy undergarments into her tote bag. I scanned the area for security mirrors. Once I found one, I waved my hands over my head to get security's attention and pointed at the woman. She lifted her head and her green eyes looked directly at me through the mirrors that lined the back of the shelves. Without turning around, the woman slowly removed the garments from the tote and returned them to the shelf.

"You better put them back, lady. Everyone else has to pay for your thieving in higher retail prices," I said while continuing to watch her watching me.

She didn't look the least bit ashamed. In fact, she appeared to be amused.

I wanted to shake the smug attitude right out of her.

Janice, unmindful of anything but her need to leave, tugged on my arm. "Who you talking to, Cassie? I'm ready to go. Please."

"Okay. Stop." Pushing Janice ahead of me, I turned back toward the direction of the shoplifter and stomped my foot in aggravation when I saw she had left the department and was now out of eyesight.

At the register, I described the shoplifter to the sales clerk. She picked up a phone, spoke into it quietly, hung up, and thanked me. I looked around for security to come running. They hadn't by the time she had finished scanning in my items.

Disappointed, I took my time paying. When I couldn't drag it out any longer and neither security nor the woman was anywhere in sight, I readied to leave and handed the bag with the outfit to Janice.

"Surprise," I said.

"Wow, what did you do to deserve that, honey?" the clerk asked.

Janice looked at the clerk for a few seconds. "I'm not your honey, and you shouldn't make assumptions. I didn't scrub her floors or wash her windows." She leaned in to the register, waved her hand for the woman to come closer, and whispered, "We're lovers."

The clerk sucked in her breath and put her hand over her heart.

Janice took my hand and laid her head on my arm as I picked up my bag and hurried off. She wouldn't let go of my hand until we were out in the parking lot.

"You traumatized the poor thing," I said through laughter.

"I know what she was thinking. All she saw was my black skin."

"Really? How do you know that?"

"I looked in her eyes and saw ignorance. Not the nice kind either. It was the hateful kind."

"There's a nice kind?"

"I remember a few years ago, when my younger sister Josie broke her leg. I took her out in a wheelchair to have her hair done, and the woman in the salon asked me what style my mother wanted. Jeez, was Josie mad. The woman saw the wheelchair and didn't look any further. She was busy and didn't mean anything by it. That's the nice kind of ignorance." Janice shook her head. "Anyways, I think we're all guilty of assuming and not really seeing, aren't we?"

"I guess so," I said and then brought up a subject she'd long been avoiding, "I want to talk about your sudden recovery from the illness that forced you to sell the tattoo parlor. You know. The one that caused you to resort to begging me to buy it. Remember that illness?"

"I'm not at all recovered, and today I'm tired. We'll talk about it some other time," she said.

Before I could nag her further, I saw movement two parking rows in front of us.

"Look! There she is. The shoplifter." I pointed to the woman calmly getting into her car. No one stopped her, security didn't run out and pat her down, and the police didn't squeal into the parking lot. She drove away without a hitch.

Janice was quiet, then once she'd started the car and we were on our way out of the parking lot, she said, "It really bothers you when people get away with things, doesn't it? Aren't you used to it by now?"

"Want the truth?"

"Yes."

"I want all the bad people locked up. I don't like having to wonder who's good and who's bad."

"That's not going to happen. You have to learn to see

through people. Good people sometimes do bad things. Bad people sometimes do good things."

I looked at her. "Wow. What you just said is so help-ful."

"Shut up, lover," Janice said.

I did shut up. Neither of us spoke until we pulled into the parking lot of the tattoo parlor.

"It's disgusting. The Big Prick. It's a disgusting name," I said.

"So you've said. Maybe a hundred times," Janice said. She got out of the car and went inside.

I walked into the shop and saw the usual rag-tag bunch. Bikers, old hippies, and a group of the gangster wannabes that hung out with the cleaning kid, RJ—then there were the clients.

When he saw me walk through the entrance, RJ wid-ened his eyes and opened his mouth into a tight-lipped "o." I grabbed the nudie magazine out of his hand. He narrowed his eyes and lifted the corners of his mouth into a smart-ass smirk.

I pointed to the cleaning supplies set up on the coun-ter near the autoclave and he lost the smirk, moving off in that wide-legged duck walk that thugs with falling-down-baggy trousers adopted.

"Pull up your damned pants," I told him.

"Why are you always so angry these days?" Janice asked when I walked by her station.

Her asking that, of course, pissed me off. She, of all people, should know the answer to that question. She was the reason I owned the place. Yes, I blamed her.

"I'm not," I answered in a passive aggressive snit as I crossed my fingers behind my back.

"Well, how about you?" she said to the person under her gun. "Do you think she looks mad?"

"Yes, ma'am, I sure do," he said.

"How would you know? You're flat on your face. You can't see me," I said.

"I can hear it in your voice," he answered, "and it doesn't sound like a healthy anger either."

"I don't believe you," I said. "In fact, I wouldn't believe any man purposely getting a pink flamingo tat on his back."

I walked toward the office to schlep through the bookkeeping and smiled as I heard Janice say in a disgusted voice, "It *is* a tiger, honey! Pay her no mind."

I began working through the books until the cleaning kid interrupted me.

"Why you got a problem with me?" RJ asked, leaning against the doorframe with his hands in his pockets. The red and black boxers showing above the falling down waist of his shorts were just one of many things about him that screamed twenty-one and trouble. Although, on second glance, I could see his face was probably sweet looking before he encouraged the dreadlocks in his auburn hair, punched holes in his left eyebrow and lower lip, and stuck in the gold studs.

"I don't like what you think you're representing," I answered.

"What's that supposed to mean?" he asked.

"Just what I said. You look like a thug, and a thug isn't my idea of a person many would like to know. Going by the way you dress and talk, it seems as if you believe their behavior somehow impresses people," I told him.

"Someone else told me something like that the other day," he said.

"Oh, what a surprise. Did it happen to be a cop?" I asked.

"Na, wasn't a cop. What I told this person was, it don't pay to look weak. See what I'm saying," he said.

"Thugs are weak. They forget about right and wrong because it's the easy way out. They are brutal and criminal and—" I stopped when my breath caught in my throat. The conversation brought up too many bad memories. I would not cry in front of this little shit.

"Just saying there's always two sides to a story. Right? Did anyone ever let you tell your side?" RJ said.

"Of what?'

"Your show. Man, that's one I watched, right? *Cruising.* Wednesday nights, nine o'clock." He had a glazed over look in his eyes for a few seconds and then he shook his head. "For real, I'd like to hear why you screwed up that last case. In fact, it'd make good press and—"

"Get out. Go do some work. It's what I pay you to do," I said.

He shrugged, then he said, "I tried," and walked away.

An hour or so later I finished the bookkeeping and got ready to head for home when I heard a commotion. I walked out front and saw someone had thrown a huge glob of blood colored paint, hitting the entrance door and the plate glass window next to it. I watched as it ran down the glass and pooled on the sidewalk below.

"Who did this?" I asked.

Most everyone found something interesting on the top of their shoes, but a girl who'd apparently left her coven that morning without bothering to change clothes, mumbled, "Someone just ran up and tossed the paint."

"I'm betting you didn't see what they looked like."

"Nope," she answered.

"Where's RJ?" I looked at the group.

"Don't even go there," he said from the back of the room.

I waited for more bullshit to come out of his mouth, but he ignored me and continued sweeping.

Janice went outside with a brush and a bucket and began working on the glass.

"Stop," I said after stepping outside.

"Let me scrub it off," she said.

"I said leave it."

"Cass—" she began.

I stared at her.

She tossed the brush into the bucket of soapy water. We both watched as it sloshed over the side and mixed in with the paint on the sidewalk.

"I like it," I said. "It looks better that way. Real eye catching."

"No, you don't."

"It covers up the name. That I like."

Janice put her hands on her hips and jutted her chin. "Why?"

"Go on in and make some money, would you?" I said.

"No one here did this," she said and picked the brush out of the bucket.

I grabbed the brush out of her hand. "Yeah, only because of their high moral values."

She grabbed back the brush. "They didn't, Cassie. Believe me, okay?"

"Sure. Anyway, I'm going home. And if you want to be out here scrubbing, scrub off that," I said, pointing to the remaining visible portion of the words painted on the front window. he ig P ck. Ridiculous. Embarrassing. Although nowhere near as embarrassing and ridiculous as before the paint flowed down the window.

"Don't be like that," Janice said.

"No, really. I own the place. You're my employee and I'm telling you to do whatever it takes to get that off the window. See you later."

I suddenly remembered the errands I had to run. I

needed to leave and get away from all the human oddities that worked here and those that came here to hang out.

I walked down the street and into the grocery store. The cashier, Janie, a woman who had rung up my groceries with a pleasant smile and innocuous chitter-chatter almost every week since the first week I moved here, stopped scanning a customer's items to watch me walk past the registers.

"Hey, you're out," Janie said when I turned to look at her.

I shook my head, walked to the deli counter, and asked for the usual quarter pound of bologna and American cheese.

"I, uh, I heard about your car and the—" Lisa the Deli Manager said after slicing the bologna.

"Don't," I said, cutting her off mid-sentence.

When the third person stopped what they were doing long enough to stare at me, I left the items in the cart and walked out of the store. I continued walking five blocks down the street and then through my neighborhood feeling as if I had a big red "F" for failure on my forehead and an even bigger "S" for stupid on my ass.

CHAPTER 3

The first thing I noticed when I finally made it home was the message light blinking on the phone. Vince had left a message confirming our dinner plans, so I changed our 7:00 p.m. reservations to 7:30 p.m. He was painting the interior of one of his rental homes and he always underestimated the time it took him to get ready.

While I paced the lanai, the phone rang.

"Cassie? Ms. Cruise?"

I didn't recognize the soft and gravelly voice. "Who is this?"

"Detective Winslow. I need to see you."

The combination of his sexy voice and the mental picture of him needing me made my heart jump into gear, and a little frisson of electricity traveled down my abdomen into my nether region.

"Sure. I mean, I guess," I said.

What could he want? I thought I had made it very clear I knew nothing significant about why or how a body ended up in the trunk of my car. Nothing factual, nothing significant. Nothing that I would bring up to him, because all I had was gut and instinct. Even when over the last year I questioned whether listening to either was the reason for my past failures, I couldn't get around it. My gut told me some important things had happened in the days before the car fire and I wanted to sort it all out before I spoke with the detective.

"Could we make it in a day or so?" I asked Detective Winslow.

He was reluctant. I was insistent. He agreed to make it later.

I sat and thought about the weeks and days before the incident, trying to figure out what, if anything, stood out. My conclusion was meeting the new neighbor, Lane Somers. That one typically normal thing stood out from all of the other mundane happenings.

I noticed her the moment she stepped out of her front door. From across the street, I could see she didn't fit the neighborhood. I guessed her to be under thirty, which is about a forty-five-year gap from the fossilized fussbudgets making up eighty percent of the subdivision. She was tall and lissome with an unaffected elegance in her walk—a woman with an assured style.

She stood out in other ways, not only because she didn't automatically reach for the handrail when she moved along her porch. Prior to her moving in, at forty-nine years, I was the youngest chick on the block. After much thought and planning, I purposely chose to live amongst a gaggle of WOOPs—well off older people—because I knew, statistically, only about one percent of persons aged sixty-five and older would be involved in violent crime. The stats were much different in my old neighborhood. Living here, statistically, I would be safe. I would be anonymous.

Safety and anonymity. Those were my reasons for moving here.

After hopping off the lawnmower, I bent down to brush off pieces of grass and dirt from my legs. As I straightened, I took in the whole picture. She looked like a young Grace Kelly. A shot of envy coursed through me and I had to remind myself that beauty was not a reason to be jealous. By my age, you should realize it was just an occurrence. An act of nature. That was what I told myself anyway.

"Cassie Cruise," I said and put my hand out.

"Lane Somers." She moved her hand to take mine and sent a light vanilla-citrus fragrance my way.

"Well, I'm here. Finally." She sighed and leaned back on her heels. "It's so exciting."

"To move here?" I asked, at that time thinking, first glance should have showed her nothing exciting ever happened in this neighborhood. Unless she counted the occasional lawn watering schedule violation.

Her eyes flitted from the hibiscus bushes and day lilies growing along my walkway to the baskets of spider plants hanging between each columned section of the porch and back to me.

"It's more than that," she said.

"Oh, really? Why's that?"

She tossed her head back and crossed her arms.

Something in her demeanor gave me pause. I tried concentrating on her face, hoping to discover some smidgen of her story.

"Do you have something in your eye?" she asked.

Embarrassed, I shook my head no and thought about explaining my theory of a person's life story showing on their face, but she beat me to the punch.

"Think you can judge a book by its cover?" she asked.

"Somewhat. First impressions are telling, you know."

"You have a point." She looked me over, starting with my feet and ending at my face.

I'd felt as if I'd been busted and didn't know what

else to say. We both became silent, not looking each other in the eye.

The temperature inched up by a degree a minute. *Lord have mercy, it's summer in paradise.*

"Well, it's great meeting you, Lane," I said and gave her my social smile. I put my hand on the mower's steering wheel and waited for her to take the hint and leave.

Lane smiled.

And there it was. Sadness. It slipped out of the edges of her smile. It touched the corners of her eyes.

Oh, oh. She had some definite baggage. Not a good thing. *Don't get involved*, I thought. I squinted at the sun, remembering the last time I had involved myself in a neighbor's emotional baggage. Some part of me continued to believe it played a part in my sister's death.

"Okay," I said for no reason other than filling in the uncomfortable silence.

"Great," Lane said probably for the same reason.

Walking up the stone pathway to the front door, I was surprised when I felt her presence behind me, and I shivered in the heat. Then, a vague, buzzing sensation started in my head and ran down to land somewhere near my belly button. This was what I called a gut feeling. Just plain God-given common sense was what my sister, Rachel, used to call these feelings. Pay attention and they might save your life, she said a year or so before her murder. Although I had some things to say to her about heeding this advice, I believed it was good advice at its core.

Lane smiled again. This time it was a face-lighting smile, and it seemed so natural and healthy I pushed the gut feeling to the back of my mind.

"Nice to have met you," I said again. Another hint.

"You too," Lane said, lowered her head, and began walking away.

That's when I noticed the tattoo.

"Hey, I remember you. Stacy did that," I said.

She stopped and turned to face me. "What?"

"Your tattoo. Stacy from my shop did that. Looks good," I said.

"You have a tattoo shop in Scranton?" she asked.

"No, I don't have a shop in Scranton. It's right down the street. I'm talking about The Big Prick."

"*What* are you talking about?"

"My shop down the street."

"Huh?" she said.

"Your tattoo," I said.

She reached around with her right hand to touch her left shoulder blade. "I had this done in Scranton."

"But I saw you…" I began. "Let me get a closer look."

I moved closer. It *was* the same tattoo. The same sketch a blonde, willowy, woman had brought into my shop a while back. There were two masks, similar to the faces of drama masks, but these were identical lush-lipped smiling female faces with exaggerated, bead-tipped eyelashes. Unique.

"We did a tattoo like that a month or so ago on a woman who looked a lot like you. Asked for it on her left shoulder, just like yours. I'd swear it was you."

Thinking back, I recalled I was in a hellish mood that day, resenting the clients and staff and the shop itself. Janice, disregarding my mental state, was giving an im-promptu lesson on tattooing. Ostensibly, I was paying attention to her blabbering, but in reality, I was adding fuel to a slow burning anger and thinking up the menu for a solitary pity party. This self-absorbed mood began the day I gave in to Janice's pleading and bullying, plunked down my savings, and started my second, second career by buying the tattoo parlor.

The bell on the door clanged and I looked away from the tattoo gun in Janice's hand and its victim—a squirrelly acting man who wanted a fire-spitting dragon on his bicep. He said it was a symbol of his inner spirit.

A woman walked past the counter, stacked with overflowing binders of stock, and headed toward me. The sun streaming through the red and black hand-painted sign on the front glass window blurred my vision and changed areas of her California surfer-girl blonde hair to streaks of pink and gray. I saw the piece of paper in her hand and knew it was a sketch or downloaded flash. I put my hand out in the woman's direction.

Without speaking, she handed me the paper: a simple pencil drawing of excessively long-lashed female drama masks. I looked up from the drawing and asked, "Where?"

She smiled reached her right hand around to tap her left shoulder in exactly the same manner as Lane had just done.

"What is it? Is something wrong?" Lane asked, bringing me back to our conversation.

"You sure it wasn't you?" I asked.

Lane sighed. "You're joking, right?"

"Yeah. Never mind. I guess you'd be sure, wouldn't you?" I had to admit to myself I didn't truly look at the woman's face that day in the tattoo shop.

"Yes, I would."

"Maybe you remember where you got the flash?" I asked.

"The flash?"

"The sketch, the drawing,"

"I don't know. Somewhere online. I liked it because I'm a Gemini, you know, the sign of the twins. So that's what you do? You're a tattoo artist?" Lane asked.

"Nope. I bought the place a few months back," I said.

"Oh," she said.

I saw the confusion on her face but didn't give her any further explanation.

"Do you have family here?" I asked.

"No. I'm the only remaining member of my family." She smoothed her hair and placed it behind her ears. "Well, other than my real father. I think that's why my biological clock is ticking."

"Oh?" I didn't think people actually said things like that in real life. I thought it was something you would only hear on a TV talk show.

"My mother and stepfather both died a year ago in a car accident."

"That's rough. I'm sorry about that."

"Thanks."

"That the reason you moved here?"

"No. They didn't leave me the house."

I scratched my head under my sweat-soaked cap. "Well, I know you didn't inherit the house because—" I began to tell her that my fiancé, Vince, had owned her house. He was a house flipper. He remodeled and sold them, usually as second homes to the winter visitors.

"It was a freak accident. They crashed into each other. I was in the car with my mother." She rubbed the spot between her neatly shaped eyebrows with the pointer finger of her right hand. "That's something I've put behind me. I don't like to talk about it."

"You were a passenger? And your mother died? That's horrible. What happened? Was she distracted somehow?" I asked.

"I was cleared of all wrongdoing," she said.

"Wrongdoing?" I asked casually, though I was very curious at this point.

"They thought I had something to do with my own mother's death. Isn't that weird?"

"Intimate violence."

"What?" she said.

"Whenever there are suspicions regarding a person's death, they question those closest to the victim. They call it intimate violence. Sounds like a catchy title for a thriller movie, doesn't it?" I waited, but when she stared at me without answering, I said, "It's not."

Her face crinkled into a look of disgust. "Why would you know that?"

"I'm a licensed PI, too." I shrugged at her. "Sometimes I wonder, didn't the victims have any suspicion? They had known their murderer. Wasn't there some sort of warning during the relationship?"

"I wouldn't know. I don't like to think about those types of things."

I didn't bother to hide my annoyance at her coyness. "Okay."

After a few seconds of silence, Lane blurted, "I teach. We aren't paid that well, but it's rewarding. Anyway Mother left me some money, so I get by."

"You moved here because of a teaching position? Not many kids around here."

"That's why I'm so excited about Del," she said.

"Who's Del?"

"My boyfriend."

"I don't mean to be rude, but why did you choose this village, this neighborhood? Haven't you noticed it's full of people much older than you? There's no night life, nothing exciting ever happens here."

"I moved here to start a new life, of course, but mostly to be near Del. His mother helped choose this area for me."

"Must be serious if his mother is involved."

"We're very serious. I feel like I know him totally. He's sexy, caring, and smart," she said in a dreamlike voice.

It was the wrong information, and it was too much information, too fast. I didn't want to know any more about her or her beau. I was selectively curious, and I was afraid she would start telling me the personal stuff, like details concerning her sex life, or confessing some embarrassing addiction, or an ulcerating health issue. That kind of talk made me queasy.

"Everything has worked to plan," she said.

I was completely lost. "What plan?"

"To be with Del, you know, to be happy."

"Oh. That plan."

Just as I had resigned myself to more tittle-tattle, Lane said, "I'll be back over in a bit, okay? I want to ask you something."

"Nice meeting you," I said for the third time, not really expecting her to return any time soon.

I ran inside to check the phone for messages, hoping there would be one from a client to tell me they needed me for research or investigating. Those requests mean money—something the shop wasn't giving. There was no blinking light and I felt a twinge of worry regarding my future finances.

After returning outside, I finished the mowing, put away the mower, and started on the flowerbeds.

I felt her approach more than saw it. Without putting down my trowel, I turned and waved.

"How's it going?" I asked. It was the type of question people generally asked and expected a one-word reply.

She stood with one hand on her hips, looking down at me. "I think it would be so cool to have a father for myself and a grandfather for my baby."

I couldn't stop my eyes from going to her concave abdomen.

"When I do have a baby, I mean." She smoothed

down the front of her shorts. "I've never met my biological father, and supposedly he doesn't know about me. Mother told me he lives somewhere in New Mexico and his name is John Lane. That's why I have the name Lane."

I nodded and continued adding potting soil to the flowerbed. "Uh-huh, that's, uh, nice," I said and asked her to hand me the flat of carnations.

She used her foot to push the tray, while fanning her face with an overstuffed manila envelope, and then she leaned down to place her hand on my arm.

"So, would you do some investigating to find my father? I want him in my life."

I didn't answer right away. I intended to say no, then I thought of my finances, and I thought about the sadness in her eyes. Not one iota of that gut feeling from earlier surfaced.

"I think I can fit you in," I told her.

I wanted to keep our conversation strictly professional. I didn't want her to think we would become chit-chat girlfriends. While I planted carnations, we talked about my hourly charges and reached an agreement on how much she was willing to spend.

"Understand I'm not traipsing around the country looking for him. I really don't like doing that. Bad things happen when I start driving around in strange places," I told her.

"Oh, I understand," she said.

"I don't think you could," I said, then smiled to cover my annoyance with the platitude.

She responded with an empty smile. "Right," she said and waved the envelope at me as if trying to dismiss anything else that could steal my attention away from it and her. "Mother didn't give me much detail, but here's some stuff I found among her things."

Instead of taking the envelope, I showed her the dirt

on my hands and finished planting the flowers.

I took the tray into the garage, lifted a bag of land-scape rock, and headed back toward the flowerbed. Lane stood near the garage entrance, so I placed the bag in her free arm.

When she stumbled a half step backward, I took it from her, set it nearby on the grass, and went back to grab another bag.

"I'm going to see Del tonight," she said.

"Oh?" I walked around her and started shaking the white rock out of the bag. I didn't really care about her personal life.

She backed up out of the line of fire before answer-ing. "Del. He's wonderful and gorgeous. Since we've been together, I've come to believe we're soul mates, destined to meet and be together." The gush of her voice didn't match the determination on her face.

"Is Dale's family from around here?"

"It's Del, D-e-l. Not originally. But I've met his mom and we get along great. It's perfect." She waved the envelope rapidly in front of her face. "Well, almost."

"Oh, do tell," I said in my best impression of Bette Davis and regretted it the second the words were out of my mouth. So much for maintaining professionalism.

"We were all in Sunset Breeze, enjoying our meal when this woman came in."

"Uh-huh."

"Del and she had some sort of relationship for a time and she was his office manager, but he fired her and I guess she went off the deep end. Right in the middle of the packed restaurant, she began yelling at Del and his mom. She made Del's mom cry. Everyone in the restau-rant noticed the scene."

"Doesn't sound good."

"That's not all. A few days later, I went to pick up

Del at his office, and she came out of nowhere. I had just stepped out of the car when she came from behind me and said stuff like, he's not right for you, he's not the person you think." Lane looked off into the distance, her eyes shiny. After a second or so, she turned back to look at me with a big smile. "Everything else is great, and I asked him to move in with me."

I got down on my hands and knees to spread the rock under the carnations. "Whoa. Why would you want to be involved in a mess like that? Let him get his life straightened out first."

"Once he moves in, she'll realize he's serious. Things have a way of smoothing over."

"It's not that simple." I knew this from experience. I'm the Elizabeth Taylor of my family, with three failed marriages and one trial basis cohabitation to my discredit. It didn't matter who was at fault, problems in relationships rarely worked themselves out. "Things like that don't just smooth over," I said.

"It'll all work out," she said.

I sat in the grass cross-legged and looked up at her. The sun was straight above, as yellow and round as a child's drawing.

The single-minded expression on her face seemed that of a child, too. I thought, didn't her parents teach her anything?

"Oh, for pity's sake. Don't be a ninny. This is how people get hurt. They ignore the warning signs of trouble." The words slipped out of my mouth. *Damn, it. I did it again. Why can't I just keep my mouth shut?*

"Look, I'm sure—" She began fanning her red face with the envelope.

Why do I care? I shook my head, turned my back to her, and reached around a hibiscus bush to twist the faucet on.

She set the envelope on the porch rail without another word and walked across the street.

I stood there wondering why I always did this. I knew I shouldn't give advice. No one heeded it, and besides that, it always backfired, as I never seemed to follow it myself.

She didn't seem very enthusiastic to see me when we met going to our mailboxes over the next few days, barely glancing in my direction.

On the third day, Lane waved.

I waved back.

"How you doing?" I asked, hoping she was still a paying client.

"Everything is great! Hey, Cassie," she said in a burst of emotion and walked toward me with a weird exuberance. "I found out who you are. You're that PI from that TV show. I don't remember the name."

"*Cruising,*" I told her, and then asked, "Have you changed your mind about hiring me?"

"Noooo," she said and took a step closer. "I feel so bad about what happened on the show."

Instinctively, my shoulders hunched and I raised my arm to ward off the hug that I expected her to foist on me. She shrugged and laughed. There was a skip in her step when she turned and walked back up her drive.

Lane spewed weird vibes, and I decided back then I would do my best to find her father and then stay as far away from her as possible.

But this was now, and I hadn't figured out how meeting her could have anything to do with a body stuffed in the trunk of my car. I just knew there was something off with her. Or maybe I was subconsciously trying to validate my gut feeling.

I heard Rachel's voice say, '*Pure psychobabble.*'

CHAPTER 4

I sat at my computer and made a list of what I knew about the car fire. I added everything I could think of that had happened to me and around the neighborhood the week prior to the fire. There was nothing but commonplace happenings on the list, and staring at it on the screen didn't bring out a lead to follow, so I walked away from the computer.

I threw on a bleached-out bikini and jumped into the pool. As I swam, I felt the tension dissipate a little with each lap.

A half hour later, while opening the sliding door to go into the lanai, I saw a shadow of something move in the side yard between my house and the neighbor's.

"Hello? Who's there?"

When I didn't get an answer I left via the pool enclosure door and walked around the perimeter of the house. I didn't find anything unusual until I was at the front where two young men were on the sidewalk, their attention on a camera.

"Is that you RJ? What are you doing? Were you guys out back a minute ago?" I asked while walking toward the two.

RJ's head jerked up and he looked at me with surprise.

"Ms. Cruise," he said, cutting his eyes to the man with the camera.

The cameraman lifted the camera, settled a stabilizer on his chest, and aimed it at me.

"You'd better point that away from me." I marched toward the camera, but stopped when I saw RJ's fascinated stare and remembered I was in my old bikini bathing suit and flip-flops. Turning in the direction of the front door, I yelled over my shoulder, "Shut it off. Now."

"Do you want to tell us about the incident that happened the other night, right here in this quiet retirement village?" RJ said, his voice imitating the style of local newscasters.

"Do you need your job?" I asked from behind the opened door.

"Come on, Ms. Cruise. This is just a warm up project. Ain't no one going to see it," RJ said.

"I give you both to the count of ten until I call the police," I said before shutting the door.

I watched through the dining room window as they turned away from the house and walked down the sidewalk toward the cul de sac. RJ appeared to talk and the camera guy filmed as he walked alongside.

All the tension I'd dissolved in the pool, returned. I swallowed some pain pills with a glass of tea and then went into the bedroom to change. I returned to the computer and pounded out a couple hours of work for a pharmaceutical company, which had hired me for investigative research on alternative medicine practices. Finding myself ahead of the time line, I decided to see if I could locate any information on Lane's father.

There were four persons in New Mexico with the name John Lane. I printed the addresses and phone numbers and thought it would be a good starting point to call and narrow them down. I had an approximate age, and Lane's mother, Maureen, had described John in one of her diaries that Lane had included in the envelope. I made some notes from the entry and other bits of information I found in Maureen's papers and stuck the bunch in a folder in the drawer of my desk.

When I closed the drawer, I noticed a white card on the floor below the desk. The card had a rose on the front and on the inside was an engraved invitation to the wedding of Sheila Anne Jensen and John Normandy Lane. I'd surmised from the other correspondence that Sheila and Maureen were cousins and close friends. It was an early June wedding and Maureen, according to the other bits of information in the envelope, would give birth to Lane a short two months later. Hadn't Lane said her father's name was Lane?

Interesting, but then something more interesting came to mind. I entered the name Maureen Somers into a search engine.

One of the links I clicked on was a Scranton newspaper article.

Woman, 62, at fault in accident injuring herself and killing her husband. A 62-year-old woman was critically injured and her husband killed this morning in a two-car crash in the upscale Ravenswood neighborhood. The accident occurred about 2:40 a.m. at the intersection of Ashland and Carter Avenues, Officer Debra Tucker said. The woman was driving a newer Lexus east on Carter when she apparently did not see a Ford Crown Victoria, driven by her husband, traveling south on Ashland.

"The Lexus pulls into the intersection and is struck by the Ford," Tucker said.

The woman, Maureen Somers, of the 4100 block of North Marine Drive, was taken to Advocate Medical Center. Her condition was not released.

The driver of the Ford, 68 year-old Charles Somers, the husband of the woman in the Lexus, was also taken to Advocate Medical Center, Tucker said. He was pronounced dead there at 4:42 a.m., according to the county medical examiner's office.

A passenger in the Lexus, the couple's daughter, Lane Somers, suffered minor injuries and was treated and released. The accident is under investigation by the Major Accident Investigation Unit. Detective Tucker added that the police had been called to the Somers' household for domestic issues several times during the year previous to the accident.

An accident. Didn't sound like there would be a reason to hold a person for questioning until you threw in the domestic issues. Lane had said police cleared her of wrongdoing. Would that mean they had initially charged her with something?

I searched for follow up information. Prior to the accident, a few articles in the society news mentioned Lane's mom and step-dad, but nothing else regarding the accident came up.

In another archive, I found Charles Somers obituary. In it, he was described as a community leader and a top gun in the steel industry. His family was founding members of a town twenty or so miles from Scranton. Then I found Maureen Somers' obituary. The obituary listed her date of death three days after the accident.

Lane's stepfather died in the accident, and three days later, her mother died from injuries sustained in the accident. Sad. Where did the domestic issues come into it? And what about the wrongdoing?

Checking the clock again, I realized I had just enough time to jump in the shower, put on a presentable face, and slip into my favorite tropical sundress.

At 7:15 p.m., I heard what sounded like a car door shutting and poked my head out the door to look for Vince. His truck was in my drive but he was across the street laughing and talking with Lane. Then Lane saw me, and she nudged Vince. He turned and smiled, patted her arm and walked over looking handsome and hungry.

We walked to his truck and, as I hopped in, I noticed Lane was still standing in her driveway. There was an edge to her face that hadn't been there before. Her eyes had dark smudges under them and her cheekbones looked razor sharp. There was a level of nervousness surrounding her, where before there was an almost childlike composure. I smiled and waved.

"It's good you and Lane have made up," Vince said once we were in the truck and driving through North Harbor toward Venice.

I didn't respond right away. It began getting under my skin to think about Lane and Vince as friends. If he could be friends with such a namby-pamby type, how could he love me? I then thought about the fact that he sold her the house. That's all there was to it.

"Cassie, you with me?" Vince said, bringing my attention back to him.

"Yeah." I smiled. "I didn't know Lane and I had anything to make up about. It really shouldn't have been a big deal anyway. She should have simply told me to shut up and mind my own business. I would have shut up, you know."

"You do come on pretty strong sometimes," he said.

"Is that what you two were talking about?" When I saw he was shaking his head in that way men did when they thought a woman was behaving emotionally or irrationally, I didn't wait for him to answer or explain. "She didn't have any problem telling me everything about her love life and I didn't censure her until I felt she was going to get hurt." I looked at him to see if he was paying attention.

He appeared to be listening, so I continued. "What would you have me do? Shut my trap? Should I not voice my thoughts when I think they might be helpful? Don't I have the right to suggest behavior modifications? You know, sort of like what you're doing to me right now."

I folded my hands in my lap and waited for his response. I looked over and smiled. It was my subtle way of letting him know that applause would be appropriate at this time.

"Look, we both know you don't have the most welcoming personality. I think you need to encourage more people into your life and suggesting behavior modifications to someone you've just met isn't the way to do it," he said.

"I have my family. I have you. I have Janice."

"You have us, yes, but only after poor Janice went through a rigorous yearlong interrogation."

"I only want certain people around me."

"Uh-huh." He always said that when he didn't want to discuss a subject any longer, but I wasn't ready to let it drop.

"Who do you have in your life?" I asked, knowing he didn't have many friends who he could call close. His friends, the two I knew about, had been his friends since grade school and they still lived in Michigan.

"It's not about the number of friends. It's about how guarded and afraid you've become."

"I'm not afraid."

"Yes, you are. You're afraid of looking soft, or weak. I guess weak is a better word. But mostly you're afraid to care about people."

"I care, but caring doesn't change the way people behave. And, as you said, it's not about the number. Quality, not quantity, right?"

"Right. But there's more to it. You don't engage people in conversation. You interrogate them. You want them to answer all of your questions—they have to pass your test."

"I don't know any other way," I said.

"You can keep a relationship casual and light for business purposes. You are a business owner now, you know. In my line of work, I have to do it every day. It's all in the mindset. Keep it at surface level by engaging in easy going conversation and don't invest yourself every time you meet someone new."

"If what you're telling me is some people are worth taking the time to get to know, then that means there are people who aren't worth getting to know. I just shorten the process. If a person seems offended by my questions and has something to hide, then they avoid me. So instead of finding out the hard way, I find out right away. I haven't wasted any of my time."

"You can't just force them to tell you everything all at once," Vince said.

"I just want enough to figure out if they're what they seem to be."

"You didn't behave that way when we met way back when."

"I know, but I thought you were rich so it didn't matter," I said.

"I am rich."

"Guess I know what I'm doing then, don't I?"

"So you're just after my money?"

"That's something you should've asked yourself a long time ago, back before being with me became so addictive."

"Uh-huh, Cassie, you think you've just proven a point, don't you?"

"Yep."

"Well, you did. You've proven mine," he said.

"Do you know you have gorgeous eyes? Then there's your perfectly hairy chest. It's yummy. Oh, and your feet. Did anyone ever tell you, you have the feet of a twenty year old?"

"It's an old trick, but feel free to go on distracting me. That way you won't have to tell me I'm right. Anyway, I'm asking you to lighten up on Lane, okay?"

His request seemed so unfair I could barely catch my breath. I felt surrounded by a gray cloud of failure. Had we changed so much that we no longer understood each other?

"What is it you want from me Vince? What do you want from life?" I asked.

"What do you mean? I want to succeed. Retire early and live the good life. I thought we wanted the same things. That's why we're a couple, right?" Vince said.

I did my best to hide my disappointment, knowing I needed time to figure out its cause. "Right."

Looking out the window the last few minutes before reaching the restaurant, I thought about the meaning of success. Perhaps that's where our problems began. We both wanted to succeed, but hadn't really discussed our definition of success.

At the restaurant, we sat at our usual table overlooking the beach during the time the movie-making industry calls magic hour, which really doesn't last an hour. Nothing beautiful lasts forever and magic hour is no different. This is the time the sun sets, the light is perfect, the sky is reddish pink, and for approximately thirty minutes, everything looks amazing.

I decided to let go of the anger I'd felt about Vince and his request regarding Lane. I didn't want anything between the evening and us.

We held hands across the table while staring out at the waves and sky. The sun was huge and red and, for a brief bit of time, I thought of the body in my car and the red paint splashed on the window of The Big Prick. They were both things an enraged person would do, and it felt very personal. *Who would do that to me?*

"Drinks anyone?" Amy, our usual server, asked. She had dark spiky hair with pink edges and a diamond stud in her right nostril. Nonetheless, her petite shape and perky attitude reminded me of Audrey Hepburn in *Roman Holiday*.

"It's so good to see a happy couple," she said.

I looked over at Vince and stuck out my tongue. He crossed his eyes. Amy groaned and held up her hand in an effort to stop us.

Vince gave his winning smile to Amy and caused her to blush.

"Seriously, you two are a great couple," she said. "You wouldn't believe the stuff we overhear. Sometimes the whole restaurant gets to hear, like a few days ago when this 'Barbie' and 'Ken' look-alike couple got into it. They came in all happy, looking and behaving as if their perfectly planned lives were just that. Perfect. And then we all got to see they're just like everyone else."

Amy shook her head and waved her hand in the air

as if to rid herself of the memory. "Working here, I've figured out the people who try to appear perfect have the bigger problems out of the public eye." She looked at Vince. "You know what I'm talking about, don't you?" She looked at Vince.

"Yes, I know what you mean." He crossed his arms over his chest and turned his head to look out the window.

For a guy who'd just lectured me about engaging in light conversation and not investing emotions, his body language was telling a different story. Although, I did appreciate how crossing his arms like that highlighted his tanned muscular biceps.

"Anyway, my bet is you two—" She pointed at Vince and me. "—will be hanging out ten years from now. I'll be right back with your drinks."

Something about the Barbie and Ken story had me thinking about Lane and her boyfriend Del. "Wait, Amy, I want to ask you—"

"Cassie, come on now. Let's have a nice romantic dinner, okay?"

He used his smile on me. As much as I should be able to ignore it after all this time, I couldn't.

I crossed my fingers. "Just wanted to know the dinner special, that's all."

"Oh, right." He made a face at me and turned to Amy who waited quietly. "Just the drinks for now."

I let it go when I looked across the room and noticed RJ sitting at a corner table, fiddling with his phone. He saw me looking and nodded. I looked around for the camera person. When I didn't see him, I gave all my attention to Vince. I was determined to have an unstressed evening.

We did have a nice romantic dinner and the mood continued well into the night. To my relief the image of Detective Winslow only flashed briefly during the midst of it all. There was something about both men that made me wobbly-knee weak.

Sadly, history had proven, when it came to maintaining relationships, I was not to be trusted.

CHAPTER 5

The next morning, after Vince left, I was too lazy to untangle myself from the bed sheets and remained snoozing for much longer than usual. At half past ten, I made coffee and sat near the pool, drinking and thinking. I remembered Amy talking about the Barbie and Ken look-alike thing. The first person who came to my mind was Lane because she looked like a living Barbie doll. Then I thought of the problem she had with Del's former girlfriend bothering them at dinner. *Didn't Lane say they were at Sunset?*

I walked down the street to see Janice.

She answered the doorbell by stepping out onto her porch and partially shutting the door behind her.

"I wondered if you wanted to go out to dinner, my treat. Last I looked you only had the one appointment and that's for some old bimbo who wants a hibiscus on the back of the neck to celebrate her sixty-fifth birthday. Should take about twenty minutes. Although, if she's a golfer like you, she could have the hide of a rhino and it could take much longer."

"I'm in the middle of something. I, uh, have a visitor," she said.

"Jeez. Sorry. I meant to send my maid down with a

calling card before popping in on you," I said while try-ing to look around her to see whom she was entertaining. I caught a glimpse of baggy shorts and smelled traitor.

"No problem. I'll call you, okay?" Janice said, step-ping into my line of vision.

"That RJ in there? What's he doing here?"

"I'll call you," she said as she backed up and closed her door.

Walking home, I brewed up a big batch of pissed-off at the dismissal. The irritation turned to mournful pity, and then I settled on annoyance. She was so anxious for me to leave that she hadn't noticed my snidely clever comments. Not one sassy word back.

"Phooey on that old bird and that gangster wannabe," I said to my coffee and cigarette. "I like my solitude."

As a distraction, I reviewed the list of John Lane ad-dresses and phone numbers and called the first on the list. He was too young; a teenager who had parents that felt for some reason he should be trusted to answer their home phone.

The second John Lane listened politely as I ex-plained the situation and just as politely called me a nut case while disconnecting. I left a message on the third's machine. When I hung up, my phone rang.

"Hello, I have plenty of cigarettes for you," I said.

"Ms. Cruise? This is Detective Winslow."

"Oh. Hi. I thought you were Janice and—oh, never mind."

"I'd like to come over and discuss the incident from the other night. It shouldn't take long."

"What incident are you speaking of?"

"Are there that many you're involved in?" he asked.

I ignored the question. "Any time today is fine. I'll be here or at the shop until about seven tonight."

"Where?'

"My shop. The tattoo parlor on Tamiami Trail."

"Really? That's yours?" he asked.

"Just meet me here at my home." I squelched the desire to snarl at him. I'd heard the presumption in his voice. I might as well have said meet me at the head shop.

"I'll be there in ten minutes."

He was prompt. I offered him a seat in the living room and he told me no thanks. He stood in the entryway, chest out, and feet wide apart. His eyes moved to areas behind me and to the side. Mindful of not making any sudden moves or drawing any concealed weapons, I took the time to admire his control over his emotions, noticing that no one would have to wonder from one day to the next how he would present himself.

"Ms. Cruise, I want you to go over what you saw the other night. Did you think of anything you might have forgotten to tell us?"

Rachel too preferred to get right down to business. They would have gotten along famously. No fooling around or wasting time.

I repeated what I saw on the night of the car fire, cleared my throat, and said, "I'm told I have a vivid imagination on top of being, um, observant, and it's not always a good combination. Anyway, any chance you checked with the neighbors about what they might've seen?"

"Why?" he asked.

"For starters, the neighbor across the street—her boyfriend usually parks his car in the street." I let that sink in. "Now, I'm wondering if any one told you someone has a grudge on him."

"We've talked to everyone around here. No one claims to have any disputes with anyone out of the ordinary," he said.

"Just wanted to make sure. Lane had told me some

stuff about her boyfriend's ex-office manager/girlfriend and, well, I don't know why, but she came to my mind." I drew in a long breath and let it out through pursed lips.

"Who came to your mind?"

"Her boyfriend's ex."

Winslow pulled out a small notebook and flipped through it. "We attempted to talk to the woman, but we are currently unable to locate her," he said.

"Did Lane tell you about her?" I asked.

"Ms. Somers called in a complaint a few days before this incident. She was concerned about the woman's behavior, wondered if we'd consider it stalking or harassment. She said talking to you had convinced her there was a problem."

"Oh. She didn't tell me that. Is that where it ended?"

"She was advised of the process for petitioning for a Harassment Restraining Order, ma'am."

"In other words, that's where it ended." I knew restraining orders meant next to nothing most times.

"We don't have anything to go on other than her name, Crystal Jane Evans, and no one knows much about her or her background. She was staying in a local motel with no vehicle and checked out on the day of the incident." He flipped the notebook shut and returned it to his back pocket.

"Then I guess you feel she's somehow a part of all this? That's the only thing that makes sense to me. Am I right?"

He shook his head.

"Do you know who the body is yet? Is it male or female?" I asked.

He shrugged. "Thanks for your time, Ms. Cruise. I've asked your neighbors to let me know if they see or hear anything unusual. You do the same."

"Wait. Will you let me know when you find out who the body is?"

Detective Winslow again shook his head. "Why do I get the idea you're going to be a problem? You understand this isn't a plot made up for a TV show, right?"

"Tell me what you think happened," I said, ignoring his reference to *Cruising*.

"Murder," he answered.

"Where do you think it happened?" I asked.

"Here," he said.

"Why my car? Why my fucking car?"

"That's a good question," he said and turned the door handle. He left without a look back at me.

Then it hit me again.

Someone was murdered. Here. In this neighborhood. I couldn't rid myself of the thoughts, time, and trouble I'd put into finding this supposedly safe neighborhood. How could I have gotten it so wrong?

After a few minutes of nervous pacing, I forced myself to sort through the information from Lane. The personal group was the largest and I reviewed the items again.

Then I made a phone call to the number four John Lane on my list.

"Hello."

"Mr. Lane, this is Cassie Cruise. I'm calling on behalf of my client, Lane Somers," I said.

"Ma'am?"

"She's hired me to locate her father. His name is John Lane and his last known location is New Mexico. Do you have a few minutes to talk to me about this?"

"Lady, I don't know you."

"Is your wife's name Sheila?" I asked.

He wasn't friendly, but he wasn't rude. "What does my wife have to do with anything?"

"Well, it's just that Lane's mother's cousin is Sheila. See, Maureen was seeing John—Maureen is Lane's mother—John Normandy Lane. That's an unusual middle name don't you think? Then John met Sheila and they married. I don't know if Maureen introduced John and Sheila or how it happened, but Maureen never told John she was pregnant with Lane."

"Uh huh," he said.

"I'm not saying it was a good decision. I mean she could have made a big stink about the whole thing, especially when she received their wedding invitation."

Pausing, I gave Mr. Lane Number Four time for a response, and when there was none, I continued. "Anyway, Maureen married someone else shortly before she had Lane and I guess they were happy, but they didn't have any children together. She and her husband died in an auto accident a year or so ago. Therefore, if your wife is Sheila and you are the John Normandy Lane who knew Maureen, had a brief, um, romantic interlude with her and Sheila has a cousin with the name of Maureen then you are Lane's father." I let out a big breath.

"You sound crazy as a loon."

I found it crazy he was still on the line. "Look, Mr. Lane, I know all this comes as quite a shock. I'm going to leave you my name and number. When you've had a chance to think about this, give me a call. I'll put you in touch with my client when you are ready."

Leaning back in the chair, I thought how normally I wouldn't vomit out all the information I had on a case. It was my tendency to dole it out only as needed and with care, but I wanted to be finished with this job. I wanted to find Lane's father and move on to concentrate on finding the killer. I waited for him to speak, but there was only silence, or in my present mood, encouragement. "Okay, here's the information. My name is Cassie Cruise and I was hired by Lane Somers, S-o-m-e-r-s, to help her find her father. You can reach me at 908-429-2319. Just leave a message. 908-429-2319. Bye now."

Pushing away guilt feelings for doing a shitty job, I focused on the feeling that I'd been talking to the correct John Lane. It would be a waiting game for a day or so. He might try to ignore the whole thing, but it would gnaw at him, and he would call me back. If he didn't, I would send him an official looking request for more information regarding his history. He would call then.

I made some notes regarding the call and added them to the folder. Picking up the envelope Lane had given me, I found that while most of the items in the envelope belonged to Maureen, there were also some of Lane's papers mixed in. Her name was on a receipt for a computer purchase and the warranty information was in the pile. She had stapled the phone number to a computer help desk onto the identification key and license to her word processing software, handwritten along the edges of it were the words, Lanesom28@netscape.net, and below it was the cluster of letters "yandr."

The thing about being nosy was it was a part of you. Actually, it was a compulsion. You had to follow through and face the consequences. Believe me, there were always consequences.

I clicked on the web browser and went to the Netscape web site, clicked on the sign-in button, typed in the user name of "Lanesom28," and entered the password as "yandr."

I held my breath while Lane's home page loaded. I clicked on the mail option and reentered the password.

She had forty-two items in her Inbox, nineteen of which were unread and looked to be advertisements and general spam.

There was email from "teach72" dated weekly all

through the previous year until the last one dated three months ago. I moved to the Sent folder of the email account and found replies to teach72. In the older email notes, they discussed various soap operas and the characters in them. Later, the two talked about issues that were more personal. Lane wrote the way she spoke—at length. Teach72's emails were short and filled with questions about Lane's life.

A few months ago, Lane sent Del's picture as an attachment and a giddy note explaining how great things were going for her. Then a few weeks later, she sent a short email asking why teach72 had stopped writing her. There was no reply from teach72.

I moved back to the Inbox and looked at the emails from "MTMan." These emails were signed Del. They began as typical introductory-type flirting and moved into more advanced "I'm intrigued and want to meet you" email.

Lane's initial replies were crowded with details of her life and were soon more personal. I found myself feeling anxious and embarrassed for her. She laid it out. She expressed her need to be near him. She wrote about her dreams of having a family and she let him know she thought he was the one she had been looking for.

Del's responses were to the point. He told her what time he would call her or gave details of his schedule.

I opened the new pieces of mail in the Inbox. Once I had read a few, I put together that Lane had posted her picture on a singles web site and had received a response from Del. It looked as though her picture was still posted and responses continued to trickle in. I clicked on the boxes in front of the previously unread email. I then clicked on the option, "Keep as New." Then the whole thing started depressing me. I knew this was snooping and I didn't have the right to look at her email account.

The depression lasted two seconds. I returned to the more descriptive of Lane's replies to Del and re-read them. A person could find out a lot about a client's personality by reading their correspondence. It helped to know what and whom you were dealing with.

Once I logged out of the email account, I began typing a report detailing my progress with finding Lane's father. I decided not to include my impression of John Lane Number Four. I would give Lane the facts and let her decide whether I should continue along the path.

Half of me hoped she would tell me to stop working on it and take over the project herself. If she took hold of it in the same way she did meeting Del, she'd have a Daddy in a matter of days and I wouldn't be compelled to snoop into her private email account. Most especially, I wanted to spend my time concentrating on catching whoever killed the person in my trunk.

After seeing Del's vehicle parked in the street, I knew, or I guessed I convinced myself, Del and his ex were in some way involved. I wanted the killer held responsible and it agitated me to think that wasn't going to happen.

Within thirty minutes, I had printed a report, stuffed it in an envelope, and walked across the street to Lane's house.

"Hello?" Lane stuck her head out and looked at me blankly. "Hello?"

"Hey. I'm pretty much finished with the research portion for locating your father."

"That's great." Her voice was flat.

"Do you want the report?"

"Yeah, sure. How much do I owe you?"

"Come on, Lane. I'd like to come in and talk to you about my findings."

After looking up and down the street, she sighed

heavily, opened the door, and stepped out of the way. "Come in. I'm getting ready to take off though."

"I was happy that Del was here for you the other night. I hope they find the Crystal woman you told me about. Have you heard anything more?"

Lane sucked in her breath. "She's nothing to be concerned about. Don't worry about her, okay?"

"Sure, but—"

"Just drop it."

"Look, Del's car is very similar to mine. Don't you think maybe Crystal tried to get at Del and mistook my car for his? I mean it's farfetched, but still what better way to get back at an ex? You know, put a dead person in their car, torch it, and call the fire department. Then the ex has to spend their time explaining how they didn't do it. Some people are that crazy," I said.

"I wouldn't know. Do you have an ex that would do that to you?" she asked.

Good point. I thought about it for a few seconds. "No, but I thought Del's ex went off the deep end. Isn't that what you told me?"

As I watched, her face reddened. "Do you have to look at people that way?" she said.

"What way?"

"Like you think you're Superwoman or whoever had the x-ray vision."

"Someone put a body in my car, and you don't seem to want to discuss the very strange fact that your boyfriend normally parks his car in the spot I left mine. Seems odd," I said.

She turned away from me and walked into the living room. I followed her in and looked around. Through the entry to the dining room, and in front of an antique-looking oak buffet, was a box with overflowing contents.

A chunky bleached oak rectangle, which most likely

served as the dining room table, was fully covered with a mish mash of face makeup, skin lotions, perfume, hair care products, canned cat food, and a bag of cat litter. Four sage-green painted, mix and match chairs were near the table, two were overturned and laying on their sides.

In a corner, near a window overlooking a landscaped island of palm trees was a white polyester sweater. A yellow and white cat was kneading the sweater with his front paws, creating a clinking noise on the ceramic tile floor.

I could see a portion of the galley style kitchen. Between the kitchen and the dining room, a door leading to the garage, left partially opened, allowed a whiff of cat urine to assault my nose. When I looked through the opening, I saw a gaping suitcase with a small amount of clothing, folded with care. Nearby was a pile of clothing that had been tossed or dumped.

Looking again at the dining room, I wondered what had disturbed Lane to the point she gave up all attempts at putting things in order.

"Want some help in here?" I righted a chair and walked toward the sweater intending to pick it up.

She moved to stand in front of me with her hands on her hips and her head angled. "Let's go in the living room."

"I didn't know you had a cat," I said.

She brought her head up straight. "What?"

I pointed at the cat. "What's its name?"

"What? Oh, um, Scooter." She walked over to the cat and tossed it into the garage. She slammed the door and went to the pile of clothes, grabbed the sweater, and pushed it into a buffet drawer. I heard her mumble, "Damn thing stinks."

If she was talking about the cat, it was my sentiment exactly.

"What is it you wanted to go over?" she asked.

"Here's the report. Why don't you take a minute to read and I'll go over it when you're done."

"I guess." She moved to the couch, brushed her hair off her face, and with stiff hands opened the envelope. She put her head down and let her hair fall back over the side of her face.

I sat uninvited at the other end of the couch. Lane was wearing her vanilla-citrus perfume, but today it had a tang. I, too, had the type of body chemistry that could change expensive designer perfumes to the smell of bug spray. Sometimes, just switching your deodorant or skin lotion would help, but I didn't feel comfortable bringing the subject up. She wasn't the same person I had met a week ago. She had changed. There was something dark and unapproachable about her. It wasn't anger. More like a cloud of depression or gloom. She had an atmosphere surrounding her similar to the mood portrayed in *Wuthering Heights, Rebecca*, and *Jane Eyre*.

Lane folded the report, placed it back in the envelope. "Let me handle it from here," she said while walking toward the door.

Startled, I tried to get her to look at me. I had wanted her to handle it, but now that she actually said she would, I felt disappointment. I thought she would ask my opinion. Maybe it was my ego, but I couldn't understand why she didn't have any questions for me. "Do you want my take on it?"

"No. It's fine. I'll deal with it now. There's no reason for you to waste any more time on it. How much do I owe you?"

"It's on the report. Didn't you see it?" I asked.

She took the report out of the envelope and glanced at it. "Okay. I'll write a check. Hang on."

She went to her purse, scribbled out a check, and held the door open before I could respond.

I was getting some strange vibes. She wouldn't look me in the eye. In fact, her hair was still covering part of her face. There was a trace of perspiration above her mouth. The bug spray smell had changed to something more acrid. She definitely wanted me to leave.

"Okay. I guess I'll take off now," I said.

It wasn't until I reached the sidewalk that Lane said anything in return.

"Hey, uh, Cassie. Just forget I asked you to do this, okay?" She crumpled the report in her hands. Her voice came out soft and sad. "I've changed my mind about wanting to meet him."

I crossed my fingers behind my back. "Sure thing. It's forgotten already."

"I mean it," she said, her voice stronger. "I know you're thinking this is a way to improve your reputation as a PI, but I want you to stop. You understand, don't you?"

"Yep," I said and continued walking away.

Like hell, I'd forget it. If anything, her change in request had permanently imbedded her flip-flop personality into my mind and melded with the thoughts of finding the individual responsible for killing the person placed in my car. The two issues at that point became one.

Lane was a changed person. In my opinion, she changed right around the time someone put a body in the trunk of my car and torched it. It didn't bother her that there was a possibility that someone had been trying to set up Del and in the process set up me. She just wanted me to drop it and go away. Sure, maybe it was a farfetched scenario, but tell me the cops' conclusion. I doubted their scenario made any more sense. If they even had one.

"Like hell," I repeated aloud.

This wasn't about my reputation, I'd put that part of

my life to bed. This was about giving a voice to a name-less dead person. This was about finding the person who took away the voice. This was about justice.

CHAPTER 6

I walked in the door, put on a fresh pot of coffee, and emptied the ashtray. As soon as I put it back down on the table, Janice was at the entrance to the lanai.

"Come on in."

"Coffee smells good," Janice said. She went to the coffeepot, added enough cream and sugar to make it look like the leftover milk after a bowl of chocolate flavored cereal, and poured a cup of straight for me.

"Sit down over here by me. I want to watch you steal my cigarettes," I said.

She lit up. "This is going to be long, isn't it?"

"I'm afraid so."

"Well, before you start, let me ask you something."

"Go ahead."

"Have you been watching your Alfred Hitchcock flicks again?"

"No. And don't—and I really mean this—do not bring up the TV thing. I'm going to tell you this one more time only. That was last year. I'm last year's failure. Hardly anyone remembers. Hardly anyone recognizes me. Except somehow, this whole thing never dies in this neighborhood and this village. Any idea why?" I asked.

"It makes for good conversation at the Association

meetings," she said and shrugged her shoulders. She tried to keep a straight face but instead let out a big hoot and slapped her thighs. When she noticed I hadn't laughed with her, she said, "Would it help to talk about it? I've never really understood what happened."

"I was set up. Reality wasn't cutting it, so they added some juicy bits and forgot to tell me."

"Didn't have nothing to do with you being in your late forties? That's what some people say."

"No. I mean that's not the whole story," I said.

"So they brought in, um, shall we say, a younger version of you, and that younger version solved the case you were having trouble solving, and you went off on her out of jealousy, on air, no less. And then you stomped off and quit. Is that the whole story?"

"Thanks for your support, Janice."

"I'm just trying to understand what happened," she said.

"Right."

"Back to my point. Don't waste your breath trying to get me involved in some half-baked scheme that comes from you watching your old movie collection. That's not going to get your show back," she said and shook her finger at me.

"They are classics for your information. And who says I want my show back?"

"Now, that's just what I'm talking about. Those movies are old. Do you hear me? Old. Almost as old as me and twice as useless. Now, if you want to talk about movies, let's talk about Clint Eastwood's classics," Janice said.

"Oh, sure. Being a follower of Dirty Harry wouldn't get anyone in trouble, would it?" I said.

"Cassie, just tell me. You need to get it off your mind, and I'm here to listen," Janice said.

"It's hard to talk about, you know. I feel so betrayed even after all this time," I said.

"Better do it now. There's no telling when you'll get another chance," Janice said.

Suddenly, I did want to talk about it. "RJ asked me if I wanted to tell my side of the story, and I told him no. I guess I do really."

"Well, go on ahead and talk, but hurry before I die of my disease," Janice said and then she had the nerve to wink.

"What exactly is your disease?"

"I'll tell you, just not right now. This is about you," she said.

I sighed and then the story poured out of me.

"*Cruising* had a great concept: the daily life and cases of a real-life private investigator. I mean, people think we sit and type names into Google, and we do. But we're also out there pounding the streets, knocking on doors that no one answers, leaving messages on phones that no one returns.

"Most people don't realize the type of cases that are our bread and butter. They tend to think we're out there solving murders and chasing down the bad guys. We're not. We're working on insurance fraud, taking pictures of cheaters, and trying to find missing people who don't want to be found. These cases can have huge time chunks of immense boredom. Problem is, people tune into a reality show and expect an exciting beginning, middle, and end, just as if they were watching *The Thin Man*." I looked at Janice to see if she was still listening.

She nodded and I continued. "Real people don't live their lives in interesting scenes, so the producer has to find creative ways to fill in the gaps. Sometimes the ending never happens. So, they make it up. Right?"

Janice spoke up. "I'm not naive. I figured they would have to 'help' with some cases."

"Well, me too. I just didn't know they wouldn't let me in on their creativity. So, anyway, I got a new missing person case—I didn't know it was a made up case—and then, suddenly I had an apprentice. Then they forced an exciting ending for the made up case."

I started to feel as though I was opening an old wound and stopped.

"Cassie? Finish," Janice said.

I got up and reached over her to grab a cigarette and a lighter from the end table. I lit up and returned to my chair. I took a sip of my coffee before talking. "It was bad enough to have another person pop up out of nowhere and find the supposed missing person while I was tirelessly looking in the wrong direction. That shit is bound to happen in real life. Yes, I had a childish and ugly meltdown in front of the 1.9 million people tuned in to the show's second season. Apparently, people want to see that stuff. They like to think how much better they would have behaved had they been in my place. But that's okay.

"What really ended it for me is that they wrote me out of the lead. I've never known how to be a sidekick. I mean, everyone was okay with watching a sore loser try to best her attractive young apprentice-turned-partner. My sniping and sarcastic comments about her inability to do the hard work involved were entertainment with a capital E. So were Tiffany's theatrical and teary-eyed attempts to soothe my bad feelings. She only wanted to help me feel necessary to the show, she said."

"You couldn't work with her? Couldn't be a team?" Janice asked.

"It was my show, for fuck's sake!" I answered.

"Jeez. Calm down," she said.

"I just didn't like being involved in it anymore. It

wasn't my style to talk over my every move and make sure I didn't step on anyone's toes while trying to solve a case.

"So, I quit. The show only lasted one more season without me. My bubblier partner tried to hang on to her five minutes of fame by running the talk show gambit and blaming it all on my supposed jealousy of her many attributes." I stood up and acted out Tiffany on the Letterman Show.

LETTERMAN: (calling) "Tiffany—come on out!"
TIFFANY (walking through the curtains and nodding as the audience claps)
LETTERMAN: "So what *really* happened, Tiffany?"
(leans in close as if the answer would be between just the two of them)
TIFFANY (fluffs hair) "Well, David."
(looks at the studio audience)
"As gorgeous and smart as Cassie is, she's also just plain envious and—" (shy and demure look) "—downright bitchy!" (cue the audience for laughter).

I returned to my chair.
Janice had her elbow on the arm of the couch and was holding her head in her hands. "You are so weird."
"I mean that's what I'm judged by. I ended up looking like a pouting bitch."
"I'm truly sorry about what happened. And I care about you. You know that, don't you?" Janice said once I'd sat down.
"I do," I said, turning away to hide an embarrassing display of emotion. Then I stood up to find a tissue, wiped the tears from my face, and blew my nose before returning to my chair in the lanai.

We finished our coffee without saying anything more about the show.

❦❦❦

Later that afternoon, we'd been at the shop for a good four hours. Every station was busy. Even RJ stayed busy. People were chatting, laughing, and enjoying each other. Clients came in excited and left pleased. There was camaraderie all around me, and I felt bad for having to pull Janice away from it. Not.

"Need to talk to you as soon as you're finished here," I told her and smiled at her client, a sweet little librarian type. Then I noticed the location of her nearly complete tattoo. *Holy shit*!

I pointed to the woman's pelvic area. "Can we do that *there*?"

Janice shrugged.

"That had to hurt," I said to the librarian-looking woman.

She sighed and gingerly adjusted her G-string.

"Nice job shaving though. Or did you have it waxed?" I asked.

"Cassie, go wait in your office until I'm finished," Janice said.

I headed toward my office when Stacey brushed by me to stand near Janice. "There's someone here who said she had an appointment with you an hour ago. She's still waiting. She said you told her you would be right with her. What's up?" Stacey asked.

"I don't know. Who is she?" Janice's eyes were wide open and her mouth pulled down into a frown.

"What should I tell her?" Stacey's face compressed into a mask of irritation.

Janice looked around, stopping when she saw the client currently in her station. "I don't know. I—"

"I'll be in my office. Come see me when you can, Janice," I said as I walked off, not wanting to get involved in time management issues.

An hour and a half later, Janice came into the office and sat in the chair across from my desk. She closed her eyes and leaned her head back against the wall behind her.

"Hellooo," I said.

"What is it?" she asked without bothering to open her eyes.

"Okay. As you know, Lane asked me to locate her father. Well, I think I located him. I took the report over to Lane and there is something weird going on over there. She wasn't the least bit interested in what was in that report. Now, she won't talk about Del and his ex-girlfriend. It's more than that, though. She is different. She talks different, behaves different, and even smells different. I could put it off to her and I having a disagreement, but it's something else. I can't put my finger on it. I don't know what it is, but it's there," I told her.

"What's there?" she asked.

"I don't know. Maybe Del is an abuser. Maybe Del's ex-girlfriend, Crystal, is threatening her. She might be in the midst of severe depression. I mean it looked as if someone came into her dining room and tossed stuff around and or maybe she just forgot how to take care of things," I said.

Janice continued resting her head against the wall.

"They weren't a man's things, but—"

"Stop!" Janice said in what I felt was an overly dramatic voice. She sat up straight in the chair and glared at me.

I rolled my eyes. "Here's the thing: something or someone has changed Lane Somers. Oh, and she now has a cat, and she definitely isn't behaving like a cat lover. There's something going on over there. She might be in danger."

"You're doing it again," Janice said and rubbed her forehead.

"No, I know what you're thinking. But I have a right to be involved in this. I think someone burned my car, thinking it was Del's car. I think someone was setting him up. I want to know what is going on over there and I need your help."

"Here you go. You haven't had any trouble for a while, so you're going looking for it. I'll tell you what I think. I think you need the chaos of your old neighborhood. I think you're bored with our little slice of paradise. I think you're not happy here. And if you're not happy, then why should the rest of us be happy?"

"That's pretty damned harsh." The sensible Cassie inside of me recognized some truth to what Janice said and it hurt. The little and mean Cassie inside said, fuck you, Janice, and believed what she'd said didn't change the facts about Lane.

Janice walked past the desk and opened the door that led into the alley. She stood in the doorway and lit up, the smoke curled over her head and then followed the heat of the outdoors as it made its way inside the office.

"The air is on," I said, knowing she would most likely continue to hold the door open and smoke regardless.

Turning toward me, she said, "You have no real reason to get yourself involved in Lane Somers' life. Everything you've said so far is nonsense. It's that gut-feeling thing again, isn't it? You can't take it to the police. They'd laugh in your face. You won't talk to Vince about it because you know what he'll tell you. You only have me, hoping I'll take you seriously and help you butt in where you don't belong. I wonder what you would do if you didn't have me. Hmmm?"

"I will find out what is wrong across the street. It may be nothing big. She might be premenstrual for all I know, but there's help for that too. I'm not going to cause a big scene or commotion. I'm just going to discreetly inquire into Del's past and find out where Crystal is. It's too weird that she wouldn't continue to stalk or harass. I think she is bothering Lane. I'm going to find out and I'd like your help."

"You're not making sense. Do you honestly think an ex-girlfriend would kill a person just to put the body in the boyfriend's car? I understand the setting him up thing. But there's much more to this than that. Someone is dead. Someone's family is missing a loved one. It's not a puzzle or a game. Can't you just tell Lane to go to the police? Do you have to do this? It seems wrong to get involved. It's like a violation or something. Do you know what I'm trying to say?"

"You're right. The police won't listen to my gut feelings. Lane is not receptive to anything I might say to her; although, after our previous discussion, she did call the police to make a report about the ex-girlfriend."

Janice put the cigarette butt in the sand filled coffee can next to the door. She came in and returned to her chair. "Well, see? You might not think she'll listen to you, but apparently, she will. What could be wrong with that? It seems like the sensible thing to do. Just give it your best shot and then drop it."

"I don't want to brag, but I did help your friend Marge when no one else could find out why she wasn't receiving her Social Security checks," I said.

"Marge? I don't remember her," she replied and rubbed her forehead.

I frowned. "Funny." I frowned.

Janice returned the frown.

"So, how about when I staked out Virginia's husband when she became suspicious after he told her he was out every Tuesday and Thursday learning yoga. Remember that?" I asked.

"That wasn't hard to do. The man is 84-years-old. They've been married for fifty odd years. You'd think she would know he had a thing for the dog track. I still laugh when I think about it." Janice hooted and slapped her thighs. "She thought he was having an affair. Jeez, the man moves as if he's wearing cross-country skis on gravel. Where she thought he'd find the energy to be fooling around, I'll never figure out."

"I thought I did a good and thorough investigation."

"Look here, now. Virginia did appreciate your help, but she asked for it," Janice said.

"If you could have seen how desperately Lane wanted to get rid of me, you'd want to find out what's going on with her too—which brings to mind something else. Why'd you want to get rid of me earlier? What was RJ doing at your house?"

"I didn't want to get rid of you. I just know you two don't get along. Sometimes I feel my age, okay?"

"That's bullshit," I told her.

"I'm not going to argue. So here is where I give in and agree to follow along with you. Right?"

"Janice, please. I just want to find out why the body was in my car. Why is that wrong? Plus, I was hired by Lane, remember?"

"You were hired to find her father. That's done, right?"

"I guess," I said, not looking her in the eye.

"Listen. You need to be extra careful that everything you do is on the up and up. You never know when someone is watching."

"What's that supposed to mean? I was in a reality show. I think I'd know if someone was watching me."

"I'm just cautioning you to use some common sense, okay?" Janice said, and now she wasn't looking me in the eye.

"Do you know something? Is there something you should be telling me?" I asked.

"I give up already. What is it you want me to do?" Janice asked.

"It's no big deal. Just go to dinner with me. We'll have to use your car, of course. I want to talk to a waitress who mentioned a 'Barbie and Ken' couple who had a disagreement in the restaurant."

"How does this have anything to do with Lane's personality change thing?"

"She looks like a Barbie, doesn't she? Del looks like Ken doesn't he?"

"Oh, now I get it," she said. And then with her eyebrows raised and her forehead crinkled, she said, "What the hell are you talking about?"

"I have a hunch Amy will be able to give me more information. So dinner first and then we'll create our game plan."

"Not our game plan, your game plan. I'm just going along for the dinner and entertainment. Drinks are on you too, right?"

"Right. Now are you going to tell me why RJ was at your house?"

"I like RJ. He's a talented young man. Quit nagging me."

"Well, then tell me about your illness," I said.

"Cassie, you done wore me out already," Janice said on her way back to her station.

CHAPTER 7

Janice dressed to the nines for dinner at Sunset Breeze in a floral print dress and matching shoes. I'd have sworn they were originals from the late 1940s. I left her in the hot-as-hell outdoor patio, otherwise known to her as the smoking section, with a cocktail and my cigarettes while I went to search for Amy. I found her inside near the bar.

"Amy, hey, do you have a break coming up soon? I want to talk to you for a few minutes."

"Oh, hi! What's up?"

"I'm doing some research on couples," I lied. "I remembered what you had talked about last time I was here with Vince. You know, how couples can look happy and you overhear them arguing and all."

"Oh, yeah. I remember that. Are you going to quote me and stuff?"

"Well, it's research and usually it breaks down to statistics." I said.

"Okay. I can take a break in about a half hour. Come back to the bar and we'll talk."

"Thanks, Amy. I'll see you then." I loved it when it looked like things were going my way.

On my way back to Janice, some women from the North Harbor Care and Share Club stopped me.

"We need your help."

"You do?" I'd involved myself in the club last year, at Vince's request, but it had quickly become a chore. I'd made excuses for the past six or so months when the bi-weekly meetings had come around. I couldn't imagine a reason they would need me. When I had participated and made suggestions regarding projects or fund raising methods, they had pooh-poohed them. Most of the women had bored me and that had put my imagination into overdrive, so I understood why they had turned down my ideas. What I didn't understand was why they would now ask for my help.

"What is it?" I asked.

"Did you hear what Elaine did to our bookkeeping?" Luella, a black haired woman with false eyelashes asked.

"I don't remember hearing anything," I said.

"If you had, you'd remember. The Club is broke and I'm not so sure she didn't do something illegal. We want you to look into it."

"I'm sure Elaine just made innocent mistakes." I couldn't think of who Elaine was, but I didn't think she could have been any worse at bookkeeping than the majority of women in the club.

"Now you're politically correct?" Luella asked.

We had never gotten along. Mostly because she seemed to have figured out, early on, the nice gene was missing from my DNA.

She smirked and tipped her head, obviously waiting for my usual rude response, but I ignored her. My attention was on the woman sitting next to her. A heavy-set woman with auburn hair and startling green eyes. Something about the woman bugged me. Did I know her from somewhere? Had she always been a member of North Harbor Care and Share group?

"Cassie? You going to help us?" I turned toward the woman who'd asked the question. Oh, bother. It was Rene, The Professional Organizer. That was how she introduced herself, and that was why I avoided her. "I'm working on this big project. Call me in a week or so, okay?" I said as I fled.

I made a detour to the ladies room, checked my hair, put on some lipstick, and walked back to the patio of the restaurant. Janice was in conversation with a couple at the adjacent table. She was happily chatting and had a Gin and tonic in her raised hand.

"Oh, you're just in time. I'm giving a toast to my birthday," she said.

"Your birthday?"

"Cassie, you know it's my birthday today. Come here, sit down, and celebrate with my friends, George and Ella."

"Of course I know when it's your birthday," I said, and I did know. It was in December, not July.

"Good. Good. Now, shit down and sut up. Celebrate," Janice ordered and I sat.

"Sit," I said.

"Yes, sit," she said.

I looked over at George and Ella and smiled.

The woman put out her hand. "Nice to meet you, Cassie. Actually, my name is Stella and this is George. Your mother has been telling us how well you look after her. We're sorry to hear about your father."

I shook her hand. "My mother? My father?"

Stella gave my hand an extra squeeze before letting it go. She seemed to be in her late seventies and looked sweet and proper. George looked older and had what appeared to be remnants of yesterday's lunch on his shirt and the ashes from his ultra-long cigarette on his tie. He was nodding his head and smiling. I recognized the behavior—he was hard of hearing. I could pretty much guarantee that he would smile and nod his way through the evening.

"It's our wedding anniversary. So it's a double celebration, isn't it, dear?"

I didn't know if Stella was asking George or me. We both smiled and nodded.

"Ask Ella what Georgie got her for their anniversary," Janice bellowed.

I reached over and moved two empty glasses from the edge of the table to the center. She kept a tight grip on the fresh drink in front of her.

"Mother dear, did you order our dinner?" I asked with my teeth clenched. I couldn't believe she would cause such a ruckus when she knew I was here on a case.

"Shhhh. Don't fuss at me. I ordered our drinks and we can order dinner when they come. Now ask her."

Stella looked at me, excitement sparkling in her eyes. "Oh, let me tell you. I'll be the envy of my bridge club. George gave me a gift certificate for a massage. It's with Delbert Welling. All of my friends are talking about him. He's a licensed massage therapist and he looks just like Dr. David Hayward on the soap opera All My Family. Well, except he's blond, but you know what I mean." Stella giggled.

"It's not shexshual, is it Ella?"

"Sexual," I said.

"Not at all! It's for relaxation and it's therapeutic. Don't you believe all those lonely widows who'll tell you a different story. That's all just rumors. Isn't that right, dear?" Stella said.

Again, both George and I smiled and nodded.

"You know how some women are. He's accused of

stimulating some of these women purposefully. One of them has complained to the Board, which governs massage therapists. I guess the story is that she had a little crush on him and then her son found out he was charging eighty dollars a visit and she was seeing him three times a week. Isn't that right, dear?" Stella said.

George took a longtime to think about it. Stella nudged him. He then looked up to say, "Yes, dear."

All ignored him.

"My best friend, Delores, goes there for a massage session once a week and she told me there is nothing sexual about it at all. It's a massage and healing therapy all blended together. She says she feels wonderful afterward. It's some therapy called Shiatsu," Stella continued.

"Blesh you," said Janice.

The three of us turned to her, smiled, and nodded.

Our waiter came to the table.

"Would you like to order dinner now?" he asked.

"Most definitely. Let's see, I'll have the oven roasted grouper and the house salad. Janice?"

"I'm thinking about it," she said with her face inches from the menu.

"How about if I order for you?"

"Oh, how sweet," Janice said.

"She'll have the grilled veal porterhouse and a baked potato. Sound good, Mommy Dearest?" I asked.

"That's great."

The waiter left and I looked over at Stella and George. They were being served and talking among themselves. Well, okay, Stella was talking and George was doing you know what.

I took the opportunity to get Janice's attention.

"What are you doing? You can't drink like that. I'm driving on the way home. And you lied to those people. You're not my mother and there is nothing wrong with my dad. You think they don't know you're making it all up? They can see I'm white. You're black."

Janice sucked in her breath and widened her eyes. "Oh, no. I'm black?"

"Janice, come on. Please?"

"Oh, relax. It's not every day I can go out and party. Don't spoil it. Anyway, you got shome good information didn't you?"

"Some," I said.

"Well, shome information is still information" she said.

"Oh, yeah, great information. I'm going to run right home and schedule a massage with an inner-thigh rubbing, blond haired Dr. Hayworth."

"It's Dr. David Hay*ward* from the soap opera *All My Family*. Dummy. The massage guy is Delbert, get it?"

"No, I don't get it. And for your information, there is nothing more irritating to me than a drunken person."

"Pay attention. Del and Lane. Delbert Welling, massage guy. Lane's Del is a massage guy." She had her head tilted to one side and was looking at me as if I was mentally slow.

Then I got it. "Oh my god, you're right. It must be the same guy."

"Of course I'm right."

"I found Amy. She's taking a break in a little bit and I'm meeting her in the bar," I told her.

"Oh goody."

"Would you do me a favor and keep a low profile until I'm done talking to her. Then you can party all you want. I told her I was doing research on couples and relationships. I just have a few questions for her and I don't want her to be distracted by your drunkenness."

"Blah-ditty-blah-ditty-blah."

"What was that?" I was getting a bit cranky.

Janice decided not to answer. She turned toward the view of the water and continued sipping her drink and smoking. Lighting one right after the other for the better part of a half hour until the server brought out our meals.

"Here's your dinner, ladies. Let me know if I can get you anything else." Our waiter was looking at Janice. She was holding her head up with her hand under her chin and her elbow on the table.

"Coffee in a few minutes. For both of us," I told him.

He nodded and left.

"Please don't take it upon yourself to monitor my drinking nor my behavior. It's offenshive to me," Janice said.

"Offensive," I said.

Janice looked at the plate of food. "Not at all," she said.

I threw up my hands.

While we concentrated on our meals, I realized Janice was right. I had no business telling her how to behave. I just couldn't think of a way to keep from doing it.

After polishing off my meal, I excused myself, leaving Janice to have coffee and dessert with Stella and George. Before I left, I asked Janice to meet me in the bar whenever she was ready.

Amy was at the bar when I walked in. I sat down next to her and ordered a coffee.

"I've only got a few minutes left of my break. So go ahead and ask your questions," Amy said.

"First question. Could you describe the 'Barbie and Ken' incident that you talked about before?"

"Barbie and Ken?"

"Yes, remember you mentioned the story to Vince and me the other night when we were here for dinner. You remember the happy couple thing, don't you?"

"Oh, sure." She pushed an order pad and a pencil

over to me. "Don't you need to write anything down?" she asked, when I didn't immediately take them.

"Thanks," I said.

Once I had the pencil in my hand, she began, "That was weird because it was this lady that looked like Barbie and this guy that looked like Ken. They were, you know, real lovey and stuff, and then this other Barbie came in, grabbed the Ken person, and told him it was time to go. She said to him, 'The fun is over. You need to leave her alone now.'"

"When you say 'this other Barbie,' do you mean she had blonde hair too?"

"Well, yeah, but I guess it was more like she had the same look as the other Barbie. You know, blonde hair, blue eyes, tall and slender. This one was kind of rough around the edges though. I guess what I mean is, she looked like what my anal-retentive mom calls a coarse person. You know, a little too much makeup, flimsy-looking discount-store clothes, that type of thing." Amy said.

I nodded and drew a doodle on the order pad.

"Afterward, we were all talking about how everyone has their twin in the world, and how some guys always go for the same looks. You know what I mean? A guy could be divorced four times, and all of his ex-wives look the same."

"What did the Ken guy do when she grabbed him?" I asked.

"He was pissed, but he tried to hide it. I could tell though. He had this vein on his forehead that stuck out and he kept clenching his jaw. My dad's like that when he's mad at me. I think it's funny."

"What did Barbie number one do?"

"She mostly just stared at the other Barbie. It was the fat older lady that made a lot of noise."

"What kind of noise?"

"Whimpering noises. Like a puppy dog or something."

"Then what?"

"This Ken guy, he tried to sweet talk her and tell her to calm down."

"The fat lady? And the first Barbie just sat there?"

"She was, you know, embarrassed like. She tried to say something and they both snarled at her and told her to stay out of it."

"Who do you mean when you say 'they'? Who snarled at her?"

"I mean Ken and the fat older lady eating dinner with them."

"So then what happened? Did they leave or what?"

"No. Ken grabbed the arm of the second Barbie and walked her outside. Barbie number one just sat there and I think she was crying a bit. The fat woman was bawling her eyes out. When Ken came back, he went over to Barbie and pulled her out of her chair and hugged her, rubbed her back, and whispered in her ear. The fat woman cried louder until Ken went over to her and calmed her down. Then they just continued on all happy and finished their meal and had a couple drinks."

"Do you know any of their real names?"

"No. Oh, wait. Hey, why don't you just ask your old man? I mean he did stop and talk to the chick when she was waiting for Ken to come back."

"My old man? Vince? Are you sure it was Vince?" My heart did a flip-flop as I waited for Amy's answer. When she shrugged and looked uncomfortable, I didn't need an answer.

Trust was such a fragile thing. Just a hint of suspicion could tear down a relationship. I didn't want to feel the way I was feeling about Vince. Why didn't he tell me about being in here when Amy brought this up before? The woman had to have been upset and probably was crying. Did he comfort her? Did he hold her? Whatever he did, I knew it wasn't something he would just forget. He chose not to tell me.

"Anyway, I did hear the Ken guy yelling at Barbie number two when they were in the hallway on the way out the door. He said something like, I've had enough, and he called her Kris or something." Amy bit her lower lip and looked up at the ceiling before continuing. "No. I'm not sure what the name was, but it maybe started with a 'K.' Sorry."

"No worries," I said and motioned for her to continue.

"Then he told her she was being a stupid bitch and that she should just wait and see how things worked out. Here's the real weird thing. I walked to the hallway to check out what was happening and I saw him kissing her. She tried pulling away at first, but I don't know if she just gave in or if he was forcing her, but then it looked like a mutual kiss."

"Did she say anything to him after?" I asked.

"She was saying something like, you know you can't do this. Oh, and she said, um, something about his mother. Well, really I didn't understand everything she was saying because by then she was really crying and shaking. I mean she looked wacko," Amy said.

I jumped in my chair when Janice slid into a bar stool next to me and sipped from my coffee cup.

Amy and Janice made nice for a minute and then Amy said she had to go back to work.

"Thanks so much. I appreciate your help." I ripped the top page from the order pad, put it in my purse, and handed the pad to her.

Janice took another sip from my coffee, and then she

made a face and added a gallon of cream and a pallet of sugar.

"Ready to party?" I asked.

"I'm a little pooped out now."

"How about coffee while we make our plan."

"Your plan, not mine," Janice muttered.

"You want a shot of Amaretto in it?" I asked with a smile.

"Just coffee is fine," she said and yawned.

While we drank our coffee in silence, I made a plan to question Stacy, the tattoo artist at The Big Prick who'd tattooed the willowy blonde-haired woman. It seemed odd to have two similar appearing women with the same tattoo. Stacy had to have some remembrance of the woman. Anything would be more that I had.

CHAPTER 8

Do you understand the concept of a fixed budget?" Janice asked as we were on the way to her appointment for a massage.

The rental was a convertible and Janice had a polka dotted scarf tied tight under her chin. It had not stopped her from making remarks about the wind messing her hair.

"Sure I do. As I've already told you, I'll expense the massage off. You schmooze with the people in the waiting room, okay. Ask them questions about the therapy and the therapist. You know, like how often they get a massage, does their insurance cover it, and their feelings about the therapist. Get the massage and pay attention to the therapist and his attitude and how he treats his staff," I said.

"You have to do this, don't you?" Janice said. "You'd fall down and die if you didn't have some way to get involved in someone's business. That's why you're a PI. You can listen to all this stuff, and really feel like you're getting the goods on people."

"That's what PIs do, and I'm not going to feel bad about it," I told her.

"I don't care. You are a business owner now. Think

about The Big Prick. You need to worry about blending your jobs. Ain't going to do anyone any good if you start blending them. What are you thinking, going in there and interrogating poor Stacey? In front of customers no less. Our clients don't need to think you're some kind of cop," she said.

I blew a kiss at her. It was the only way to handle her when she had a hangover. "Probably right. Especially since Stacey didn't have much to say other than the woman who got the tattoo was pretty, blonde, and nice. Whoop-dee-do. I already knew all that," I said.

Janice glared.

"Anyway, I have an appointment with the guy to talk about alternative therapies, and when you're finished with your appointment, you can take the car and go wait for me over at the outdoor cafe downtown. I'll walk over to the cafe when I'm finished and we can have lunch. How's that for a relaxing day?" I asked.

"You're not the one that has to deal with some soap opera star look-alike putting his hands all over you," Janice snapped.

"Look, I thought you'd enjoy a massage. It's not 'shexshual' remember?" I said.

"I believe the word is sexual. And, maybe that's my problem. Maybe then I could look forward to a massage."

"Too much information."

"Oh, there's more," she said.

"I'm begging you to keep it to yourself."

⋍⋍⋍

Pulling off my sandals, I spent my hour at the beach, looking for shark's teeth. I walked into the warm water and sifted the sand to my heart's content.

When I drove back, Janice was waiting under a palm tree at the edge of the parking lot.

"How did it go?" I asked while tossing the keys to the car.

"He took a lot of time asking questions which are none of his business. I ended up telling him I was poor and at the mercy of Social Security. I told him a friend paid for my visit. He didn't have many more questions after he heard that," she said.

"Were you able to talk to anyone in the waiting room?"

"Yes. They all love him. That is one smooth man. Watch your pocketbook. He could charm it right out of your hand."

"Speaking of pocketbooks, which by the way, no one calls their purses pocketbooks anymore, here's my credit card. Start a tab and I'll be there as soon as I can for lunch." I could tell by the look on her face she was going to argue about the credit card. "Shut up and take it. I'll expense the lunch too. Don't quibble about it okay."

"Where am I going?" she asked.

"Anywhere downtown. I'll find you," I said.

In the reception area, I signed my name to a clip-board with a pencil tied to it. I waved at the receptionist who had a phone tucked between her ear and her shoulder, and I sat in a chair in the waiting room.

The waiting room looked like a social gathering. Chatting over the top of each other were two were mid-dle-aged men and three active-looking women in their seventies and eighties. These women weren't wearing the typical, heavily embroidered short set that seems to be the outfit de rigueur for most women in North Harbor. They were wearing dresses, and more surprising yet, some had on panty hose. These women were out to impress.

That's just one reason why RJ stood out. I sat next to him.

"What the fuck are you doing here?" I asked in a whisper.

RJ continued messing around with his phone, not looking up. "Huh?"

"Ms. Cruise?"

There he was. It was Del—Lane's Del.

"Good morning. Nice to meet you. I'm Delbert Welling."

"Cassie Cruise." I stuck out my hand to shake his.

He took my hand and placed it between his hands. He patted it, gave it a quick squeeze, and let it go.

"I assume your receptionist explained why I made an appointment to see you?" I asked.

"Yes, she did. I'm happy to be of assistance in your research, although the pharmaceutical industry might not be so happy with your findings. Come this way, so we can talk privately." He took my elbow and led me down a hall to a room arranged as a break room.

"Would you like something to drink?" he asked. "We have coffee, tea, and soda."

"Coffee would be great, just black, please."

"You know, you look familiar. Have we met before?" He put the Styrofoam cup in front of me and sat in the chair across from me.

"I think we have a mutual friend. I think you are Lane's Del. Am I right?" I raised the cup and took a sip. It smelled scorched and tasted of hot Styrofoam. "I'm her neighbor, across the way."

"Oh, yes. I remember you now. We've never officially met, just waved across the street. Great neighborhood, isn't it?" He was smiling at me, but his green eyes didn't sparkle and his demeanor had changed to something close to a used car salesperson who found out his customer had bad credit.

"Yes, it is. How is Lane doing? Is she handling the stress of moving and getting settled in okay?" I asked.

He scratched his neck. "She's fine, doing well."

"Are you all moved in?"

"Not totally," he said, erratically tapping on the table.

"And the old girlfriend thing? Have you heard any more about her? Is Lane dealing with that okay?" I asked.

He stopped tapping. "Again, Lane's fine. No need to worry. She's put it behind her and everyone else should too."

"Tell her she doesn't need to feel bad about my car. We all know it was mistaken for your car. Tell her I said to come over and chat with me some afternoon soon, would you? School starts in a few weeks and then she'll be too busy." I kept my eyes on him and watched a bit of the color drain out of his face.

He licked his lips, and then suddenly clapped his hands together. "Your theory is incredibly far-fetched. Anyway, we'd better get down to business. As you noticed, there are people waiting for me."

"I did see that, and one of my questions is related to that. Is this a typical day? How can one person do it?"

"It's getting to be typical. I offer a great service. But I believe some of the people out there have brought friends or relatives to wait with them. They're not all waiting for therapy and I do have staff members to help out."

"But they can't do the actual massage, can they? You have to be licensed in Florida, right?"

"Oh, definitely you have to be licensed. No, they can't do the massage, but you have no idea how much paperwork and filing and scheduling is involved."

"How long have you been licensed?" I asked.

"Going on two years in Florida," he said.

"And before that?" I asked.

"Before that?" He raised his fist to cover his mouth, cleared his throat, and then crossed his arms over his chest. "Before is a whole different story and we don't have time for it today," he said, and again began tapping on the table.

Liar, liar, pants on fire. I recognized the telltale signs of lying. An instructor covered it in a Life and Detection course I took. I wished I could remember what you were supposed to do to drag the truth out of a liar.

"Tell me about the types of therapies you offer, and are they considered to be a replacement for medicine or drugs in any way?" I asked, mostly to stop him from drumming his fingers on the table.

"Good questions. I'll go over it briefly because of the time constraint, but before you leave, ask the lady at the front desk for some brochures."

"Does the lady at the front desk have a name?" I felt my face heat up. *How rude.* I'd been the "lady at the front desk" a time or two in my life, so I knew what it felt like to be a position without a name.

"What? Oh, yes. She's my mom, just started a week ago. You can call her Tillie," he said.

"Nice of her to help out. Lane told me you fired your office manager."

"Lane sure is chatty." He knocked on the table and laughed. "Momma's having a little trouble, but she'll catch on. I hope. Anyway, to answer your questions, massage therapy is a holistic, drug-free healing art, which recognizes and incorporates the scientific approach to healing of the West with the energy-based, intuitive, approach of the East. We do deep tissue massage and a method of massage therapy called Shiatsu." I looked behind me. Surely, someone was holding prompts for him to read. "Shiatsu is a traditional hands-on Japanese heal-ing therapy, is a deeply relaxing experience, and regular Shiatsu sessions help to prevent the buildup of stress in our daily lives." He continued talking as he stood and walked toward the door. "So, there it is in a nut shell," he said once he reached the doorway.

"How much do you charge? And how does this differ from a sensual-type massage?" I remained sitting out of pure orneriness.

"I charge anywhere from $80.00 to $125.00 a session. It depends on the massage and the individual. My work is top quality and I need compensation, right? I'm sure you understand. What is your line of work again, Ms. Cruise?"

"I'm a freelance investigator, and I own The Big Prick," I told him.

"That guy, Vince?" he asked.

"No. No. No. Vince isn't a prick. Why would you think that? I'm talking about my tattoo shop," I said.

He nodded. "Oh. Okay, a tattoo shop. Then you do understand. Time is valuable."

"Hey, how do you know Vince?" I asked.

"Business. He sold his house to Lane, remember?" he said.

"I couldn't forget that, believe me. Just didn't realize you two had met."

I squelched the urge to ask him for more details of their meeting. I needed to stick to the case that brought me here.

"Now as to your second question. Massage therapy focuses on muscles, while erotic or sensual massage would focus on the skin. It's more like foreplay. Nice, but not something you should expect from a Licensed MT. All set?" Del asked.

I stood and strolled toward the door. "What happens when someone crosses the line?"

"I really don't know." He again took my elbow and led me out through the hallway. This time his hand was like a steel clamp.

"Oh, one more quick question." I wrenched my arm from his hand and smiled at him. "Sorry, I know you're busy, but who determines how often to schedule an insured person for therapy? What is the norm, once a week, twice a month?"

"That is determined by me, with input from the client." He took a file folder from the ledge next to the door and maneuvered me out ahead of him with his hand. "Here we are. Hope I've been helpful. Have a good day."

I turned to make sure he wasn't going to kick me in the rear as I left and saw he was no longer focusing on me.

"Mr. Cranston. Good day. Come on back with me."

His smile was big for Mr. Cranston, aka, RJ, and bigger yet for the little old lady in the floral print halter dress who blushed and batted her lashes when Del came near. He rubbed her arm as he passed by. I thought she was going to faint. I thought I was going to puke.

I gave RJ the evil eye as he scooted by me to follow Del into the hallway.

At the reception area, I knocked on the plexi-glass to get the woman at the front desk's attention.

So this is Del's mom. Lane's future mother-in-law.

Tillie was a rotund woman with three wobbly chins. She held up a finger and pointed to the phone at her ear. Her profile looked familiar, but I couldn't place whom she reminded me of other than if she lost a hundred pounds she would look like an overweight Maureen O'Hara. She replaced the phone and opened the sliding window.

"I'm sorry. I just love these people. They're all so sweet." She sniffed and reached for a tissue. Her hair was auburn and softly styled. She had dark green eyes and beautiful skin.

She also looked highly excitable.

"What people? Who do you love?" I looked around the waiting area.

"Everyone. I just love people. All the clients here." She nodded at the waiting room. There were tears in her eyes and she had her hand over her heart.

"Oh," I said.

"Do you need another appointment with Dr. Welling?" Her voice was quavering and she let out a ragged breath that caused her chins to wobble double time.

"He's not a doctor, is he?" I asked.

Her eyes popped open wide. "No, I guess not really, but I call him that." She put her hand to the side of her mouth, looked from side to side, and whispered, "And, in case you didn't notice, the ladies all think he's that gorgeous doctor on TV."

"Is that so?" I said.

"Yes. That's so," she said in an overstrung voice.

"Tillie, Del told me I could get some brochures from you. He also told me I could talk to you about the practice. Do you have time to answer some questions?" I crossed my fingers behind my back. "He said you were very helpful."

"He said that? He told you I could answer questions?" She narrowed her eyes and tilted her head to the side.

As if I would lie.

"Yes, he did. Could you tell me how many people are on his staff?"

Tillie released a big breath of air through her lips, and then said, "There's me and a file clerk that comes in for the afternoons. Her name is Marisa. She gets all the patient files ready for the next day."

"Are you typically this busy? It seems like a lot of

people waiting at one time. Doesn't each session take about an hour?"

She inhaled a theatrical breath, grabbed a tissue, and answered, "I did that. I messed up the schedule, and that's why I love everyone here so much. They're being very patient with me, even the clients who have to wait extra long." She sniffed into her tissue for a bit and then set it on the desk in front of her. All the while, her eyes stayed on me waiting for a reaction.

Then I remembered why she was familiar. I had watched her shoplift on the day Janice and I went shopping, but on that day, she'd had an odd burgundy color of hair. And, oh my god, she was the green-eyed woman sitting next to Luella at Sunset. More important, she was a thief. I bet the apple didn't fall too far from the tree.

I felt disgust and I needed to hide it. I panicked and forced a smile through a clenched jaw.

She watched my face for a second or two, and then she honked her nose into another tissue, leaned over, and reached around her girth to the side of the computer monitor. She grabbed a few brochures from a pile, and stuck them out the window.

I used my thumb and pointer finger to take them from her and dropped them into my bag. "Thanks. Can you handle one more question?" I asked while pumping the sanitizer from the container on the counter into my hands.

"Quickly, please. I have to straighten out the schedule for tomorrow," she said in a new and efficient manner.

"Who does the insurance billing?"

"I'm just learning," she said.

"Who did it before you?" I asked.

"The previous office manager."

"What was her name?" I leaned in closer, hoping to encourage her to confide in me.

"I don't remember," Tillie said and scooted her chair an inch or so away from the reception counter.

"Have you met Lane?"

She raised her chins and stared. "Of course I've met Lane. Why do you ask?"

"How about Del's ex-girlfriend? Does she ever pop in to see Del?"

"I don't know. Sorry, I have to get busy now." The tips of her ears suddenly turned red-rimmed and there were new bright dots of color in the center of her cheeks. She swallowed three times and looked out into the waiting room.

"She hasn't harassed him at work? Wasn't she the office manager he fired?" I asked.

Tillie turned back to me with tears in the corner of her eyes. She raised her voice. "Why are you asking all of these questions? I don't have any more time for questions."

"What did you say the afternoon file clerk's name was? Marisa what?" I quickly asked, realizing I was pushing it and she could get overly emotional again. If that happened, I feared the people in the waiting room would come to her aid. They were now watching the two of us. I smiled in their direction, but got glares instead of smiles in return.

"Johnson. Good bye now."

She shut the window and put the phone to her ear. I debated on knocking on the window she so rudely shut in my face. Instead, I left and didn't tell her about the moist green object she had hanging out of her left nostril.

I really didn't like her and I felt sorry for Lane having to deal with her. Del and Tillie were a shifty set.

I found myself grateful for the three-block walk to the outdoor café. I wanted to be alone and walk off my bad mood. Unlike Tillie, I didn't pretend to be a people lover. I find people to be aggravating most times, and I include myself in that group.

Why was I involving myself in this? In what exactly was I involving myself? Del was a jerk and probably unethical. If not, why would he put his shoplifting ditz of a mother in his office?

Every day, clients and patients paid for the privilege of being crammed into a waiting room to wait for their allotted fifteen minutes of service. It wasn't anything new. It was expected. Whatever Del was up to involved more than allowing Tillie to overbook.

Del, in my opinion, ranked damned high on the overall sleaze scale. He was smooth, though. I could almost understand why a young person such as Lane fell for him.

Tillie didn't seem to be Lane's type of person. Or was she? Lane seemed enamored enough with Del, she would probably do anything he asked of her. And anything Del asked of her could be something such as liking his mother.

Why did I care? Really, what was it I cared about? Lane? That would be honorable, but to be truthful, I knew she and I would never become more than neighbors. We were very different people.

So, no, I didn't feel any great connection with Lane.

What I cared about was that somehow, someone was getting away with something. Somebody killed someone, torched my car, and walked away without getting into trouble over it.

I guessed that was it. I was just a big, overgrown tattletale. I was all about finding out what someone did wrong and telling on him or her.

෴

Janice was waiting for me at a table under the cafe's

large, green awning. She had a smile on her face and she was looking off into the park across the avenue. The crepe myrtle trees were in bloom along with hibiscus of every color. A breeze from the Gulf drifted across the table and lifted the paper napkin on her lap. Without taking her eyes off the beauty of the park, she caught hold of the napkin before it blew away into litter land. She turned as I sat down opposite her.

I wanted to talk about how much of a jerk I thought Del was. I also didn't want to ruin Janice's peaceful mood.

"Hey," I said.

Janice blinked and looked toward the street. "Are we going to work?" she said.

I laughed. "That can't be what you were thinking about. You had the most idyllic look on your face."

"No, I wasn't wasting my thoughts on that," she said and lowered her head.

"The massage was good for you, wasn't it?"

She looked up. "I'm not sure."

I groaned, irritated by her lack of enthusiasm. "I think it can be really therapeutic. Can you imagine how many of the elderly aren't touched for months at a time? Just being touched is therapeutic in itself, you know," I said and decided not to bring up the fact I had done some research regarding the healing aspects of touch. I didn't want to sound like a know-it-all. Again.

"I bet it is," Janice said.

"They come down here to Florida to retire, to live a stress free life in the sunshine. The rest of their families are in another part of the country working toward the very same thing. All of the sudden they're on their own. No hugs from the grandkids, no kiss on the cheek from the kids for comfort. That's why I hate it that he's playing with people's emotions and trying to get rich off of them."

"Was it that obvious to you?" Janice asked.

"Well, I'm going to see if he's had any complaints. The Florida Department of Health has a web site and a log of discipline reports. Didn't that Stella lady at the restaurant say something about him having a complaint made against him?"

"Who?"

"Okay. Ella. But didn't she say that?" I didn't want to correct her about Stella's name. I was beginning to feel as if we couldn't have a conversation without a disagreement.

"She did say something about that, I think." Janice appeared to concentrate on something over my head.

"Ready to order lunch? You need to perk up." I waved at the waiter, feeling concerned about Janice's demeanor. "You okay?" I asked, and then noting her bloodshot, teary eyes, I remembered the amount of alcohol she'd guzzled the night before. "No booze for you today."

She smiled but it didn't reach her eyes. "Okay."

I wanted to ask her if she felt booze was worth feeling the way she was feeling, but some things just aren't worth arguing about, I decided. And most likely, for the same reason, I forgot all about wanting to ask Janice what she knew about RJ. And had she seen him in the therapist's waiting room?

CHAPTER 9

I finished a draft of the pharmaceutical research project, attached the document into an e-mail, and sent it off to the pharmaceutical company for review. I printed off a hard copy and filed it in my cabinet. It was always a good feeling to finish a project, even better when you could look forward to a decent sized check afterward.

Instead of logging off the computer, I went to the Florida Department of Health web site and clicked on the Medical Quality Assurance link where I learned that every twenty days the agency ran a discipline report. All licensed healthcare practitioners regulated by the Department of Health's Medical Quality Assurance division, who have had a discipline in that period, were in the report. The final disposition, listed in the report, showed the highest penalty taken by the board or department.

It took only a few seconds to find Delbert Welling, Lic. MT.

Listed under the column heading Action Taken was the phrase "Obligations Imposed, other major penalty imposed."

There was a notice at the end of the report stating that if further information was wanted regarding the complaint and the final order, you could write to the Department of Health and request a copy.

Oh, man. That could take days. I wrote a short request and placed it in the pile for the next day's snail mail. For the time being, it felt good to know the Department of Health had disciplined Del.

In celebration, I grabbed the ragged afghan my mother made for me years ago, shut the blinds, turned on the air, popped *Shadow of a Doubt* into the player, and settled into the couch.

It turned out *Shadow of a Doubt* was not a good movie to fall asleep to. I woke up with a shaky, scared feeling around midnight. Glancing around the lanai and seeing nothing out of place calmed me a bit. There didn't seem to be a reason to be afraid, all seemed right in the house. I flipped the television to a local news station and sat up to watch the weather report. Its normalcy further calmed me.

I shut off the television and admired the clear night, the moon big and low in the sky. Shadows of the palm trees played on the white walls. Then a shadow moved and turned into a stretched out human shape.

Someone was in my back yard.

I went to the desk drawer and pulled out my gun and a large flash light. I slid open the lanai door, stuck my head out, and aimed the light around the pool area and back property.

Nothing moved or made a sound. I came back in, secured the lock on the door, and went to the living room window to make sure that nothing outside had been set on fire. Everything looked normal and I considered going to bed, but checked out the front window one last time.

Then I saw RJ walking along the sidewalk. The familiar duck walk gave him away. I opened the front door, stuck my head out and hollered.

"Hey, RJ."

He turned toward the sound of my voice.

"Come here," I said.

"Hey, Ms. Cruise," he said once he'd moved to the walkway in front of the porch.

"What are you doing on my street? You didn't bring that camera guy, did you?"

"Nunyor," he said.

"Huh?"

"Nunyor business."

"Were you out back? I saw someone out back of my house. I believe that would be my business," I told him.

"I took the shortcut through the golf course. It ends at the fifth hole, but you can call it your backyard if you want," he said and turned to leave.

"Wait. Where you headed?" I asked.

"Why do you want to know? This is a free country, ain't it? I figure I can go down any street I want. Right?"

"I've seen you here twice in a matter of days and I never saw you in this neighborhood before," I said.

"Before what?"

"Before someone freaking stuffed a body in the trunk of my car and set it on fire." I was all out of patience.

"Yeah, that's fucked up," he said and visibly shivered as if the thought grossed him out.

"How'd you hear about it?"

"A friend lives down there a ways." He pointed toward the cul-de-sac a block to the east.

"Yeah? Who's your friend?" I asked.

"Nunyor," he said and walked away. When he'd walked ten feet or so to the corner, he yelled out, "See you at the shop."

"Why not? I see you everywhere else," I yelled in return.

He shrugged. Then his mention of The Big Prick reminded me of something I'd wanted to ask him for days. "Wait. RJ, please come back."

He turned and stood under the streetlight.

"Please?"

He walked up to the house as I waited on the porch.

"Come in, okay?" I asked when he stood in front of me.

He shrugged and then followed me inside. "Hey, put that away," he said when he saw the gun.

"Sorry." I went to the desk and tucked it back into the drawer. "Want something to drink? Coffee?" I asked when I returned.

He wrinkled his nose in disgust and shook his head. "My friend is expecting me."

"Have a seat." Because I needed something from him, I realized I had to be polite.

"My friend is expecting me," he repeated.

"Okay, I just want to ask you if you remember someone who came into the shop."

"Lots of somebodys come into the shop," he said.

"There was a blonde lady that came in. Stacy gave her a tat. It was a unique one—at least I thought so at the time. Female drama masks. Do you remember her?"

"No," he said and started for the door.

"Wait. Hang on a minute. She was pretty and you stared at her and—"

"I don't remember no blonde lady. They all look alike to me, anyway," he said.

"Blondes?" I asked.

"Yep," he said.

"That's stupid," I said.

"Whatever. I'm sayin' I don't remember."

"What about the paint on the windows? Happen to remember who did that?"

"You accusing me of something?" RJ asked.

"You bet I am. I think you know exactly who did that job on the windows. But right now I want to talk about the lady that got the tattoo."

"Tough luck for you, cuz I don't feel like talkin' to you. I sure don't remember nothing about a blonde and I don't know nothing about the damn windows," he said as he walked through the doorway. "See ya."

Frustrated, I locked up and went to bed. I tossed around and re-plumped my pillow enough that I realized I wasn't going to fall asleep. So instead, I went to the kitchen and put on a pot of coffee.

While it brewed, I walked into the dining room and, this time when I looked out the window, lights radiating from Lane's house across the street caught my attention. Her silhouette showed through the filmy drapes outlining the picture window of her living room. I watched as she opened the curtain an inch or so and looked out onto her front lawn. Then she turned quickly and just as quickly raised her hand and slapped the face of what appeared to be a man's silhouette now standing next to her.

Maybe she needs help, I thought as I headed for the lanai. 'No. *You're just being nosy*,' I heard Rachel's voice say. She was right, of course.

I went out the back way and circled around to the front where I stayed in the shadow of the trees as much as possible, avoiding the streetlights. I stopped when I reached the bushes in Lane's front yard. From there, I watched as the garage door opened and Del walked to his backed-in car. The interior light flashed on and I saw the frustrated and worried look on his face when he sat in the driver's seat.

He didn't start the car immediately, but put his hands to his face and rubbed them up and down in the way that some do when they're tired.

Then he sped down the street. I didn't stop watching

until he turned the corner and I could no longer see the lights of his car.

I hunched down and ran to the side of Lane's window. Looking through the small opening between the sheer draperies into Lane's living room, I saw she was sitting on her couch. I watched as she arranged cards on the glass-topped dinghy that served as her coffee table. It seemed to be a game of solitaire and the look on her face suggested she was winning. I was amazed at the smug and contented picture she made after slapping Del.

I tried hard not to judge her for being physical with the person she claimed to love. I was not innocent to the mean and hard side of life. I had resorted to slapping, and once in my younger days, I had been slapped. It's ugly. There was no getting around it. One thing I could guarantee was that I had never sat down and calmly played a game of cards afterward.

I waited for a few seconds to see if she would do anything interesting, but when she continued with her card playing, I returned to my house.

Once inside, I grabbed a cup of coffee. While drinking it, I thought about her action or reaction, whichever it might have been, possibly to something Del had done or said. I hadn't pegged her as a physical person. I had thought she would have used other means to get her way or get her point across to others. But what I saw definitely changed my mind. Who knew what another was capable of doing?

Returning to the lanai, I logged into a background check web site. Then I did a skip trace type of search on Lane Somers. As I had already suspected, nothing of value came up. She had good credit. She didn't have a criminal record. She had lived most of her life in Scranton with her parents.

I did find a list of a few of her hometown friends and neighbors, and printed out the information.

I wouldn't be able to figure out Del or Crystal's role in the car fire until I figured out Lane. No matter how I rolled it around in my head and no matter that no one else seemed to notice, I knew she wasn't what she appeared to be. Some discreet questioning of her neighbors and former coworkers was definitely in order. I also would have liked a chance to talk to Detective Tucker who was quoted in the newspaper article I'd found regarding the accident between Lane's parents.

What was Lane hiding from? I just couldn't believe a happy, well-adjusted twenty-eight year old would plop themselves down in a neighborhood like this.

I had told Lane I wouldn't be traipsing around the country, and when I said it, I meant it. I hated traveling to strange places, trying to figure out directions to this place or the other. There was no navigation system without its fault. I'd tried most and realized the majority of the problem lay with me, and I couldn't seem to fix it.

In a momentary lapse of common sense, knowing something bad would happen, I logged into my online travel account and booked a flight to Scranton. Lane's hometown.

CHAPTER 10

The next morning, as on any other Monday, I kept The Big Prick closed. So even though I had only a few hours of sleep, I jumped out of bed in an energetic mood and did my laps in the pool. After coffee, I turned on my CD player, put in Aretha Franklin, and did forty minutes of water aerobics.

My phone rang as I headed in to shower.

"This is Cassie."

"Don't hang up. We should, I mean, I would like to meet with you. There's something I need to talk to you about—"

I recognized the voice. "Tiffany? Are you kidding me? What are you thinking? I'm not talking to you," I said through clenched teeth, and then disconnected.

I was ready on time for golf with Janice, and I allowed her to give me pointers on my game while I pretended to take her seriously. Rather than listening to Janice, I was reliving *Cruising* and remembering how I'd publicly thrown a tantrum whenever Tiffany came near. That, and every other mistake I'd made in my life thus far, rolled through my head like a never-ending movie in which I was the embarrassingly untalented leading lady. Bitterness as an art form.

It didn't matter, I couldn't learn.

After nine holes, instead of spending our usual hour or so in the club bar, Janice drove us back to the house in the golf cart. The time was around one in the afternoon. We intended to lounge around the pool and drink margaritas for the rest of the afternoon and later in the evening convince Vince to come over and barbecue steaks for us.

It wasn't until I walked up to my door and turned to look across the street that I noticed Vince's truck parked in the grass next to Lane's garage. *What the hell?* I stood on my porch and thought about going over to find out what he was doing. Instead, I went inside and waited for him to come to me and explain why he was at Lane's house. *It's all innocent. Don't make an ass of yourself.*

The house was quiet and I paced back and forth in the kitchen, feeling antsy and nervous. Janice came into the house. "Vince said to tell you he'd see you tonight." She immediately walked to the spare room to change into her bathing suit.

When she came out, I stopped her before she went out to the pool. "When did you talk to him?" I asked.

She looked around the room. "Who?"

"Vince. Didn't you just say he'd be coming by to-night?"

"Sure," she said.

"Did you see him across the street?"

"Why?" she asked.

"Go to the pool." I waved her on without answering her. She took Vince's side on everything. To her he could do no wrong.

"Hurry up. Go change into your suit," Janice said. She picked up her phone and went out to the pool area.

While I made margaritas, I thought how strange it was that Vince chose now to be at Lane's home. He knew it was normal for Janice and me to be at the golf course for at least nine holes and then hang out in the club afterward for lunch and drinks. Usually we were gone a total of three or more hours. It seemed he'd purposely chosen a time when he thought I'd be away to go to Lane's.

Why would he do that?

He wasn't the type to double-dip, at least I'd never thought so before.

I put my old standby black halter suit on and walked out to join Janice.

"Cheers." Janice and I clinked our glasses together, took sips of our drinks. She smoked and I abstained.

Snubbing out her cigarette, she jumped into the pool. I picked up Janice's phone and dialed the number to Del's office.

"Hello," a sweet sounding voice answered.

"May I speak to Marisa Johnson?"

"Speaking," she said.

"Hi, Marisa. This is Janice Lily," I flinched when I realized Janice would scold me for using her name. "I had a massage scheduled with Mr. Welling, and—"

"Oh, I'm sorry. No one is here right now. I wouldn't have answered the phone, but I forgot to switch it over to the answering service, and, anyway, I'm not supposed to touch the schedule. There's been some sort of fuss about the schedule."

"What was the fuss?" I was just making conversation. That's what the nosy do, make and encourage conversations that have the potential for rewarding you with juicy tidbits of information.

"Mr. Welling said the schedule needs to be refined. He said he didn't want any more complaints. I didn't ask for details, because that's not my job anyway. I just do the filing and stuff. I wish Crystal would come back."

"Crystal? Did you say Crystal?"

"Crystal. She's not here right now; she's on vacation

or something. I don't really know when she's due back in town, but I wish she would hurry," she said.

"Oh, yes. Crystal. What's her last name again?" Hey, if it works once it should work again. There aren't that many people named Crystal. It had to be the Crystal the police were looking for, the ex-girlfriend.

"Evans. Anything else? 'Cuz I got a lot to get done here, ma'am. I could maybe take a message and leave it for Tillie if you need to reschedule. Just be warned, she's new and it seems to be taking some time for her to catch on," Marisa said.

"No, but thanks for your time. I'll call in the morning."

Janice was back in the chair, looking at me.

"You won't believe who Del's assistant is, or was," I said excitedly.

"Jeez, I'm not deaf. It's Crystal. She's the one that was bothering Lane and Del, right?"

"Right. What does it mean? He had to have known she would be a problem and fired her. Don't you think? Why isn't he telling everyone he fired her instead of saying she's on vacation or out of town? He's hiding something."

"Big deal. So he fired her and isn't telling everyone about it."

"Look, I've got to get this straight in my mind. Let me talk it out. Lane meets Del through the Internet. They have their home town of Scranton in common, and they hit it off right away. Lane decides, well, mostly Lane, going by the e-mail of hers I've read—I know it was wrong, so don't look at me that way—decides Del is the man for her and moves to Florida. He knows Lane is coming to Florida and encouraged it or at least agreed to it."

Taking a drink of my margarita, I continued thinking aloud. "Meanwhile, Crystal is working for Del, is maybe infatuated with him, and maybe thinks they have a special relationship, and maybe they did. Del has to tell Crystal at some point Lane is coming down to Florida and let her know he is involved with Lane. It doesn't sit well with Crystal. Crystal follows them and harasses them. So even though Crystal has helped him get his practice up and running, Del fires her. Crystal acts out by setting fire to Del's car; only it's my car. Makes sense so far, doesn't it?" I said.

"If you take away the dead person," Janice said.

I thought it through. "You're right. That doesn't make sense at all. Why would Crystal kill someone? What would she gain from that?"

"No, it doesn't make sense. That kind of behavior shouldn't make sense. These young people watch too many soap operas on TV, see too much on the internet, and play too many computer games. They think it's okay to have affairs with their sister's husband, have an abortion once a year, and marry someone out of anger, and so on and so on. Someone dies and miraculously come back the next season. It's like you and your damn movies. Those things rot your brain. So, no, it doesn't make sense to me." Janice picked up her margarita and took a long swallow.

"I don't think you can compare television to classic movies."

"I guess I wouldn't know. You'd be the expert."

"Did you know Lane likes soap operas?" I asked.

"I could tell by looking at her."

She ignored me, put her swimming cap on, and jumped into the pool. I raised my voice and continued.

"The problem is, I mean, what I can't figure out is, where is Crystal? I had a client once who had a stalker. So I did some research and came to know that a stalker or a person who behaves the way I believe Crystal behaved is not going to just go away. Violence is most likely going to happen when there is a rejection or a betrayal, real or imagined. That would explain the car fire, but would it go so far as murder? And what could be next?"

I heard Janice mumble something that sounded like, "You and your research."

"What? Did you say something?"

"I said I need to go to church," she yelled and flipped under the water.

"Stalkers do need acknowledgment, even negative, that's how they continue to feel connected to the person they are infatuated with. I think she'll be back for more." I looked at Janice.

She was in the deep end of the pool, doing some sort of water ballet.

"Are you listening?"

She laughed at me. "Barely."

"Fine. I'll remember this," I said. "Next time you need someone to talk to, don't come here and try bending my ear."

"Don't pout. You know white people's skin breaks up and cracks when they make those faces. Freshen my drink and I'll be right by your side listening with everything I have in me," she said and added in a lower voice, "which ain't much."

She did work her way to the steps in the shallow end, so I went inside, brought out the pitcher of margaritas, and filled her glass.

"I'm going to ask something of you," Janice said and now she was serious.

I felt my stomach tightening up and my jaw clenching. Already, I made up my mind to dig my feet in and I didn't know what she was going to ask of me. This wasn't a conscious decision. I guess it's part of my makeup. I didn't know where it comes from other than genetics. I did know stubbornness can cause problems in relationships, so I forced myself to relax.

"I'm willing to consider anything you ask of me." I felt proud of myself for saying it, and I tried to be sincere.

"I was thinking about family and how we act as though we have all the time in world, you know, to see our families. Well, jeez, we really don't have all the time in the world. So, anyway, I would like to go see my sisters. They're all meeting in West Virginia at my baby sister's horse ranch. But I don't feel comfortable driving all that way by myself."

"And?"

"I thought maybe you would fly up there with me. West Virginia is so pretty and you'd love the horses and the ranch. My sisters are a riot too, if you're not afraid of obnoxious old women. Would you consider it?" Janice looked at me, batted her lashes, and put her hands together under her chin as if she was praying pretty please.

I felt surprised by her request, and touched by it. Janice was so independent, never asked for help, just dug in, and did things on her own. She must have really wanted to go if she gave in and asked me to go with her.

"Sure, I'll go with you. When did you plan on going? Fall?"

"Good. We leave Friday," she said as sweet as could be.

"Friday! I can't be ready by Friday—" I started to tell her of my trip to Scranton, but she interrupted.

"Why not? You said yourself you're finished with your project for the drug people. You're in between projects, so why not take a vacation. The Big Prick is self-sufficient for the time being. If it's the money, I already paid for the tickets, and we'll be staying at Josie's so there will be no hotel costs," she said.

"It's not the money—wait! What do you mean you

already paid for the tickets? What if I had said I wouldn't go? You'd be out the money for the flight." She had planned on me going all along. She knew I wouldn't make her feel bad and say no.

"Jeez, you have the rest of the week to get ready. It's not as if you have a big social calendar to rearrange, now is it? Just throw some jeans in a bag, call the shop, and tell them where they can reach you. Vince already knows, so you don't have to worry about arranging anything with him."

I sat up straight and gave Janice the evil eye. "What! You told him before you even asked me. What is this all about?"

"I saw him in the grocery store the other night and I mentioned it, that's all," she said, not looking at me. She patted her hair and shook the water off the swim cap.

"You are a rotten liar. Vince goes to the grocery store as often as I watch football. It doesn't happen."

"Well, I did talk to him. Maybe not at the grocery store," she said.

"What's this all about?" I had started to catch on, but I wanted to make her say it. "I'm going to push you in the pool and ruin your fancy-schmancy coiffure if you don't start talking. Out with it, Janice."

"Okay, okay. It's this Lane thing. You're all wrapped up in it. All the things you've said about Lane, Crystal, and Del, they're more than likely true. What you said about Crystal not going away—well, it may be true too. But you're not qualified to handle this. You're running around questioning people and pretending to be some rough and tough private investigator, and it's not getting you anywhere, is it?" She looked at me and waited for an answer.

I crossed my arms over my chest and scowled. "I am qualified," I said.

Damn it, I was qualified. Very few people knew I went through the training at the Michigan State Police Academy. Well, most of the training. It had been many years since I got the boot from the academy but I remembered it all like it was yesterday. I did very well with the physical and psychological tests and I really would've made a great cop. It was all so unfair. All over a lousy driving record, a couple speeding tickets, a small accident where I neglected to yield the right of way. I took an illegal left turn when I forgot to wear my glasses and didn't see the big No Left Turn sign. They were not very forgiving. I mean a few points on your record and bam! It was over.

Janice stood in front of me, interrupting my thoughts. "Be sensible. You've found out Del is a jerk, and you think Lane has changed somehow, but you're not sure how. And Crystal might be out there somewhere getting ready to bother Lane and Del again, but you have no way of knowing that. You said yourself the police are aware of Crystal, so let them look for her. Lane is a grown woman, Cassie. She has to help herself, you can't do it for her," she said.

"But Lane is not Lane anymore." My nose had a sneezing feeling and tears were building up in the corner of my eyes.

"See what I'm talking about. Now what is that supposed to mean?" she asked.

"God, Janice, I don't know. It's just how I feel. I can't explain it." I wished I had something to say, something concrete.

"But you don't know why you feel that way."

"Nothing I can do about how I feel, and no one believes me," I said.

"I believe you. I mean I believe you truly feel something is wrong, but as I said, you cannot do anything about it. You are not qualified in any way, shape, or manner to handle a murder case. No one hired you to do this. You are your own damn client." She leaned over, picked up my hand. "Just call the police, talk to that detective that came around to everyone after the car fire, and let it go."

I grabbed my hand away from her, went inside, and shoved *Suspicion* into the player. Janice came in after a time and we watched the second half before Vince showed up.

"Hey, guess who I saw yesterday?" he asked after pouring his rum and coke.

"Don't know," I said, barely managing not to say, "and don't care."

"Tiffany Holland," he said.

"Oh, fuck. Where?"

"At the airport." Vince swallowed a large gulp of his drink and began crunching an ice cube.

"She was leaving, I hope."

"Just getting into town."

"Really? How'd you happen to be at the airport?"

"Had to pick up a snowbird and shuttle him back and forth to available houses," he said.

"Whatever," I said, wondering why I had to suffer through hearing her name again and again.

"Excuse me?" Vince said.

"Whatever about Tiffany, not about you and your snowbird," I said, noting the deep lines in his forehead and his narrowed eyes. "I don't want to hear about her. Don't want to hear her name, okay?"

"Just thought you'd be interested. Should have known better." He dropped his head and stretched his neck from side to side, before lifting his head to look out the patio doors.

I watched as his expression changed from irritation

to resignation. Out of frustration and for want of a reason to fight, I started up a conversation with him about Lane.

"Vince. Tell me. Would you believe me if I told you I saw Lane slap Del's face? From what you know of her, that's not something she would likely do, right? You wouldn't have thought she would do that sort of thing, would you? But I saw her do it. Only it wasn't the same Lane you probably know, it was a different Lane. This Lane liked slapping. It didn't bother her in the least. In fact, she sat down and played a card game after. It was almost as if she'd had sex, you know, and then smoked a cigarette afterward. Do you understand what I'm trying to tell you?"

"I'm out of this discussion." Janice left the lanai through the sliding doors. Once in the pool area she pulled her flower-laden swimming cap over her pomade waved hair, adjusted the seat end of her suit, and jumped back in the pool.

Vince watched Janice for a bit, and then answered. "What is really irritating to me is that you act like you know Lane. You are assuming things. You don't know people after only meeting and talking with them a few times. How is it you can make a judgment on a person before you even know them? And why wouldn't she slap Del? From what she's told me he's a jerk."

"Oh, I wasn't aware the two of you were that close."

"Christ," he said. "I sold her the house. She calls me to fix things. That's all there is to it."

"How long of a 'warranty' does she get? Seems like mine ran out months ago." I felt melodramatic and out of control as I said it, and I wouldn't have continued if he hadn't flopped back in the chair and shook his head in that certain way, implying that he thought I was melodramatic and out of control.

"Maybe you don't realize it. There. Is. Something.

Wrong. With. Lane. I know it in here." I tapped my gut. "And another thing, I am qualified. Why do I have to prove it to you? Just as qualified as anyone else around here. Maybe more since they aren't doing a damn thing to find out who made a bonfire out of my car," I continued.

"Did I say anything about you not being qualified?" he asked.

I then repeated, "I am qualified."

Vince stood. "I'll come back another day."

"Yes, run across the street where everyone is nice. But don't go away thinking I don't know about the things you've hidden from me. Like seeing the 'Barbie' scene in the restaurant. Like being over to Lane's when you think, I won't be home to notice. Apparently, you prefer to honor her 'warranty' over mine," I said.

"You'd be better off making it easier for me to be here instead of accusing me of wanting to be somewhere else," he said.

"If you weren't so busy correcting my behavior and trying to make sure I'm nice to Lane, you might have noticed that I've needed your company and support. Instead, you're with her," I said, all the while knowing my anger was probably misplaced.

"I didn't realize you were so unhappy." He shook his head and left.

Leaning back in the rocker, I closed my eyes. I was unhappy. I didn't know all of the reasons why, but I did know it had to do with feeling as if I could never measure up. And as if there could be no fixing any mistake I made.

Grabbing Vinnie's glass, I gulped down the remainder of the drink. After a minute of contemplation, I understood I should be honest with myself and face the fact it wasn't any wonder that no one believed I was capable of handling a murder case. Why should anyone trust my instincts? It was not as if I had a degree in psychology and I wasn't a sociologist. I sure as hell hadn't ever worked on a murder case. I had a license for investigating. Something almost anyone could apply for and get. I never was a police officer or detective. I didn't have a great record of accomplishment of believing in myself or trusting my intuition. Why would anyone else?

But really all everyone seemed to remember was the stinking TV show.

So, as far as calling the police and talking to them about Lane, what purpose would that serve? I was sure they considered me nothing more than a nosy old has-been. I didn't have much to say to them that wouldn't confirm their image of me, and I couldn't stand the thought of hearing their patronizing voices.

What more could I do to figure out the puzzle? Lane wasn't interested in talking to me about her dad, let alone Del or Crystal. I had to find out if I could trust my instincts. Would the friends and neighbors in Scranton validate my thoughts? What was there to lose except the cost of the flight? After I returned from Scranton, maybe I could let it all go and forget about Lane and her changing personality. Taking a vacation was the answer. I could see the sense in it. Lane could deal with her life and I would deal with mine.

Then I would work on figuring out Vince and me.

Returning to the pool area, I said to Janice over the noise of her splashing, "Maybe, you are right. I should just get away for a while. A change of scenery never hurts."

"I'm always right," she shouted back.

I remembered I hadn't trusted my instinct about people since Terrence killed my sister. Before that, I'd bragged about seeing the real person. I swore I could spot a fake or a liar in a heartbeat. Since then, I hadn't said it, let alone believed it, and it now wasn't true.

I had to start from scratch. I had to believe it myself. Only then would others believe. I was keeping my flight to Scranton and to hell with two-timing Vince and crabby old Janice. They didn't need to know about it. It was my life and I didn't need their permission to live it the way I chose.

CHAPTER 11

I appreciate your taking time out of your day to talk to me, Jennifer. I understand you're busy." I looked around her living room and moved a box of diapers before sitting in a floral, comfortable-looking chair. She sat on the couch opposite me, surrounded by various baby items. She had wet circles on the front of her blouse and dark circles under her eyes—telltale signs she was breast-feeding.

"No problem, Detective Cruise. Is Lane in any trouble?"

"You can call me Cassie. No, she's not in trouble. This is just an employment background check."

"What's she applying for? She's still teaching, isn't she?"

A nervous jolt ran through me. I hadn't prepared for any questions and didn't have any ready lies. "That information is confidential."

"Can't you tell me the type of work?"

I gave her a pointed look.

She contracted her lips and shrugged.

"You and Lane went to high school and college together and were pretty close, right? Tell me about Lane. What do you know of her and her family?" I asked.

"They're rich. Or they were. Now Lane's rich," she said.

"Define rich."

"I mean filthy rich. Her great-great grandfather on her father's side was a founding member of this city. The family was big in the steel industry for many years."

"You're talking about Charles Somers' family?"

"Yes. I did say her father's side, didn't I? I meant stepfather. Well, evidently, they invested all that money through the years and Charles inherited it and made more. From what Lane told me, he was definitely tight. A real skinflint. The only person he spent money on was Maureen, Lane's mom. When he died in the car accident, it was all to go to Lane's mother, but she died days later. Everything went to Lane. You should drive by the family house, I think, then you'd understand how rich they are. I mean were."

"Who lives there now? Any family left?"

"Oh, no. Just Lane. She donated it to the Chamber of Commerce or something like that. It's a museum or on the historic home tour anyway."

"Wouldn't Charles have made provisions in his will to take care of Lane regardless of Maureen dying?"

"I'm not sure. They weren't very close. In fact, I heard they did nothing but fight the last year or so of his life."

"What were they fighting about?" I asked.

"I don't remember. Maybe you could talk to the woman that lived next door. I think she was pretty close to Lane's mom."

"Have you and Lane kept in touch since school?"

"Not really. It's the typical situation. I'm married with a baby and all. Just don't find the time to keep up with everyone."

"Okay. Is there anything else you can think of to tell

me?" I was struggling and didn't know what other questions to ask. I wished I'd taken the time to write a script.

'*Just play the part*,' Rachel said. Straightening my spine, I forced a serious, intent, expression.

Jennifer narrowed her eyes and raised an eyebrow. "Are you okay?"

"Yes. Why?"

"For a minute you looked like my baby, Dustin."

"Oh? In what way?"

"He's colicky at times. Has gas. The way you were looking just now reminded me of him."

I readjusted my expression. "Oh. No, I'm fine."

"Good. Let's see. You said this is an employment check. Regarding her work habits? I never worked with her, but I do know that once she makes up her mind to do something, she'll get it done come hell or high water. As far as her background? I know she's never been in trouble, never needed or wanted for much."

"Sounds too good to be true," I said.

"This might be kind of bitchy, but she's had the perfect life and she never seemed completely happy. Seemed like she wanted more from everyone around her. She wasn't sad or anything, just not happy. She didn't have many friends because of that."

"Hey, did you name your baby after Dustin Hoffman?" I asked.

"Who?"

A baby began a low hesitant cry.

"Never mind."

"Got to go." She got up and moved toward the sound.

"Thanks for your time." I was at the door when she turned back to me.

"I just remembered something. The neighbor lady I told you about?"

I nodded.

The baby's cry was no longer hesitant. It had become a confident wail. She headed down the hallway toward the crying baby, still talking. "She might not talk to you. She and Maureen had a falling out before Maureen died. Something about Charles messing around with some- body's daughter. Just rumor. I haven't hung out with any- one from that area of town since I got married."

"Thanks again, Jennifer," I said and let myself out.

As I opened the door to the car, she opened the front door, stepped out with Dustin at her breast, and said, "Hold on. I've got something."

I waited in the driveway. She returned with a book, Dustin still attached to her breast. "I don't know if it'll help, but here's their high school year book."

"Whose year book?"

She flipped some pages and pointed at a page. "That's my mom." The baby squirmed and jostled the book.

"Here?" I took the book and she adjusted Dustin. A woman at the edge of the page caught my eye. A very sexy looking young woman. Loretta Evans. I thought about being seventeen or eighteen and looking like that. Couldn't have been a good thing. I looked at Jennifer and knew it wasn't her mom.

She took the book from me and placed her finger be- low a different picture. I looked at Arlene Elvin. Nice looking. Jennifer looked a great deal like her mother. *So what? Why would I need to see a picture of her mother?*

She flipped the pages and pointed at Maureen Jensen. "Here's Lane's mom. Beautiful, wasn't she? Mom and she went to the same high school."

"This is a public school yearbook. You and Lane went to a private school." She nodded and I took the book from her and studied the picture of Lane's mom.

"That was important to my parents," Jennifer said.

That's really why I brought the book out. To show you that we're just regular people. Everyone but Charles Somers, that is. Nothing he had came from hard work. That's makes a person different, don't you think?"

"Will you send Dustin to private school?"

"I don't think so. Right now, I think it's better to keep things real. Don't you agree?"

I thought about the public schools in my old neighborhood, and I wasn't sure if I agreed. And that's what I told her and left.

As I drove away from Jennifer's subdivision, I decided I wanted to drop off my overnight bag at a hotel and freshen up. I looked for a hotel in an area central to the couple of visits I had scheduled in my head. My return flight was at six the next morning, so this afternoon and evening would be full.

The problem was I was directionally challenged. If I didn't take the time to figure out a driving plan, something bad would happen. Most times, I ended up with a ticket for some obscure traffic violation. Sometimes it was worse. Every time I drove somewhere new it happened, and this time was not an exception.

Right away, I made a left on Adams Avenue when I saw a sign for a Hilton even though the GPS was giving me other directions. Turned out it was a one-way street and not the way I was going. Looking back, I guess the situation could be a metaphor of my life.

I screamed and jerked the wheel, aiming for the side of the road when I saw the police car headed toward me. Then I understood and I stopped. The officer jumped out of the car like it was an emergency.

When he stood at my car door and glared, I pushed the button to put the window down.

"This is a one way street, ma'am."

"I was only going one way," I said and smiled very big.

The officer didn't return the smile, instead he continued glaring.

Then he asked for my driver's license and when I pulled it out of my purse, Rachel's badge plopped into my lap.

"What's that, ma'am?"

"A badge. It's my sister's."

"Hand it to me."

I did and took note of his badge. Officer Todd Davis.

He held it next to my driver's license and then put the license behind the badge and looked at the badge by itself.

"Where is your sister?"

"Dead."

"Why would you have this?"

"I brought it with me for good luck and it came out when I reached for my license."

"Why did you need good luck?"

"It's a long story."

"I'm listening."

"Really?" I didn't want to explain everything, and tried to think of a reason a normal person would need a good luck charm. Nothing came to mind.

"Ma'am?"

"I was doing a background check on a client. I came here to talk to an old friend of the client."

"You had this with you? That's impersonating an officer. In some states it's a third degree felony," Officer Davis said.

"But you don't understand. I never technically said that I was a police officer. I never showed her the badge." I made myself breathe in deeply through my nose. I let the breath out slowly through my mouth. "Did you say felony?"

"Where are you headed," he barked.

I told him and he seemed understanding about me being from out of state and in a strange city.

"Is Officer Tucker still around?" I asked, wanting to keep his attention off both the badge and writing tickets.

"Officer Tucker?"

"Debra Tucker."

"Do you know her?" he asked.

"I know of her. She made a statement to the local newspaper about my client."

"Let's go down to the station. You can tell me more about why you're here and maybe we'll run into Officer Tucker."

Resigned to my fate, I got out of the car, turned, and put my hands behind my back.

Officer Davis shook his head, puffed out his cheeks, and blew out a breath of air. "Just get back in your car and follow me."

Once at the station, I told him the story of my car and Lane's odd behavior changes. He left me in the lobby and returned, saying nothing. He wrote up a ticket for driving the wrong way down a one-way street, or careless driving or something of that nature, and handed it to me. He didn't bring up the impersonating an officer issue and neither did I.

"Hang out here. I'm leaving, but Officer Tucker's coming on shift and I'll ask her to stop in here to see you." He left without giving back Rachel's badge.

After fifteen minutes or so of waiting patiently, I got up to find someone to give me the badge. Then I would leave.

A female officer stopped me on my way to talk to the officer at reception. She didn't have a shred of makeup on her face and her chin length hair had been wet-combed and left to air dry. Her uniform was tight and it appeared uncomfortable.

I watched her eyes move down to my shoes and back up to my face, taking in my strappy leather sandals, my tan legs, and short, cotton dress with the matching leather belt. And everything else in between.

"Officer Tucker," she said and put out her hand.

I shook her hand.

"Ms. Cruise?"

"Yes?"

"Step back in here so we can talk."

"I need my sister's badge returned to me. Can you get it from Officer Davis before he leaves?"

"I have the badge, don't worry. Have a seat. Would you like something to drink?"

"No."

"I need you to do something for me before I let you have the badge and send you on your way." She had a calm smooth look on her face. She opened her eyes wide, blinking every other second, and she bent her mouth up at the edges, creating just enough of a smile to indicate how serene she was feeling. It came across as patronizing, but I could tell Officer Tucker thought she was giving me a very patient and loving smile. I'd seen the same look on people everywhere who felt the call to serve the great unwashed.

I was getting that clenching feeling in my jaw and stomach, an early indicator of potential stubbornness, and I felt all the necessary make-an-ass-out-of-yourself hormones flowing through my veins. But because I was unwilling to walk away without the badge, I talked myself into listening.

As long as she didn't touch me, I could do it. No pat on the hand. No lightly touching my arm in that gentle caring way I was sure she'd convinced herself was a part of her nature. If she did that, I might snap.

It seemed safer to mimic her behavior. I knew from a past relationship that if you faked something, other people might start to think it was real. Sometimes, you could even convince yourself.

"What is it you need from me?" I asked kindly as I sat in the chair.

She rested her navy blue polyester ensconced hips on the table and looked down at me with all of Mother Theresa's leftover love.

I pulled out a nearby chair and patted the seat. We needed to be on the same level. No one needed to look up to the other.

I smiled very big at my new best friend. "Oh, please sit down and relax."

Moving the chair three feet away from me, she sat with a groan. She leaned over, put her elbows on her knees, and rested her face in her hands, her attention on my face. Concern oozed from her pores. "Tell me a little bit about why you're here."

I told her all of it. I told her about seeing her name in the newspaper article regarding the accident involving Lane's parents. I mentioned the calls for domestic issues.

"So you wanted to talk to me and get some insight into Lane Somers's, umm, personality issues. Is that it?"

"And to try to find out who killed this unknown person, put the body in the trunk of my car, and then torched my car. I know whoever did it must have been trying to get at Del, Lane's boyfriend, or maybe even Lane."

"Uh-huh."

"Can you just tell me why the police were called to the Somers' residence throughout the year prior to the accident? You mentioned that to the reporter after the accident. It was in the article."

"If I remember correctly, there had been a few nuisance calls."

She left her head in one hand and brushed lint and white animal hair from her slacks with the other.

"What were the nuisance calls?"

"You know what? Let me go pull that record and refresh my memory. You wait here, I'll be right back," she said.

She left and returned in under five minutes carrying a manila folder.

"Here's the info I have," she said as she sat. She opened the folder and while looking at the papers inside, said, "On one occasion a call was made because they saw someone walking around the property. Someone set the alarm off trying to get in the house on one occasion. There were one or two calls from the neighbors stating they heard loud noises and arguing coming from the Somers's home. Nothing else."

"Do you remember if you ever caught the person? I mean maybe they were trying to get to Lane."

"No. We never arrested anyone."

"See. It could be the same person. The person that started my car on fire could have been the same person who was bothering Lane and her family a year or more ago. Have you ever heard of Crystal Evans?"

She looked at me now without the syrupy sweetness. "Did you say Evans?"

"Yes. She looks very similar to Lane, as I understand. Blonde hair, blue eyes, slender."

"Blonde hair, blue eyes and slender?"

"Yes."

She nodded. "Look, Ms. Cruise. Here's what I wanted to talk to you about. Wait. Let me ask you first, do you live by yourself?"

"Yes."

"Okay. Now do you have any hobbies or groups or clubs you belong to?"

"Not really."

"Kids?"

"Nope."

Officer Tucker nodded. "You need to get involved in something. Go back to Florida and meet some people. Start a book club, something like that."

"What are you trying to say?" *Breathe slowly and deeply.*

"Quite frankly, you're coming off as an old lady snoop, talking to her cats, and stepping all over the police detective trying to do his job. On the television, it's somewhat funny. In real life, it's not funny. It's annoying and you could get your butt thrown in jail. You need to give your family and loved ones a higher priority. In other words, you need to find something else to do with your spare time."

"I have The Big Prick," I said.

"That your boyfriend?" she asked with a new type of interest.

"Let's just say The Big Prick takes up my spare time," I told her.

She looked disgusted for a few seconds and then scooted her chair closer and put her face near mine. "Listen to me. I think you need to go home and let the police down there in Florida do their job. There's some underlying reason that you're putting so much importance on this. I'm trying not to be harsh, but maybe there's someone there you could talk to. You're too old to be living this way. Talk to someone. A professional."

My eyes traveled over her brown-gray hair made fuzzy with a home permanent, her crusty-looking post-menopausal liver-spotted skin, and her cow udder boobs that no bra would ever work miracles on, and the vest and uniform shirt would never hide.

She was calling me old? And how dare she imply I needed to talk to someone?

"You think I'm a lonely old lady? You think I'm old?" My voice screeched on the last word.

"I'm not calling you old. I don't judge people by appearances. I judge them by their actions," she said.

"You're older than me."

"Am not."

"Are too."

"Am not."

'Cassandra! Grow up!' I heard Rachel yelling at me. I heard it loud and clear.

I rubbed the area between my eyes and Officer Tucker sighed. Really, it was more like a tornado, smelling of burnt coffee and non-dairy creamer.

'Suck it up, Cassie,' Rachel told me. *'And get my badge back.'*

I smiled a soft smile and laid my hand gently on Officer Tucker's arm. "Sorry," I said. "Tell you the truth, I'm nearing that certain age that tends to make women oversensitive, if you know what I mean."

"I understand, and that's why I'm suggesting you talk to a professional."

"I'll certainly take your advice to heart. A part of me appreciates what you're saying. Now, may I have the badge?"

"You are leaving now, am I right?"

"Yes. I think I'll go directly to the airport and put myself on a stand-by list." I crossed my fingers.

"Good. Good." She stood and put her hand on the small of my back. The pressure, intended to encourage me to stand and leave, worked. Peripherally, I could see she had the badge out of her pocket and was busy fondling it. She rubbed her thumb up and down the front of it in a rhythmic motion and hummed softly and tunelessly.

I wanted to rip it from her hand and run. I turned toward her, looked her in the face, and saw that was exactly what she wanted me to do. She wanted me to grab it from her. It would've given her pleasure to throw me in jail.

"I do have one small, teensy-weensy question. Just for my own curiosity. I promise it's not to interfere," I said.

"Yes?"

"It seemed to me—now I know I could be wrong due to my surging hormones and such—but it seemed as if you recognized the name Evans."

"Ms. Cruise." She slowly shook her head and her face was full of concern again. She returned the badge to her pocket, keeping her hand holding the badge inside her pocket.

"Did you? If you did and you told me, you certainly would help my confidence level, which has gone right down the toilet, as I'm sure you can tell by my recent petty behavior. I think sometimes that I am going a little crazy." I said. Then I whispered, "I even hear my dead sister talking to me."

"Really? What does she say?" She brought her hand and the badge out of the pocket. She dangled it along her side, holding it with her thumb and finger.

"Mostly she tells me to shut up."

"Pardon me for saying, but that's probably good advice."

"So, did you recognize the name?" I asked.

"What name?"

"Evans." I said.

"There are Evans's in this town."

"In connection to the Somers's, I mean." I bit my bottom lip in order to keep from showing my impatience.

"No slender, blue-eyed, blonde-haired Evans was connected to the Somers as far as I know." Her hand was on my back again and we walked down a hallway toward the exit. "Take care now. Go right to the airport, you hear?" She turned and walked back down the hall.

"Officer Tucker?" I stuck my hand out and waited for the badge.

She stopped and looked at me. Her face showed her exasperation and her eyes turned to an officer behind an intake window. The officer smiled at her in sympathy and shook his head.

She handed me the badge. "Go," she said.

I dropped the badge into my purse and zipped it shut. "Do you have a cat?" I asked.

"Yes. Why?"

"I don't own a cat."

"What?"

"And I'm not old."

Blood rushed to her face and turned it red. "It's in your best interest to go straight home, Ms. Cruise."

I left and, ignoring Officer Tucker's advice to go straight to the airport, I found a convenience store nearby. I bought coffee and a pack of cigarettes, and chain-smoked all the way to Lane's childhood home.

"Screw that old biddy," I said aloud. I'd wasted a lot of time with her, and I knew from experience, no matter how I finagled I couldn't get the wasted time back.

CHAPTER 12

The Somers' house, a surprisingly easy find from the Scranton Police Department on Washington, was a true indication of wealth. Old money. The Federal style house wore its years with elegance. A sign near the columned porch marked it as an historic home, built in the early 1800s, and in the Somers family until the previous year.

I parked at the end of the drive behind a row of eight or ten other cars. Women were walking from the cars loaded with shiny wrapped gifts, greeting each other and laughing as they entered the house.

A man dressed in chefs' colorful baggy pants and a white jacket passed me as I got out of my car. He opened the rear doors of a catering van parked at the curb and began pulling out foil-covered trays.

I stepped behind him.

"Let me help," I said, holding my arms out for him to load.

He turned, gave me a quick glance, and set a huge tray in my outstretched arms. When his arms were loaded, he kicked the van door shut and gave me another once over before heading to the house. I followed him through the entry and down a hall into the kitchen.

"Wedding shower?" I asked as I set the tray on the kitchen island.

"Yes, this time. Tomorrow a baby shower. They never rent it out for anything interesting. Um, who are you?" he finally asked.

"A friend of the family that owned this house. The Somers. You know them?"

"Nope. Probably, too snooty for me if they owned this house. Not my kind of people."

"Mind if I go join the others?"

"Why would I care?"

I meandered into the parlor and sat in a chair near the fireplace, ignoring the few questioning glances sent my way. I sat there, listened to the gay chatter, and tried to figure out a way to ask questions about the Somers family.

"Are you from the groom's family?" A woman in a chartreuse blouse asked. Her mouth caught my attention as her lipstick had bled into the fine lines around her mouth, making an undefined red blur. Her eyes were a cloudy blue. Before I could answer, her unfocused eyes had drifted off to the left of my shoulder.

"I'm a distant cousin." I smiled to encourage conversation. "This house is amazing, isn't it?"

"Yes, it is."

"Do you know anything of its history?"

"I've lived in this town all my life. This house is always a part of the Scranton tours I take my visiting relatives."

"How about the Somers, what do you know about them?"

"Tragic. That accident was tragic." She allowed her eyes and her attention to wander about the room.

"Tell me about the accident." It came out sounding like an order, and she jumped in her seat and looked at me with surprise or fear, I wasn't sure which. And maybe she wasn't sure either, but I had her full attention now. "I didn't hear about an accident," I said in a kinder tone.

"It was horrible. The whole family involved like that, never heard of such a thing before. He died, and then she died. Just terrible."

"I heard he was a difficult man to live with. Do you think anything weird was going on in this house? You know, behind closed doors, so to speak."

She didn't respond and I saw that I'd lost her attention again. "Yoo-hoo!" I waved my hand in front of her face.

"What's that? Oh. I heard he was a mean man. He was a womanizer too."

"He was?"

"Well, that's what I heard." At that point, I lost her totally. She initiated a conversation with the woman on the other side of her, one I'm sure she wouldn't finish.

"Are you with the groom's family?" I heard her ask.

I got up and wandered around, said hi to a few women, and asked questions about the house or the Somers. Soon all I got was a group dismissal.

Climbing over the velvet rope blocking off the staircase, I wandered around upstairs picking out the room I thought would've been Lane's. They were all beautiful and any one of them could have been hers. Bored with the idea and giving up, I looked out a window and caught a glimpse of the nearest neighbor's house. The house was just as impressive as the Somers family home.

I decided to visit, walked across the landscaped lawn, and knocked on the door.

"Hi. I'm Cassie Cruise, an investigator, and Lane Somers is my client. I want to ask you some questions about the Somers family." I didn't make up a lie or beat around the bush. If she was going to shut the door in my face, I wanted her to get it over with immediately.

She gave my face a quick look over. "Come on in," she said.

I followed her down a hall and through a quiet swinging door into the kitchen, noting her appearance. She didn't look as though she was much concerned with fashion or style. She covered her slim body with casual, throw on type clothes—a loose knit shirt over equally loose fitting denim jeans and a pair of runner's shoes.

She motioned for me to sit on a bar stool next to a granite topped island. "Coffee?" she asked.

"Please. I can't think of anything better than a real cup of coffee right now," I said.

She poured coffee into a thick white mug, placed it in front of me, and returned to pour herself a cup from the pot. She sat across from me and took her time stirring sugar and cream into her mug. "What is it you want to know?" she asked when her coffee was stirred to her liking.

"I want to know about the Somers family. Charles, Maureen, and Lane."

"Why?"

I gave her the whole story. She listened with her elbows on the counter and her chin in her hands, occasionally dropping one hand to pick up the mug of coffee and sip.

"Oh," she said when I completed the story. She looked off toward the area of an oak door, seemingly deep in thought.

I took the opportunity to study her. She most likely was in her early sixties, her gray hair, shining and nicely cut into a low maintenance bob and her makeup, equally low key, gave her a look that said she was comfortable with her appearance and who she was. She seemed to be the type of person I would enjoy having coffee with under most circumstances.

"Did you come here to talk to the owner of the house?" she asked eventually.

"Yes."

"You're stuck with me. Mrs. Feeney is the owner and she's in rehab. She had a stroke last month."

"Oh. Well. Who're you?"

"I'm Sally Kennedy. I guess you could call me the housekeeper, although I've done much more than keep house these last ten years. I've done it all, from planning parties, to holding hands, and wiping asses. But that'd be my title, anyway." She smiled.

"Do you know anything about the Somers?" I was a little pissed. I didn't want to waste any more time. My plane was scheduled to leave at six in the morning and I would have to be at the airport at four-thirty to turn in the car and go through security. It was now seven-thirty in the evening. I had no more time and I wished she had shut the door in my face rather than getting my hopes up.

"You happen to be in luck. I probably know more about the Somers than Mrs. Feeney does. Know why?" she asked.

"Why?" I asked.

"Because I didn't like them. Not one of them. More importantly, I didn't trust them so I kept my eyes and ears open."

"Do tell," I said.

"Maureen Somers was a self-involved bitch and she had one friend and one friend only. That was Regina, Mrs. Feeney. That's because they're like two peas in a pod," Sally said.

"But why would you stay and work for a bitch?" I knew it wasn't the time to interrupt, but I couldn't suppress my curiosity about this nice, capable, and independent-appearing woman working for a self-involved bitch for ten years or more.

"As I said Regina Feeney is selfish and spoiled, that meant I was almost invisible to her most of the time. As long as I did my job and stayed out of her way, I could go about the rest of my life as I chose. I knew too, there would be a pension to fall back on. That's something we agreed on in the hiring contract. You don't get a guaranteed pension in very many jobs these days."

I nodded, ready for her to continue with talking about the Somers even though she hadn't fully satisfied my curiosity about her life choices.

There was more to her life than she was letting me know.

But I was here to get information on the Somers, not Sally Kennedy, and time was wasting.

"Since I was invisible to both Maureen and Regina, they weren't any too cautious about what they said in my presence. That's how I found out Charles was a pig, and Lane was a little more than neurotic most times."

"I know of Lane's neurotic behavior, somewhat anyway. Tell me about Charles and Maureen," I said.

"Maureen was disgusted by Charles. She put up with his sick ways because of the lifestyle it afforded her. It was amazing how she could go about her life and forget whom she married as long as the money was there. I don't think she ever gave a thought to what it did to her daughter to live that way."

"In what way was he sick? I've heard he was a womanizer and a tightwad. Is that what you're talking about?"

"Yes. It was more than womanizing, though. He had a compulsion. He had to touch and fondle whatever and whoever attracted him. It was a disgusting thing to witness. He was constantly in trouble one way or the other. If it weren't for his money, he'd have landed in jail more than a few times. I'm surprised someone didn't kill him long ago."

"Kill him? So you don't believe the accident was an accident?"

"The only question in my mind is whether Lane planned it or whether Maureen did."

"Wow. You seem very certain."

"They both had something to do with it, probably."

"I read in a newspaper article about the accident that there had been domestic issues at the Somers' during the year before. Apparently, people had called about hearing loud arguments and yelling coming from their house. Did Maureen, Lane's mother, ever say anything about that to your boss, Regina?"

"Not that I overheard. Mostly she was concerned about some notes or letters that someone was leaving her. Once she found a note in her purse, which meant that whoever was leaving them had gotten close enough to drop one in her purse and remain undetected. That frightened her, but since the notes were all about threatening to make Charles' behavior public if she didn't pay up, I doubt if she called the police about them."

"Why would someone blackmail her rather than Charles? He had the money, not her."

"I wondered about that too. I don't know the answer, but I know someone blackmailed Charles early on in the marriage. One day Maureen and Regina had a good laugh over what Maureen called 'his stupidity.' Evidently, he had paid a woman to keep quiet about him fathering her son. He was so in love with Maureen way back then that he didn't want any hint of his past to cause her to change her mind about marrying him.

Later when they went to the doctors to find out why they couldn't conceive, they told Charles he was sterile. He had mumps during his late teens and the infection caused infertility. Evidently, he ranted and raved over that for months. He'd been taken to the cleaners and didn't like it one bit. She said losing money had more of an effect on him than the sterility."

"Did he ever do anything about the blackmail?" I asked.

"Going by what I overheard, no," Sally said.

"And he didn't press charges or make a complaint to the police?"

"He didn't. The only reason he ever did anything was for money. He must have avoided that for something that had to do with his money," Sally said.

"Do you think Lane knew about him being black-mailed?" I asked.

"I couldn't say for sure. One thing I can tell you is that if there was any yelling in that house loud enough for someone to call the police, it would have come from Lane. On more than one occasion I was lucky enough to witness as her neurosis took over." Sally twirled her finger in a circle around the side of her head.

"Loco," she said.

I knew it!

"That sounds like one effed-up family," I said. Amazed at the breadth of some people's greedy and cruel behavior, I compared Lane's life with my own. My parents—my truck driving father and my lawyer mother—had their issues and oddities, but nothing in my childhood would come close to what Lane's would have been like.

"That's the truth," Sally sat quietly sipping her coffee.

"Did the Somers have a housekeeper?" I asked, suddenly thinking I should be talking to that person, too.

"No one lasted in that house for long. They mostly used a service and kept who they could for however long they could."

"Sally?" The voice sounded female and far away.

"In here," Sally called out. She slid off the bar stool

and walked toward the oak door at the opposite end of the kitchen and held it open. A woman climbed the last few stairs and turned to shut the door.

"Oh. We have company," she said as she faced the kitchen.

"This is Cassie," Sally said. "She's investigating the Somers."

I didn't bother to clarify.

The woman bent and kissed Sally on the tip of her nose. Then she turned to me and smiled. "I'm Ronnie. Are you staying for dinner?"

I stayed for dinner, and since I never did make a hotel reservation, I slept on a couch in their den for a few hours before dragging my butt to the airport.

CHAPTER 13

Once I arrived home, my thoughts were mostly on how I'd treated Vince earlier. The more I thought about it the more I convinced myself Officer Tucker was right. Running around the country, trying to solve a case—one that wasn't even mine—at the expense of a relationship was sad and ridiculous.

I called Vince and, when he didn't answer, I left an apologetic message. Then I saw the message light blinking on my phone. I retrieved the message and sat at the desk to listen.

"Ms. Cruise. This is John Lane. I'd appreciate it if you'd let Lane Somers know I called. I'll call you again soon."

As I got up from my desk, I noticed the glass door leading to the pool was open a crack. I looked around the lanai and office to see if anything was missing or out of place.

The desk looked as disorganized as I had left it. The file drawer was open a slice, but I had pulled out the envelope from Lane and taken it with me on my trip to Scranton. It could be I had left the drawer open. I looked through the other drawers in the desk and nothing seemed to be out of place or missing. Most importantly, the top drawer was in the same order as I had left it—locked. And the Colt .38 Diamondback was in the rear left side corner of the drawer. Very rarely have I ever carried the gun. In truth, I only used it on the job once, and that was during *Cruising,* which doesn't count.

Still troubled, I went through the rest of the house, room by room. I found nothing missing or out of place, but something I couldn't name gave me goose bumps and made the hair on the back of my neck stand up.

I returned to the lanai and called Janice, but got her voice mail. I tried Vince's cell again. Same thing. There was no way I was going to call the police. What would I say? "I might have left my door open when I went out of town. Nothing's missing or disturbed, but I have a creeped out feeling." I didn't think that would be taken seriously.

Rubbing my neck, I tried to dismiss the feeling, but it wouldn't go away. After locking up and double-checking the locks, I decided to go to the shop and, when I was ready to leave from there, I would ask Janice to follow me home and wait while I went inside to make sure all was safe.

As I drove, I began to feel foolish. Maybe Janice or Vince had come over and found that I wasn't home. They both had keys to my house. Maybe one of them forgot to shut the sliding door. That was probably what had happened, I decided, and resolved to check with Janice.

Then thinking of Janice and Vince, I went over in my mind the things they had told me about not being able to help Lane. Both had said the same thing. They believed and trusted my instincts. And, I'd been right. There was something "wrong" across the street. Whatever was wrong with Lane probably stemmed from the disgusting life she lived with Charles and Maureen. There wasn't much hope anyone could fix that, but I believed being aware of someone being on the short side of sane was important. Especially, if they were your neighbor.

Once I'd parked in the alley, I let myself in the back door to the shop. Instead of going out front to find Janice, I picked up the phone in my office and dialed. I had a big need to know the answer to something.

"Hello," a female voice answered.

"Mrs. Lane? Could I speak to Mr. John Lane?"

"Who's this? If this is sales, I want my number removed from your list immediately. If I want to buy something, I'll call you, understand?" She sounded as if she meant it. Either I answered her or she would come through the phone line and choke the answer out of me.

"I'm not a salesperson. This is Cassie Cruise. Is this Sheila? It's important that I talk to John," I said.

"What for?" I heard the click of a lighter and she inhaled with a quick, sharp, breath. "Oh, I know who you are. You're working for that sweet little Lane, aren't you? She's trying to find her long lost daddy, right?"

"Look, I'm just trying to do my job. Is John some place where he can be reached?" I asked.

"Oh, you're just doing your job, huh?" she said. "Do you have any idea what you're really doing? You're stirring up a mountain of shit. That's what you're doing."

I didn't answer her. I could hear ice tinkling in a glass and a clunk when the glass was set down. She caught her breath, and she began to cry a slow cry. There was silence. She blew her nose, and ice tinkled on glass again.

Okay, I believed there was a twelve-step program for this type of illness.

"Hey, Cassie," she said in a softer voice.

"Yes?"

"It never was like she said it was. Everyone fell for her act. She lied all the time. She let Charles believe the baby was his and she let her family believe it was John doing the leaving. She lied to her little girl, too. I never lied to mine. I saw what it does, that lying all the time. I didn't betray her. She did it to him. You understand that?"

"I think I do." I had no idea what she was talking about but I did remember something I had heard while watching *Beauty and the Beast*; "Children believe what we tell them, they have complete faith in us…they believe a thousand other simple things." To lie to children was the worst thing a parent could do. It was true in 1946 when the film came out and it was true today.

"You know what it's like to be second choice? It's hell, that's what it's like. John, he doesn't understand. He says it ain't like that. But I know what I feel. I've been feeling it all my life."

"I'm sorry you're feeling so bad. You shouldn't be by yourself when you feel that way. Is John going to be around tonight or maybe your daughter could come by and sit with you until you feel better?" I wanted to talk to someone coherent.

"It wasn't that she was pretty, I was pretty too in my day. It was something else. I heard it all the time. She just sparkles. She's so lively. You should smile more often, Sheila. Be more like Maureen, they told me. But I never wanted to be like her. I don't want my little girl to go through that. Ever."

"You're right. You should never try to be someone you're not. Do you want me to talk to John about it for you?"

She inhaled and I heard ice clinking as she brought the glass to her mouth again. I was close to hanging up. I really didn't have the patience to listen to a drunk. *Does everyone drink these days?*

"I'm going to tell you the truth. Maureen did it. It was her. Not my John and me. She told him to get lost.

Maureen knew damn well she was pregnant, but she had her eye on someone bigger and better and she was going after him. So who did John turn to? Good old Sheila. How stupid everyone was. Poor, poor, Maureen. That's what everyone thought. They thought I stole John from her out of meanness and jealousy and no one believed me when I told them different. Why? Because they wanted to believe her. She was the good witch and I was the bad witch."

She inhaled and continued. "You know, I really lost my whole family to her. No one talked about it, but I knew what they were thinking. Sweet, brave, Maureen. I was an outcast. They didn't see that it was all about her getting what she was after. And good for her. She did get him and he was rich and handsome. Too bad he screwed everything in a skirt behind her back. I don't think she cared, though, as long as she could keep playing the part of sweet Maureen. And I bet the apple didn't fall far from the tree."

"Are you talking about Lane?" I remembered thinking the same about Tillie and Del.

"You bet I am." She sighed and I listened as she blew her nose.

Her voice was stronger when she said, "John's on his way to Florida and he's going to drag my baby girl into the mess. I told him, you leave her outta this. Crystal doesn't need to be involved. She doesn't need a sister like that."

Whoa. I had called to ask John his daughter's name, and Sheila had given it to me. Crystal. My heart was pounding. Lane and her half-sister, Crystal, probably looked similar. Their mothers were cousins, and they supposedly had the same father—my god, it was possible they would look like twins. Barbie number one and Barbie number two.

"Wait! Sheila, does Crystal know about Lane? Did you ever tell her?"

"Yes, I told her when she was in her teens. And a long, time ago I brought it up to John, but he said he didn't believe it. I wish I'd never told Crystal. For a few years, it seemed as if that's all she ever wanted to talk about. Where is her sister, what did I think her sister was doing. I tried my hardest to be nice about it, but it drove me crazy. She out grew it, I guess, after she went to college and got married. She didn't bring it up anymore."

"Is she still married?

"Oh, no. That didn't last. He was a jerk. I told her if you want out, then just get out. Don't be miserable your whole life over some man."

Great advice coming from her.

"Where is Crystal now?"

"She packed up and said she wanted to spend her summer traveling. She had saved her money from teaching and there was no stopping her. Last we talked to her she was in Florida. She said she was enjoying herself and not to worry, she'd be back in time for school to start."

"Did she say anything about meeting someone? You know, such as having a boyfriend here in Florida?"

"No. I don't think she's interested in meeting anyone right now. She never was able to trust too many men after her divorce. Why? Do you know something about her?"

"I think she…listen, this is all speculation, but I think she was seeing a man down here. It didn't go so well and they broke up."

"What?"

"The thing is I think he's now Lane's boyfriend."

"Jesus."

"When did you last talk to her?" I asked.

"A week ago. She didn't say anything about a guy," she said.

"It's odd that Crystal came here and then Lane moved here, isn't it?"

"What are you saying?" Sheila asked.

"Do you think there's a possibility that Crystal knew Lane was moving to Florida and came here to meet her?"

For a time, the only sound I heard was the faint crackling and static on the phone line. Then softly, Sheila said, "I suppose it's possible. She always wanted to meet her."

"She knew Lane grew up in Scranton, right? That's where your family is from, isn't it?"

"So? A lot of people are from Scranton. A lot of shitty people. Crystal's ex is from there."

"Did Crystal use the computer a lot in her spare time?"

"She seemed to. Especially after the divorce." Ice clinked on glass. "You'd better tell me what you're getting at."

"I think they've been emailing and communicating on the internet for some time now. I don't think Crystal let Lane know they're half-sisters, though. Can you think of a reason she wouldn't tell her?"

"I told you she didn't trust people anymore," Sheila said.

"Do you think she'd follow Lane? You know, try to get to know her maybe and then tell her?"

"What do you mean follow her? Anyway, why don't you ask her?"

"I don't know where she is. Do you?" I asked.

"She's in Venice. If you wanted to do something useful, you'd go 'n' find her. She'll tell you how crazy you are," Sheila said.

She was right. I should find Crystal, but if the police couldn't find her, how could I? I needed to find a way. Soon.

"I'll let you go. I hope you feel better," I said and then I heard a few beeps and clicks from the phone before we were disconnected.

Maybe Crystal had been stalking Lane for a long time. She was a teacher and Lane was a teacher. I didn't believe it was coincidence. She was the Teach72 in the e-mail correspondences, and she knew everything about Lane and her life.

Maybe Crystal wasn't after Del because she wanted him or loved him. She was bitter about Lane in the same way as her mother was bitter about Lane's mother. Maybe she had come to Florida to meet Del purposely, knowing Lane was making plans to do the same thing. It could be an attempt to keep Del away from Lane. She went to work for him, ingratiated herself by turning around his office, and tried to prevent Lane and Del from meeting each other.

Del had to hold his share of the blame, in my opinion. He was crooked somehow, I could feel it, and he was probably unethical, but did he know about Crystal and Lane's relationship? Did he realize they were half-sisters?

Or maybe Crystal wanted to ruin Lane's life. Or maybe Sheila was right about Lane—the apple didn't fall too far from the tree.

Frustrated at being unable to tie all the information together, I walked out front looking for a distraction. I wanted to think of something other than Lane or Crystal or Sheila and John.

Of course, I got my wish.

"Jeeeez-us H. Christ. Are you tattooing? You can't do that. Don't you have to be certified or something?" I yelled, without thinking it through.

Luckily, the person under RJ's gun didn't flinch.

"How can you own this shop and not know the answer to that?" RJ said without looking up or stopping.

No question the kid had nerve. I walked away feeling foolish and went to find Janice to ask about the door to my lanai. I found out she hadn't been to the house and she hadn't realized I was gone.

After an hour more of sitting around the shop, I realized I was avoiding my own home. My pride kicked in and I decided I didn't need a protector. I've always taken care of myself. I drove back home, not bothering to ask Janice to follow me.

Walking through the house this time, everything seemed fine. I checked for new messages. There was one.

"Cassie. Listen, it's Tiffany. I want to meet with you—"

I pushed nine to delete. There was no way I wanted to meet with Tiffany the Twit. Ever.

I crawled in bed and slept the night through.

CHAPTER 14

The next morning, I remembered John Lane's message.

I walked across the street to Lane's house and rang the doorbell. I stood on the porch and waited for an answer long enough to feel foolish. I also had the feeling someone was watching me. The hair on my arms and neck stuck out as if someone had rubbed a balloon over them.

The feeling was most likely one borne out of guilt. If there were anyone who watched people standing on their doorstep rather than answering the doorbell, it would be me. I wouldn't want the word to get out, but salespersons and those running for city and county political campaigns had been a source of entertainment to me for years. You'd be surprised how many people talk to themselves, and I won't bring up the number of men who adjust or dig at their private areas while waiting for someone to answer the doorbell.

I looked in the windows of the garage doors to see if Lane's car was in it. Scooter the cat stood in the middle of the garage and he was not happy. He arched his back, puffed up his tail, and made a hissing noise. He didn't look healthy. His hair looked matted in spots and there were puffs of it all along the edges of the wall and floor.

I couldn't see any food or water. I walked around to the side door of the garage and checked the lock. I felt bad for Scooter, but I convinced myself Scooter would probably attack me and claw my eyes out of their sockets. Then there would be the big problem of blindly making my way to a phone to call Animal Control and having him put down. I decided to forget about the cat.

I walked back to my house and sat in front of the computer thinking about how I could not tell Lane about her father. I would let him call and tell him she was no longer interested in meeting him. Something I knew I should have done earlier. But no, I wanted to finish the job I'd started.

It took me almost thirty minutes to type a simple note. I kept adding to the information, and deleting it. Ultimately, I ended the note by asking Lane to call the police and let them know the new information regarding Crystal. I told her that I'd be home if she wanted to talk. I signed it and put my phone number under my signature. Underneath my number, I added a postscript regarding Scooter needing water and food.

Now it was afternoon and, once again, I walked over to Lane's house and rang the doorbell. Again, there was no answer. I took the note to the mailbox and turned around to see if anyone was looking out a window at me. I saw nothing and no one, so I walked to the side of the garage and pushed at the door. It took two hard shoves to open it, but I'm pleased to say I didn't damage the door. I stepped inside and Scooter's litter box stench hit me. Instead of attacking me, the cat hissed and ran behind a plastic storage container.

I walked across the garage and found Lane had left the door leading into the kitchen unlocked. I grabbed a bowl, filled it with water, and set it on the garage floor near the container where Scooter was hiding.

I didn't leave. Instead, I went back through the kitchen and into the dining room. The dining room was no longer a mess. It was neat and orderly. None of the articles I had seen before were in sight. The buffet drawer held crisp linen napkins and a tablecloth. I almost missed it, but I heard a clinking sound as I began to shut the drawer. Underneath the tablecloth, I found a white sweater with a plastic nametag. It spelled out Crystal in block letters.

Why would she have Crystal's sweater? They must have met after the restaurant incident. Did she already know Crystal was her sister? Or maybe Del had brought it from his office. Perhaps Crystal had left it there.

While debating on doing a quick check of the rest of the house, I peeked through the living room curtains and saw Lane's car as she stopped in front of her mailbox. I ran through the garage and out the side door. I stood flat against the stucco siding until I heard the garage door open and the vehicle enter the garage. I ran across the street and nonchalantly sat in the rocker on my front porch.

Now, as before, the neighborhood was quiet, except for the sound of Lane's garage door rolling down. There were no cars coming or going on the street, not one person was out walking or riding a bike, and I didn't see one other sign of human life.

The sun went behind dark rain clouds, and I laughed. Of course, no one was out. It was a humid ninety-seven degrees outside and it was time for the normal ten minutes of afternoon rain. It was the rainy season, and who wants to be hot and wet? Janice was right. I had watched a few too many Hitchcock movies.

I waited for the first drops of rain, went in, and

locked the door behind me. That was something I didn't normally do in the daylight. I told myself I was behaving like a character in a B movie. Regardless of my mental chiding, I walked away and left it locked.

It was silent in the house except for the soft chuck-a-chuck noise coming from the ceiling fans. I had turned the air down to 68 degrees on that morning in anticipation of the weather station's predicted humidity index. Now the house was cool, but too confining. I couldn't hear the birds, feel the sun, or see the sky.

When the rain stopped and the sun came back out in front of the clouds, I changed into my swimming suit and went to the pool through the lanai's sliding doors, making sure to shut them behind me.

I felt the heat immediately, but I also heard the birds and smelled the salt water on the breeze. I never wanted to take these things for granted. I wanted to appreciate them and be grateful for them, because I knew not everyone had the opportunity to live in this way.

While soaking up the sun, I thought of my previous home. Right after failing the state police training, I entered a community college and began training as a court reporter. Once through with the training and after passing the state's certification exam, I moved to a Detroit neighborhood located off one of its main arteries. My Victorian style house had beautiful, original oak-wood trim and floors, and a lot of character—which really means it needed a lot of work.

I didn't know why I chose the neighborhood, other than the convenience of the location's proximity to downtown.

Really, there wasn't much to draw people into the neighborhood. The majority of the houses on the street were rental homes and in a depressing state of disrepair. For whatever reason, I stuck it out and ended up enjoying the gritty, stand-on-your-own-two-feet spirit of the neighborhood and, after a time, I felt I belonged.

When the old man next door died, a new landlord took over his house and some other rental houses on the street. Eventually, that landlord, Vince, moved in and began an overhaul on the house next to mine. He made improvements, brought them up to code, and made them neat and tidy. He canvassed the neighborhood and initiated an association.

Falling for him didn't have much to do with the fact that his rear end looked incredible in paint spattered, faded blue jeans, but it did have everything to do with his warm puppy-dog eyes and the laughter crinkles surrounding them. After only five minutes of our first conversation, I felt he was a genuine, caring man.

When I met Terrence's mom, Julia, she worked at the hospital down the street from the courthouse where I worked and, when the weather was nice, we walked to work together. During our walks, she talked about her life as a single parent and I listened. I felt her son Terrence had a chance to do better things in his life, and tried to help Julia concentrate on his future rather than their past.

Occasionally, I would keep Terrence with me while Julia did her grocery shopping or wanted a night to herself. On one such night, Terrance and I were playing charades in the living room and hadn't noticed when Rachel slipped into the house.

Terrence had chosen animals as the category and was supposed to be acting out the word mink. I found out later he thought he was flouncing around like a woman in high heels and pretending to flip a mink stole over his shoulder. To me, he appeared to be throwing a fit.

"A bear!" I said for the third time, not because he acted like a bear, but because I couldn't think of another damn animal. I'd been through the alphabet twice, each time matching an animal to a letter.

He shook his head the first two times and concentrated on refining his charade. But this time he said, "No!"

"Don't talk," I blurted out, frustrated at my inability to get his mime.

"Fuck that," he said.

I stared at him, not knowing what to say or how to discipline him. "It's against the rules. You can't talk."

He'd balled up his fists and held his arms straight down against his thin body, his shoulders hunched as if ready to charge. Then, I thought he finally looked like an animal. A bull.

He was eleven years old but I think until then I'd thought of him as much younger. Now, his anger and hurt made him seem like an old man. I didn't know much about kids. I didn't understand what I'd said was the worst thing you could say to him. I didn't know that someone had said this to him countless times before.

"Terrence, come here," Rachel said.

Both Terrence and I jumped at the sound of her voice. She was leaning against the oak archway leading into the living room. She'd been working out. I remember how her face glowed with health and energy. Her hair, a dark auburn, looked damp, and she'd pulled it into a tail at the back of her neck. Loose strands curled behind her ears and down her neck. How could she be that beautiful and not let it change her, I thought.

"Why should I?" Terrence said.

She smiled. "It's all about strategy, my friend."

"Huh?" Terrance sneered at her.

"Come on, two minds are better than one, right?" She held out her hand to him as if she fully expected him to take it.

He went to her and they put their heads together. He came back and acted out the mink using their strategy.

I got it within a minute.

"Wow," I said.

"It's all about strategy, my friend," Terrence said. He couldn't stop smiling and didn't take his eyes off Rachel the rest of the night.

I didn't know how it came so naturally to her. Kids gravitated to her wherever she went. There was just something about her. Maybe because she never allowed herself to think they wouldn't like her.

Things were good until the day I found out who Terrence's father was. Just as Julia had told me, he was the repeat offender, the defendant, and the no-good father. He was the Cooper in State of MI vs. Cooper. I was the official court reporter and I was shocked to look up and see Julia and Terrence sitting in the first row of benches directly behind the defendant.

"This is where you sit when you support the defendant," I told her during a break in the court proceedings. "You and Terrence shouldn't be here. At least move to the other side."

"Averill's not all bad," Julia said, drawing a line in the sand with her words. "I feel sorry for him. He didn't do what they say he did, anyway."

"I don't think you're giving Terrence the right message," I said.

"You don't know everything," Julia said.

"This isn't how life has to be, Terrence. It's not supposed to be this way," I told him, stopping when I realized he wouldn't hear me unless Julia backed me up.

Terrence scowled at me and then looked at his mother, waiting for her reaction. But she busied herself by digging into her purse and didn't look me in the eye.

I was upset that she wouldn't listen, but I wasn't

overly concerned about our friendship, we had disagreed, and that was that. It was normal for friends to have differences.

Back then, I didn't know normal things could screw up your life. I didn't know you didn't get a warning, and there was no ominous music playing in the background like in the movies.

I returned to my place at the front of the court near the judge's box. The State was giving the closing argument.

THE COURT: Okay. We're back on record. Let's proceed where we left off, Mr. Beacraft.

MR. BEACRAFT: (Assistant Prosecutor) Ladies and Gentlemen of the Jury, as you know, the defendant, Averill Terrence Cooper, is charged with the first-degree assault of George Frank; first-degree assault of Jolene Frank; and burglary. Cooper's defense lawyers want you, the jury, to believe that you shouldn't find Cooper guilty of the offenses. The defendant, citing a long history of alcohol abuse, pleads not guilty. And, as you know, the State has the burden of proving, beyond a reasonable doubt, that the crimes were, in fact, based on the evidence presented at trial—uh, excuse me. Your Honor. May I approach the bench?

THE COURT: All right. Go Ahead.

The prosecutor, Mr. Joseph Beacraft, and Judge Richard Bean had a discussion outside of the court reporter's hearing.

THE COURT: Ladies and gentlemen of the jury, if you-all would step out briefly at this time. We have some other matters to take up.

(Jury excused from courtroom while a discussion was held in their absence.)

MR. BEACRAFT: I want on record the official court reporter's inappropriate behavior displayed in full view of the jury. She's flirting with the defendant, for Christ's sake!

THE COURT: The prosecutor claims he saw an exchange between the defendant, Averill Terrence Cooper, and you, the court reporter, Ms. Cassandra Cruise. Can you explain, Ms. Cruise?

I set aside my stenotype machine, pulled out my back-up tape recorder, and turned it on before answering.

"Here's what happened, Your Honor. The defendant, Mr. Cooper, smiled and winked at me as I recorded the State's closing argument. But since the Prosecutor, Mr. Beacraft, found it necessary to speak beyond his normal speed of 300 words per minute, while at the same time pick lunch out of his teeth, I, in my effort to concentrate and take the words down verbatim, automatically and without thinking, responded with a return smile. I meant nothing by it. It was reflex. I wasn't flirting with the defendant. In truth, I find him repulsive."

MR. ROSS: (Defense Attorney) Objection!

THE COURT: We're off record. Shut that damn recorder off. Now!

I got away with a note in my employee file, in which also was mentioned my brief discussion with the defendant's family during a break. Julia never returned my calls and Terrence didn't come around after that day. Not even for Rachel.

The DAs and my co-workers treated me differently after that. Or, it could've been me seeing everyone in a new and jaded way. Either way, I ended up behaving a wee-bit unprofessional and threw a couple punches at a Clerk of the Court who wouldn't shut her festering gob about the whole thing. I had a choice to give notice or talk to the clerk's lawyer.

I moved on to a second career.

Private investigating. Not a career choice that endeared me to many, especially Vince. We'd had our ups and downs. Same as any other couple.

The job, the TV show, moving to Florida—those were rough times. Through it all, to my surprise, we remained a couple.

CHAPTER 15

I plunged into the pool to cool off, did a few laps, got out, and fell asleep in the sun while listening to the birds chirping.

Scooter woke me up by clawing at the screen behind my lounge chair. I turned to look and he raised his back and began hissing at me.

"Look, you little bag of fur," I said, "you're in my territory now."

He jumped at the sound of my voice and froze midway between another hiss and running away. I got up out of my chair, went into the lanai, opened the sliding door to the kitchen, and came back out with a bowl of water and an opened can of tuna.

He smelled it immediately and began meowing. I walked over to the entrance and opened the door. He ran over to the door, hesitated, looked up at me with disdain, and walked in.

Cats are different from dogs. A dog would have run head first into the food, snarling and growling along the way. A dog's intent would be to get the food into his gullet as fast as possible and deal with any obstacles after.

Oh, but Scooter—a cat who was obviously a direct descendant of Royalty—sidled over to the tuna with slow, graceful, pre-eminence. He had the nerve to sniff it and look up at me as if I had purposely brought him the generic brand. I believe if his hunger hadn't overcome him, he would have waited for me to taste it first to ensure that it wasn't poisoned.

I propped the door open so His Hind-end-ness could leave after partaking of his pauper's meal and walked back into the kitchen to make a meal for myself. Tuna salad sounded great. I chopped the onion and celery, added them to the bowl of tuna and mayonnaise, and grabbed a box of crackers.

Sitting down in the lounge chair, I expected Scooter to be gone. However, he was in the lounge chair next to mine, spread out like a centerfold, licking his privates with abandon.

"I have some rights here, Mister Scooter," I said. "One of my rights, in my own home I might add, is to not have to look at you while you're doing that, especially, while I'm eating." He stopped his acrobatics long enough to look at me with annoyance and then resumed.

"Okay. That's it. You need to go home."

He didn't bother to look up. He moved on to a more disgusting area of his anatomy, rearranging his legs for easier access.

I decided I was finished with my salad and picked up the tuna can and the water bowl. I went inside, dropped the bowls in the sink, rinsed out the can, and took it out to the recycling bin in the laundry area. While there, I pulled a big suitcase down from the shelf above the washer and stuffed it full of clean clothing. I wanted to be ready to go on the trip with Janice well ahead of time.

Returning to the lanai, I bumped smack-dab into Lane.

"Oh! You scared me. I had no idea you were here," I said.

"I'm sorry, I didn't mean to scare you," she said, looking terrific in a white tank top and low-slung navy shorts. She seemed relaxed and happy again. She smiled and put her hand on my arm. "The door to the enclosure was open, so I came on in."

"Were you looking for Scooter?" I asked.

She crinkled her eyes. "Who?"

"Your cat. To be honest with you, I think you should give him to someone who wants a cat. He doesn't seem very well taken care of," I said.

Her mouth opened and closed. Something hard flickered in her eyes and disappeared before it became full-blown. "Okay, you're probably right about that," she said with a forced sounding laugh.

"Does Del like cats?" I asked.

"No, it's not Del's. I found him, and I should have taken him to a cat shelter or whatever you call them. I'll do that tomorrow," she said.

Well, that's settled. I understand completely not having it in you to take care of a pet, but there's no excuse for neglect or mistreatment, I thought.

"You want some tea?" I asked.

"Sure."

I went into the kitchen and turned to see Lane had followed me. She leaned against the counter across from the refrigerator.

I opened the refrigerator door to get the tea and was reaching up into the cupboard to grab the glasses when she said, "I got your note, Cassie."

Her voice was pleasant and soft. No reason for me to shiver. No reason for the goose bumps running up my arms.

"Oh, good." I poured the tea. "You don't seem surprised about having a sister."

"No?"

I picked up both glasses of tea and headed out to the lanai. Lane followed.

"I hope you understand what I was trying to tell you. I hope you and Crystal can work everything out. I think you should know it will probably take some time and a great deal of professional intervention," I said once we had sat down.

"A great deal, I'm sure," she said.

"Let me ask you. Did Del know Crystal was your sister?"

"She would be my half-sister," she said and took a sip of tea.

"How much do you know about Crystal? Or Del for that matter," I asked her.

"About as much as anyone can really know about anyone else," she said. "We're from the same home town basically."

I looked at her, hoping I wasn't on the verge of seeing the Lane with the dark and gloomy aura.

"Who's all from the same home town?"

"Del and Crystal and me," Lane said.

"I thought you met Del on the internet. And Crystal's from New Mexico, right?"

"Del and his mother are from Scranton. They moved around a lot before settling here. I never knew Del before talking to him on the internet. Probably because I went to private schools and he went to public schools. Crystal's mother is a cousin, so I consider her home town to be Scranton, too."

"Are you happy to be meeting your father? I know you told me to forget you wanted to meet him, but I had already called him by then," I said.

"When is he going to call you?" Her voice was flat like before. *Oh, oh, here we go again.*

"Tomorrow."

"What if you're not here to take the call? Does he have my number?"

"I didn't have your number to give him. Anyway, I'll be here. Janice is booked solid, so we're not golfing tomorrow. Vince's working on a house in Sarasota, I think. Anyway, I don't have anything planned with him." At the thought of Vince, I swallowed and blinked away the feeling of impending tears.

"He is," she said.

"What?"

"Vince. He's working in Sarasota. I spoke with him earlier," she said.

Without thinking, I let her know how much it bothered me that they spoke. "Why?" I asked.

She wore a smile that mimicked Mona Lisa. "Why what?"

I sucked in a breath. "Why did you speak with Vince?"

"Oh, house stuff," she said.

"I see," I said.

"Does he know where I live?" she asked.

"Who?" I forced my mind to let go of the Vince and Lane thing. "Oh, your father? Only if Crystal told him. Like I explained in the note, he's going to call again. Obviously, he doesn't have your number, but I gave you his number. Just call him and make arrangements about meeting him."

She put her hand on her hip and narrowed her eyes. "Ohhh-kaayy."

"I know, I know. But you did ask me to find your dad, initially I mean, didn't you?"

"What did you tell your friends? Did you say something to Vince about this?" she asked.

"I just thought it was odd how much you changed, how different you were. I didn't know if Del was abusing you, or if Crystal was threatening you, or what. I wanted to find out, and you know, solve the puzzle. Vince and Janice asked me to stop and let you deal with your own issues. I intended to do that when your dad called me back."

"When did you figure out that Crystal was my half-sister?" She was composed and cool as she smiled and waited for my answer.

I moved to my chair and motioned for her to sit opposite me. "It just came to me. I started thinking about John Lane and his wife Sheila, and Sheila told me they had a daughter, so I put it all together. Anyway, I know my cousins and I are very similar, even though I don't like to admit it. I thought you and Crystal would look similar, and then there's the tattoo coincidence—"

"How did you know that? You never saw her. You couldn't know."

I raised my chin and looked at her. I didn't want to explain it to her. "I asked around."

Lane leaned forward in her chair, putting me on edge for some reason. "Who? Who did you ask?"

Loosening my grip on the arms of my chair, I forced myself to relax. "I'm sorry you're upset by all this, but taking out your frustration on me isn't going to do any good. I didn't create this mess. Seems to me you did."

Her eyes popped wide open. "Excuse me?"

Lane's hair was covering half of her face, and when she raised her hand to push it out of the way, the ceiling fans caught her odor and sent it my way. There wasn't a hint of vanilla-citrus. It was a smell closer to Scooter's litter box.

"You have to be the nosiest person on this earth," she said.

"I'm not taking Crystal's side. If she stalked you and harassed you, she was wrong. She needs to be stopped and she needs to get help." I grabbed my cigarettes and lit up, not caring if the smoke was offensive. It was my house, and her funky, mildew smell was offensive to me.

When she laughed, I jumped. "You really don't know anything," she said. "You don't know a fucking thing," came out of her Princess Grace mouth.

Then, I thought, *My God, where is Crystal?* In my mind, I saw the white sweater with the nametag in Lane's buffet drawer. I heard Janice's voice saying people assume too much. I gulped in air and a scene from *A Shadow of a Doubt* flashed through my mind. "You think you know something, don't you? You think you're the clever little girl who knows something. There's so much that you don't know...so much. What do you know really..." Uncle Charlie said this to his young niece, Charlotte Newton. Uncle Charlie was a murderer and Charlotte was figuring it out.

Why would I think of this now? Maybe Crystal wasn't the bad witch, and maybe it was Lane. I pushed the question away and tried to concentrate on Lane.

"You don't know anything. You don't know about making plans or bringing order and sense to your life. You know nothing about letting no one or nothing ruin your plans. Do you?" she was saying as she paced back and forth in front of me. "If I don't have a schedule, everything is messed up. People need to stick to the plan." Her eyes were tracking everything in the room, and her hands looked like bundles of bone and skin.

"It's not too late to get help. Things aren't as bad as we think once we've asked for help," I said.

"I don't need help. I need people like you to stay out of my business." She looked around the room, flipped her hair over her shoulder, and looked hard at Scooter who had wandered in through the doors. Scooter froze, arched his back, and hissed.

"You should calm down and think things through. Everything will look better if you're calm." I said. My stomach tightened up and my teeth clenched together.

I lowered my hand and wiggled my fingers. Scooter came to the chair and I rubbed his forehead.

"I need time to think. Can we just be quiet and think? Do you think you can manage to do that for a few minutes? Can you shut the fuck up?" She sat in the chair with a sigh.

Gee-golly, telling someone to shut up sounds so nice when a face like that says it. "Pass me the sugar and shut the fuck up, sweetie," I could hear her saying to Del.

I put my cigarette in my mouth to keep from screaming or laughing.

"Oh, do shut up," Bette Davis's voice popped into my head.

I must have laughed aloud.

"You're a bit odd, aren't you?" she asked me in all seriousness.

I choked on the smoke I'd inhaled. "I am," I said, and then I shook my head. "But wow, you've got your nerve. You're as barmy as Baby Jane and you're asking me if I'm odd?"

She snorted and stared at the ceiling for a second, and then she looked at me. "Who's Baby Jane?"

"You should leave. This is my house and you're here uninvited. Whatever issues you have don't involve me." I knew Janice would laugh at that one.

"Let's handle things my way," Lane said.

"Here's a better idea. You go back across the street, reorganize your plans, whatever they are, and deal with whatever is wrong in your life."

She shrugged and remained seated. "I should be here when my father calls. I can only depend on myself to get things done correctly."

"You can't stay here." I raised my voice and looked her straight in the eye. "Look, go home. Don't make me toss you out."

"I want to be here when he calls."

"Leave me your cell phone number. It's as simple as that," I told her.

"I don't want to yet," Lane said.

"Now you're being irrational. Think about what you're doing." I put out my cigarette and waited for her to think it through.

"I don't think I'm asking much," she said.

"I can tell you right now, no one stays in my house when they're not invited. Are we clear?"

She didn't answer, just looked at the tile floor.

I had some experiences with irrational people. Then again, anyone who'd been through a couple of divorces could say that. But I had learned the best thing to do was to try to reclaim the situation. I needed to make sure I was calm and there should be an opportunity for each of us to think and have our say.

"Tell me why you feel you have to sit here and wait for your dad to call," I asked her.

"I don't want him to talk to you," she said.

Then I remembered the opened door. "Did you come into my home when I was out of town?"

"If you want something done right, do it yourself. Did your mother ever say that? I can't rely on you to follow my directions. You've proven that already." She picked up her hair from the back of her neck, flung it over to one side, adjusted the strap of her white shirt, and froze. "Uggh! Why did you allow that gross creature in your house?" She picked a cat hair off her navy shorts.

She stood, grabbed Scooter, and tossed him out the door. He landed inches away from the pool and ran under a lounge chair, backing himself in the corner of the enclosure.

"Not nice." I counted to ten under my breath. I didn't want this to get any uglier and if I lost my temper, it would get very ugly.

She hadn't admitted to breaking in, but I knew she had. It didn't upset me much. I'd done the same to her. What upset me was her inability to comprehend how wrong her present behavior was. She shouldn't get away with coming into a person's home uninvited and ignore an order to leave. No one else would get away with that behavior.

"If you don't want him in your life right now, I won't answer the phone or I'll tell him you don't want to talk to him. I'll tell him you've changed your mind," I said, barely able to keep myself from yelling.

"That could be an option." She seemed to think about it, still not moving from the chair.

"I am so trying to be understanding and patient, Lane. But it seems to me that you do not understand this is my home. You heard me tell you I'll toss you out, correct?" I was holding on, trying to rein in my anger. But I hadn't moved to this neighborhood of the near comatose to end up as a whipping dog for a disturbed child. *This was my home. Mine. I am in charge in my own home.*

"I really don't think you'll do that," she said. As if the decision was hers. As if I should wait for her to make a decision.

I didn't want anything from her other than to hear her say, yes, you're right, Cassie, this is your home and I'm here uninvited and behaving atrociously. If she did that, we'd be fine.

"I asked you a question," I said.

Lane smiled a smug smile, remained in the chair, and didn't answer.

I jumped up and lifted her out of the chair by grabbing the front of her shirt with both hands. When she tried to fight her way out of my grasp, I tossed her toward the living room. "Enough! This is my home, Lane."

She landed on her knees on the tiled step-up to the living room.

Trying to calm myself, I walked to her and pulled her to her feet. "Don't say I didn't warn you."

"You can't—" She turned toward me with her mouth open. Her face was splotched red and she was breathing hard. "You don't understand. We should work this out."

I couldn't believe her arrogance. "Now you want to work it out? Nah. Nope. Now it's too late."

"No. You don't understand," Lane said and tried to return to the lanai.

I snatched her arm and twisted her around to face the door. Pushing her toward the front door, I said for what felt like the hundredth time, "This is my home. My home, do you understand? You will never come uninvited again." I shoved her ten inches closer to the door. "I control what happens in my home. I won't have this ugliness in my home ever again."

And then both of our phones rang.

I froze. She closed her eyes for a second and took a deep breath. Then he reached into the back pocket of her shorts and pulled out her phone.

"Hello," she said. Her face changed, smoothed out and softened, and I knew who had called her. Del. "I know, baby. I lost track of the time."

There were tears forming in the corners of her eyes. I no longer existed. She focused on the caller.

The doorbell rang. Before I decided which to answer—my phone or the doorbell—she walked to the door. Without attempting to open it first, she reached beneath the handle and unlocked the bolt, which told me she knew it was locked and had tried opening it earlier from the outside. When she cracked it open, I saw Tillie, Del's mother, standing in the entrance. Lane saw her too and quickly slid through the opening in the doorway.

I pulled the door completely open and saw Tillie had Lane by the arm, leading her across the street. I also saw RJ standing on the sidewalk in front of my house, looking at me with big eyes, his phone to his ear.

I heard my phone ring one last time. RJ took his phone away from his ear and flipped it closed.

I wasn't certain any longer of who was the crazier, but it seemed by the way RJ was looking at me, he'd decided on me. And right then I thought that might be okay. I felt on the verge of being dangerous to others.

Wanting to explain, I yelled out, "Tillie. Come over and talk to me, please?"

"You leave her alone," she yelled back at me.

"Leave her alone? How about her? She fucking came to my home—" My voice cracked and I stopped shouting.

Turning toward a gasping noise, I saw Sammy standing at the corner of his yard, looking at me with his mouth and eyes opened wide.

Just great. I waved at him and he turned and walked toward his house as fast as his legs would let him.

RJ came up to my porch. "You okay?"

"I'm fine. You can carry on with whatever you were doing."

He shrugged and began walking away.

"Hey. Wait. What were you doing?" I asked.

"Later," he said and kept walking.

Across the street, Tillie and Lane had reached Lane's porch. Tillie patted Lane's back and gave her a quick hug. Lane went into her house and shut the door. Tillie reached into her navy blue Taurus, took something out of the front seat area, and returned to Lane's house.

Bette Davis slithered back into my mind. "Fasten your seat belts. It's going to be a bumpy night."

Enough, already. She's gone.

Re-locking the door helped stop my hands from shaking. Only then was I able to draw the blinds over the windows and shut the sliding doors in the lanai. After locking them, I made fresh coffee, poured a cup, and plopped down in the chair.

While lighting the eighth cigarette of the day, I thought about how much I'd always hated cell phones. I'd thought they were just another way to make it permissible for people to annoy you at all hours. I'd always said they were an invention for people who were afraid of being alone.

I liked my peace and quiet. A cell phone was an intrusion to me.

The people who carried them to the grocery store, the doctor's office, the mall, while driving, even while in public bathrooms, seemed like robots. Either it was at their ear continually or they were searching for it in their bag after hearing their special chosen ring tone.

It never seemed to bother them that the people around could hear half of their conversation and generally the things they talked about seemed very trivial.

Always seemed to me it was about something that they could have saved for when they had the time to share a pot of coffee and enjoy each other's company.

At this point, I was extremely grateful that they existed and that there were people such as Lane who felt a strong responsibility toward answering them at all times.

Always thought they were good for emergency purposes, and I was right. If she hadn't answered her phone at that point in time, I couldn't be sure that I wouldn't have hurt her.

I tried calling Vince and again got his voice mail. I

didn't bother with a message, but when I hung up, the phone rang.

"Cassie? You call me?" Vince asked.

"I've been missing you," I said.

"I'm sorry. I have to finish up here or I don't get paid," he said. "You know, there are plenty of people around you who would enjoy keeping you occupied until I can get back there."

"I'm not sure why you think I need to be occupied. I'm not a mischievous child."

I didn't want to be angry, but he wasn't saying anything near what I wanted to hear. We had left too many things unsaid and I didn't know where to start or if I should start.

What had been so easy now seemed difficult.

I winced when I heard his sigh.

"Hey. You okay? Anything going on we need to talk about?' I asked.

"Have you let go of the Lane thing?" he asked.

"You know what? I think *you* should let go of the Lane thing. First of all, you really don't know half of what I know about her. But apparently, you're going to stick to your version of her, even when your fiancé— that's me in case you've forgotten—tells you different. You see a problem here? I do."

"I don't have the energy right now to argue with you," Vince said.

"Right there is a big part of the problem. This shouldn't be an argument, it's a discussion."

"Then can we discuss it when I finish this job? I am really worn out, Cassie," he said.

"Sure. We'll talk when you've rested. Any idea when that'll be?"

"Couple days. I'll give you a call later okay?"

"Bye, Vince." As I hung up, I realized he did sound

tired and he probably was exhausted. The question was what was exhausting him. His work or us?

After checking the locks on my doors again, I looked out my window and decided I needed to talk to someone with a level head. Someone who would listen in a professional manner and someone who wouldn't let emotion cloud their judgment. I went to the phone on my desk and punched in Detective Winslow's number.

CHAPTER 16

"Would you mind looking at me?"

"I believe I am, Ms. Cruise."

"Cassie, okay?"

He nodded.

"Do you ever relax? You sit facing the door and check out everyone who comes through it. You look like a cop, walk like a cop, and talk like a cop. You can't help it, can you?"

"No, ma'am."

"Makes me miss my sister," I said, and then held my breath. Missing her was a day-to-day thing, but it shocked me when I realized I'd said it aloud.

"I bet you do," he said and made no effort to look up from writing in his notepad. His way, I believed, of letting me know we weren't going to bond over the subject.

"I just told you some very weird stuff about my neighbor—well, in my opinion it's weird. Don't you have anything to say?"

He pocketed his pen and picked up the tablet from the table, putting it with the pen. "I've taken the report."

"Damn it. I want to hear you say I was right to call you. Or tell me you're writing me off as a dramatic idiot.

I don't know." I shook my head and looked down at the plastic table. I tried to put my thoughts together. The clanging of dishes and clunk of the cash registers slowed down the process. "I want you to understand why I called you."

"You need to understand. I cannot go in and arrest or question someone without probable cause. You did not witness a crime. You're not even sure what the crime is," Winslow said.

"But—"

"I'm not working the case anyway. It's gone back to North Harbor."

"See, I don't need coddling, I need to hear from you whether you think I'm full of claptrap or not."

The server working our side of the cafe came toward me and I waved away the pot of coffee she held up in my direction. She freshened Detective Winslow's coffee.

"In fact, I wish you would tell me I'm full of claptrap," I said after she left our booth.

Winslow added a packet of sugar and a dollop of cream to his freshened coffee. He concentrated on stirring it and clinked the spoon on the side of the cup enough times I had to put my hand on his to stop him.

"Sorry," he said, looking down at my hand.

Moving my hand away, I picked up my cup and took a drink of the now lukewarm coffee. "You should have told me you weren't working the case."

"I just did."

I started to feel uncomfortable. His short responses felt like a hint. He wanted to leave. He wanted me to stop bothering him. "Look, I guess I can assume I've done my part here. Right? I mean, you have my statement or whatever you call it."

"What do you want me to do with it?" he asked.

"I don't know, I'm scared," I said.

"Of what?"

"Of me. I could have hurt her. I wanted to. And now I'm ashamed. A little too late, right?" I laughed, but it came out sounding like a cough.

He wasn't laughing. He wasn't even smirking.

"What about Lane? Aren't you afraid of her?" he asked.

"Well, only if she has a weapon or—"

"You're not a freaking Amazon. Stay as far away from her as possible."

"I guess."

"Anyone can see you're in great shape, and, yes, you might know self-defense, but you yourself said she's loony. Okay? Just stay away from her. Completely," he said.

I tried to pretend I wasn't flattered by what he'd said about me being in great shape, but I felt my face heat up into a blush. I lowered my head so he wouldn't see it.

After a few seconds, I said, "Then you do believe me when I tell you she's not right in the head."

"We need to concentrate on the cremated body and the arson of the vehicle, that's all." He glanced at his watch, and gulped the coffee.

"We who?"

"Not you. Not me."

He was ready to leave.

Don't leave yet.

"Can't you just say car fire?" I asked.

"What? That's what I said." He wrinkled his brow and I noticed patches of gray along his hairline and a few wiry and unruly gray hairs in his eyebrows. They needed trimming, but I couldn't picture him concerning himself with that type of grooming.

"You said arson of the vehicle."

"Oh." A small smile was on his lips.

"Cop talk," I said.

He pushed his cup away, and I took his hand in mine. He seemed a little spooked, but didn't pull away.

"She could be really violent, now that I think about it. She throws a great tantrum," I told him and laughed. I kept a hold on his hand, even though it embarrassed me to be feeling this needy.

"You'll be fine. Just make sure you don't interfere. That doesn't help, it only causes problems. Let everyone do their job," he said.

No one could ever call him warm and fuzzy. I let go of his hand, fished my keys out of my purse, and prepared to leave. My breath caught in my throat. "Oh, wow."

"What?" he asked. When I didn't answer, he said, "Ms. Cruise. Sit down."

"Cassie." I told him before I sat.

"I knew I didn't lock the car that night, but I didn't remember I'd left the keys in the trunk." I showed him the whole key ring. I then went through the keys on my ring, holding them up one by one. "Everything is on this ring. All of my house keys, the keys to the shop, even the remote garage door opener. They're all here. Except the keys to the car. They were on Rachel's holder and I'd hooked it to my set with one of those separable clips. I never thought about it until now when I looked for them out of habit. Stupid, huh?"

"Not so stupid," he said. "Go home. Go get some sleep."

"That's it?"

"That's it, okay?"

"Yep."

"Good." He nodded.

"You know, no one believed me when I said how much she'd changed from day to day. I knew something like this would happen," I said.

Winslow stood up and I followed him. He held the door for me and I headed toward the rental in the parking lot. He caught up with me and we walked side by side.

"You don't know what's gonna happen from day-to-day. No one does," he said as we walked. He stopped next to his car, an old Chevy Impala.

"No, but you can try to change what might happen next," I said.

His sigh was tired.

I looked down at the pebbles and crushed sea shells that made up the cafe parking lot, trying to think of a way to tell him I felt bad for asking him to meet me and for showing up needy and weak. Looking up, I caught him watching me. He smiled. Without thinking, I reached up, ran my finger across his lips, and then smoothed his bushy eyebrows into a straight line. Slowly and one at a time.

Winslow grabbed my wrist and I started to apologize, but he leaned in and kissed me. Soft and slow until I put my hand at the back of his head. Then with an urgent roughness.

Noise wafted out of the diner as someone opened the door. It clunked shut and there was the sound of footsteps on gravel, a car door shutting, tires crushing shells, and finally only the whirring of the nearby traffic.

He dropped my wrist.

When I looked at his craggy face, I saw a reflection of my need and I walked to the passenger door of his car, waiting for him to unlock it.

We didn't talk until he parked in the driveway of one of the many unremarkable stucco homes in a community called The Villa.

"Are you okay with this? Should I take you back to your car?' Winslow turned off the ignition and looked straight ahead while waiting for me to answer.

I got out and waited for him on the small, covered porch. He followed, unlocked the front door, pushed it open, and stepped aside. I took his hand and pulled him into the house with me, turning to face him once we were inside. Winslow grabbed my arm and pulled me against him. Catching a whiff of his spicy and woodsy cologne, I laid my head on his chest and felt his heartbeat and the warmth radiating from beneath his starched button down shirt. He felt safe and familiar. I wanted to stay wrapped in his arms.

But it's not Vince, I thought. And then I thought, just don't think anymore. It wasn't until later, about the time I lifted myself off Winslow, that I began again to think.

I flopped down on the bed next to Winslow, stared up at the ceiling, and tried to catch my breath. He put his arm beneath my shoulders and pulled me close.

After a time, I said, "I've been wondering why Crystal hasn't shown up. I keep saying a stalker doesn't just go away."

He took his arm from underneath me and turned onto his side to face me. "I'm not following you."

"The body in the car. I'm betting it's Lane Somers' half-sister Crystal. I just don't know who killed her and put her in the trunk." I started to get up from the bed. He pulled me back and turned my head so that I was looking at him.

"If you think you can do this on your own, you're wrong. You need to leave it alone, Cassie."

The tone of his voice felt like a slap aside my head. His message hit an exposed nerve. Tired of people telling me how to behave, I moved away from him, trying to think of a way to leave without having to ask him for a ride.

"What makes you believe the victim is Crystal Evans?" he asked.

I smiled. *So much for leaving it alone.*

"Because no one has heard from her or seen her since that day. They fought over Del, I think, and either Del or Lane killed her."

"You have no facts, no evidence. Nothing." He watched me, waiting for my reaction.

I nodded. "Yes, you're right. I can prove nothing, but I have a motive."

"What?" He had an impatient look on his face.

I turned toward him. "Lane has money. According to a high school friend, she is filthy rich. Her stepfather left everything to Maureen, Lane's mother. But Maureen died three days after this weird car accident involving the whole family. Maureen had a will too, and in her will, she left everything to Lane. Whoever marries Lane will marry her money."

"She's engaged to that putz, Welling, isn't she?" Winslow asked.

I nodded. "Now, one thing I know about Lane is she has a low tolerance for people getting in the way of her plans. And I can't imagine Del wouldn't be worried about someone getting between him and Lane's money. If Crystal was interfering in their relationship—I'm talking about Lane's and Del's relationship—I think one or the other would've done almost anything, including murder, to get rid of her."

"This is all supposition," Winslow said.

"But you believe me. I can tell." With my finger, I traced the tattoo of Superman bursting through a brick wall on his bicep.

"You're not as much of a psychic as you'd like to think." He gave me a peck on my forehead, sat up on the side of the bed, and pulled on a pair of jeans. He stood near the dresser, buttoning his shirt, and then grabbed his wallet and keys.

"Hey, Winslow. I guess I'm ready to go home now. Thanks for asking," I said.

Winslow nodded without turning toward me, not appearing to catch the sarcasm. "You can call me Brick," he said.

"Don't count on it," I said.

cɔcɔ

After Winslow dropped me off at the diner, I drove the rental home without thinking about the act of driving. Once there, I remained in the car and tried to gather energy and a purpose to go inside. It wasn't until the light from the automatic garage door opener shut off, that I got out of the car. I hit the button on the wall next to the kitchen entrance to close the garage door.

Inside, I noticed the message light on the phone blinking.

One was a hang up. Probably RJ, I thought, remembering him earlier with his phone next to his ear and the worried look on his face. Next message was Vince. "Hey, just wanted you to know, I love you. We have to work some things out, that's all."

It seemed more like days ago instead of hours ago I was out by the pool lounging and wondering when Vince would call and tell me he loved me and accept my apology. I sat down and cried—something I'd needed to do for a long time.

Eventually, I could think of only one thing to do about what I'd done. Confessing to Vince seemed the best and right thing to do and I resigned myself to dealing with the consequences. Whatever result Vince chose for us, I would concede without argument, accept it, and move on.

After splashing cold water on my face, I got back into the car and drove to The Big Prick. There were people there and, for a change, I felt the need to be around people. Many noisy people.

When I walked through the back and into the front, the noise level dropped a few decibels.

"Hey," I said to no one and everyone.

There were a few nods and halfhearted hellos. That was the extent of it. Then I finally got it through my thick head. The problem wasn't this place and the people here. It was me. I was the problem.

"I just wanted to fix The Big Prick lettering. That's going back on the window," I said before returning to my office.

There wasn't much enthusiasm for my idea at first, but once I started scraping off the remaining red paint with a butter knife I'd found in my desk drawer, a few people began looking for objects to use and joined in.

"I thought Janice was working on this," I said after a time. "Where's she at anyway?"

"She probably forgot," Stacey said, and then clapped her hand over her mouth.

"Shut it, girl," RJ told her.

"What's that about?" I asked Stacey.

Stacey shrugged. "She missed an appointment or two this month." Glancing at RJ, she moved to an area on the other side of the window.

"That's not like her. Do you know where she's at now?' I asked.

Looking at me RJ said, "Janice's at home. Why?"

"Oh. I called and she didn't pick up." I shook my head. "Anyway, I just remember telling her to scrape this all off. I wasn't in a great mood that day. She must have figured out I didn't mean it."

"I guess," he said.

We decided to paint the letters outlined in yellow and

filled in with purple paint. RJ made a trip to the 24-hour Super Wal-Mart, and returned with the paint and Janice. She wiggled her fingers toward me and went to her station.

He handed the paint to me. While I scraped the old paint, he stood nearby. Every few seconds he would clear his throat or sigh.

"Did you need something?" I asked.

"Sort of. I mean I need to tell you something."

"What?"

"I might know who messed up the windows," he said.

"Oh?"

"Yeah, um, this person who might've done it probably feels bad about it. And for sure whoever it was that, um, motivated that person, feels bad," RJ said.

"I know how that is. I've felt bad about some things I've done too," I told him.

"Do you want to know who did it?" he asked after a few seconds of silence.

"No, not really. I don't imagine it'll ever happen again."

"Probably not," he said.

"Anything else you want to talk about? Like why you seem to be everywhere I look these days?" I said after a bit.

"I'm gonna ask you again. Don't you want to tell your side of the story?"

"What would be the point now?" Shaking my head, I began painting the outline of the letters.

"People should know the truth."

"What's the big deal? Why the interest in people knowing the truth about a television show that's done and gone?"

"Ever heard of a come-back?" RJ asked.

"You have got to be insane." I put down the brush

and the paint, and turned to face him in order to give him the full-blown effect of my incredulity and wrath.

"Why you gotta be like this? I mean, this could be a good thing. Tiffany is up for it," he said.

"Good for what? And for whom?" I turned away, ready to be done with the conversation. And then, "Wait. You said Tiffany? Tiffany who?"

"You know. Tiffany Holland. From *Cruising*," he said.

"Holy shit. I don't believe this. I want nothing to do with that twit. Oh my god. I can't tell you how angry I am right now." I was right in his face.

He gave me a light push on my shoulder and I backed up. Closing my eyes, I counted to ten in an attempt to calm down. I opened my eyes when RJ said, "Listen. How can you stand people thinking you're a screw up? The plan is to tell your side, you know, and show them some proof an' all and then they'll want to bring *Cruising* back."

"I really, really doubt it. You don't have any idea how these things work. What's in it for you, anyway?"

He crossed his arms in front of his chest and stuck his chin out. "It's what I want to do."

"What? Be stubborn? Is that what you want to do? Because you are doing it very well right now," I said.

"No, I'm going to direct. Working here pays for film school."

Who was I to discourage anyone from attempting to do what he or she dreams of? But he shouldn't be relying on using me to get his foot in the door. I was a nobody and I'd gotten nowhere. "You're wasting your time with this idea. If you and little Miss Tiffany want to create something, make sure it has nothing to do with *Cruising* or me. Just keep me out of it." I took a deep breath and began painting in the lettering.

"My time to waste," he said.

"No. Keep Tiffany's dumb ass away from me and stay out of my way, RJ. That's final."

"I ain't planning on being in your way." He picked up the paintbrush he'd used and went into the backroom.

I waited a few minutes for RJ to return before I continued painting. By the time I finished the last letter on the window, he hadn't come back out front. So I cleaned up the brushes and left for home, thinking how I'd have to keep my eye on RJ from now on. Even more than I had previously. He wasn't the type to stop doing something just because someone told him to.

I tried to think who he reminded me of, but couldn't place a name.

CHAPTER 17

The room was dark. I didn't remember turning off the light. I remembered reading. The book was under my hand. I felt the smooth surface of the cover. I wiped a trail of drool from my face, stretched, and hurriedly sat up when a combination of vanilla-citrus and unwashed-bodies-in-a-closed-elevator smell hit my senses.

Lane was in the entrance to the room, her body outlined by the nightlight in the hallway. I screamed and threw the book at her. "Damn it! What are you doing?"

My sister had done this to me when we were kids. She'd wait until I least expected it and jump out at me. I was always frightened, then embarrassed she had witnessed my fright, and then I got angry.

When Lane didn't move, I began to think I was having a strange dream. I rubbed my eyes.

Lane walked to the end of the bed. "Get up."

"Didn't I make it clear to you how I feel about you coming here uninvited?" I sat on the edge of the bed. Now that my eyes were accustomed to the dark, I could see there was light from a full moon peeking through the slats of the window blinds.

She raised her hand and something gleamed. A gun.

Shit. *Does she somehow know all the stuff of my nightmares?*

"Get some clothes on," she said.

"What?" I looked at my nakedness, unable to figure out why it would matter.

"Here, put this on." She reached one arm into the closet and threw out a dress. It landed on the floor near the bed.

"I don't think it's appropriate. The neckline is too low and the slit up the side is too daring for this type of event," I told her.

"Stop with the smart ass comments. Just put it on," Lane said.

While still sitting on the edge of the bed, I bent down, picked up the dress, and pulled it over my head.

"Now tell me what you want." I felt it important to try to find out what she wanted, other than seeing me dead.

Lane grabbed my arm, pulled me in front of her, and shoved me toward the hallway.

"I can walk on my own." I shrugged her hand off my shoulder. Everything my eyes landed on I measured for use as a weapon.

"Go sit."

I walked to the lanai and flipped the light on.

She flipped the light off and grabbed my hair to steer me toward the chair.

The moon was huge, white, and in position with the tops of the palm trees. I blinked and slid my eyes toward the closed and barred sliding doors.

"How'd you get in?" I asked.

"Jimmied your side garage door. You really need a deadbolt on that if you're not going to lock the inside door."

"Well, shit." I couldn't believe I'd been so concerned

with the sliding doors and not the side door. After all, it's how I got in to her house.

"I'm sorry to have to do this," she said and gave my hair an extra twist. "I just couldn't think of a cleaner plan."

"I could help. There are nicer plans. Maybe you didn't give it enough thought?"

"You're so weird all the time," she said.

Moonlight radiated from the barrel of the revolver, a Ruger Single Six. I hid my panic while Lane backed in to the chair next to mine. She still had my hair in her hand, pulling out hair and stretching my scalp with each inch she moved. Tears came to my eyes, and then she let go of my hair.

"Do you think anyone would be surprised if you're found floating in the pool?" Lane asked, once she situated in the chair and had the revolver aimed at me just so.

"Well, I do know how to swim and pretty much anyone who knows me is aware of that. Is that what you mean?"

"Just kidding, of course. But really, no worries. I'm just here to talk to you. I have the gun for persuasion purposes only. What do you think? Are you persuaded?"

"Yes," I said, although persuaded wasn't the correct emotion. I was afraid. And I didn't believe she only wanted to talk. Anyway, I wanted her to stick to talking rather than getting right to the point and shooting.

"Good," she said.

I decided now would be the time to ask her to explain her past. Get her to talk, and keep her talking until I could figure out how to get out of this mess. "Tell me why the police questioned you about your mother's accident. Why were they at your home that year for domestic issues?"

"How would you know that?"

"I'm a PI, remember?" I said.

"You have to understand by now. It's your nosiness that gets you into these types of situations." She looked at me for agreement or confirmation.

"I don't believe I've ever been in this type of situation, but we can agree that I tend to get involved when I think someone is going to get away with doing something wrong," I said.

She adjusted her arm holding the Ruger and I jumped. I could tell she didn't know a damn thing about the gun.

"It's not up to you to figure out if I've done anything wrong," she said.

"Unless you impose your wrongs on me, of course," I told her.

"Why don't you tell me about these wrongs?" She suddenly seemed interested in my answer.

I moved a few inches out of her reach. "I think this all starts with lies. Your mother shouldn't have lied. She should have told your father she was pregnant. She should have told him she was interested in marrying someone else and not made it seem as though she was the victim. Your mother told him to get lost and then let everyone believe she was the one hurting." I didn't realize until I said it that I had believed what Sheila had told me on the phone. "I think maybe because of your mother—"

She was at me so fast I didn't see anything but a flash of moonlight reflecting off the gun's barrel. Then she was kneeling in front of me with the gun at my forehead. "Don't say another word about my mother," she told me. Her voice was soft, but her breath was coming in ragged gusts. There was spittle gathered in the corners of her mouth. She grabbed a fistful of hair with her free hand and gave my head a yank.

I closed my eyes when I felt the barrel bite into my skin.

This is how I die? Because of her? How humiliating.

I heard her sigh, and then the gun was gone. I opened my eyes and saw she had walked to the sliding doors and was leaning her head against the glass. I stretched my neck to the side until it cracked and then concentrated on not puking.

"She was mean. I was such a good little girl, and she was so mean to me. I miss hating her. I miss loving her," she said.

What did you do to her, Maureen?

The room darkened when clouds covered the moon. I started to stand, but the clouds moved again, re-lighting the room.

Lane continued talking. "But she was right about a lot of things. I mean you do have to plan ahead and be prepared for the unexpected." Her voice turned squeaky as she turned and came toward the chair.

When she walked past me, she slapped the side of my head with her open hand. It made a loud crack, but didn't hurt. It served no purpose other than to give her a jolly and royally piss me off.

Okay, you did it now. I don't feel bad for you at all. Watching them haul you off will be such a pleasure.

"Are you waiting for your dad to call?" I asked, still wanting to keep her attention on something other than shooting me.

"Yes, and there's this other business to take care of."

"What time is it?" I asked again and turned to look outside. Still dark, but the moon wasn't shocking white.

She didn't answer.

"Tell me about your plan," I said.

She shook her head and waved her free hand at me. "You know most of it. House, husband, kids. Life. Or I guess I should say life the right way."

"But living life the right way doesn't include killing people."

"Sometimes it does. You can only give so many chances for people to change."

"I don't think you mean that. You're a better person than that," I said in as soothing a voice as I could conjure.

"I'm not cold hearted, you know. I regret what happened, but it had to happen."

"Well—"

She stuck her face directly in front of mine. A purple vein on her temple was throbbing "What's done is done," she said.

"What about your plan?" I asked.

"I hate what happened."

"What do you hate?" I asked.

"Everything. The accident. Her. Him. The mess. Damn it. Everything is ruined," Lane said. She ran her hand through her hair and paced. "I don't know how it all went so wrong." She returned to the chair with one white knuckled hand gripping the gun, only to stand up and again begin pacing.

She returned to the sliding doors. "She's heeee-re," Lane said, looking at her reflection in the glass door. "Heeeere's Lane."

"Whoa," I said under my breath. *Somebody's gear slipped.*

She was holding the gun in a downward manner at her side. I scooted close to the edge of the chair.

"Lane Somers, the apple of her mother's eye, her little princess," she said, and then she turned to me, "until it wasn't convenient." Suddenly, she was crying, tears hovering and pooling, and then dropping onto her shirt.

A low scream filled the air and then a sharp wail. "I told her he put his hands on me. I don't do things like that. I'm a good girl. I told her it wasn't my fault." She walked by me, sat in the chair, and hung her head, holding the gun between her knees.

I stood. "Then you—oh my God, he molested you? She knew about this?" I moved a step toward her in the pretense of comforting her.

Her head snapped up, her eyes were bulging.

I froze in place.

"My mother? Yes, years ago. All the horrible things he did and it didn't matter to her until much later when some high school girl told her parents he'd been molesting her. And someone began leaving notes to my mother, telling her that Charles was a pervert, and asking for money to keep it hushed and out of the media. It all became too much for her. "

I was kneeling in front of her, my heart alternately pounding and skipping a beat. "In what way?" The words came out in a croak, and I quickly cleared my throat and repeated the question.

She shivered and swallowed a couple times, but she didn't look up when she began talking. "She was afraid Charles was going to run and take his money with him. We were on the way to talk to the police—she thought that would stop him—when the accident happened."

"Oh, it was an accident?" I asked, trying my best to keep the disbelief out of my voice.

Lane looked at me as if she hadn't had a gun to my head minutes ago, as if we'd all along been chatting at a Tupperware party. "We were at the stop sign. She was looking my way and arguing with me when I saw his car speeding toward the intersection," she said.

I knelt in front of her and she continued talking. "I wanted to stop him. I put my hand on her knee and pushed her foot down on the gas." She put a hand over her face.

I grabbed her wrist holding the revolver with my right hand and bent her hand downward with my left. She jerked and tried to pull away. My grip around her wrist tightened, and the veins on her hand stood out in a bloated blue against the whiteness of her skin. I again felt nauseous. If the gun was in fact an old model Single Six, and she hadn't loaded it with the hammer on an empty cartridge, simply jarring the damn thing would make it go off.

"One of us is going to get hurt. Bad. That gun goes off; nothing in here will stop the bullet. Nothing. Ever heard of ricochet? Give it up," I said through my clenched jaw.

"No," she said.

I pushed down harder on her hand, keeping a tight hold on her wrist.

Lane screamed and dropped the gun. The gun fell on its side, the barrel facing the wall between the lanai and the living room. I heard the bullet when it hit the impact resistant glass in the front window. Lane screamed again. I pulled her down to the floor and held her head to the tile.

"Shut up," I said.

Keeping her head mashed into the floor, I reached to pick up the gun. I saw it had three screws on the body and knew it was the old model.

Standing up, I put my foot on the side of her head. "Don't move. I've got the gun now." I hauled her up and into the chair.

"Where did you get this gun?" I asked.

"At a garage sale," she said, her voice muffled and weak.

"What the fuck? You're lying," I said.

"I'm not!"

"Whatever. Those were Crystal's boxes of stuff in your dining room, weren't they? And Scooter was hers, wasn't he? So where is she?" I asked her.

Lane turned away from the revolver. "I killed her," she said.

"Crystal?" I shivered when she looked at me and nodded. "Why did you do it?"

"I saw her. She was hiding out in the pool house, waiting for Del to leave I guess. I had to talk to her. She was my sister. I told her everything. She said it was okay, because now I had a new family." She gulped in air and I thought she would weep again, instead she continued talking.

"I didn't think about Del. When he got there that night, he was so angry. He said she would ruin it all. All of our plans were going down the toilet, he said." She caught her breath, and began crying.

"You didn't think you would get away with killing her, did you? Del knows for one thing. How are you going to keep him quiet? The first time you do something against his wishes, he'll rat you out."

"I don't know!" Her face went white. The hollows under her eyes filled in with dark smudges. Tears hovered at the edges of her eyes and ran down to pool at her mouth. "I don't know. I don't remember. It happened so fast. I didn't think. I didn't plan. It just happened. She was there one minute, telling me she was my sister and she was looking out for me. Then it seemed like she was ruining my chance at having a normal life." She stopped talking and stared in my direction.

"What chance did you give your sister?"

"It was not my fault!"

"Well, whose fault was it?" I asked.

"She would not listen. It would have been so nice to have a sister," she said.

"But why would she ruin your plans? I mean you can still have your house, husband, and children. You'd just have a sister too."

"She said Del was her ex-husband. She told me about things he and his mother had done. I yelled at her. I didn't want to have to choose between them. I wanted everything. Just as I'd planned. And he was yelling at her and saying she had better shut up." She bent her head and sobbed again.

I waited for her to finish before I asked, "What happened?"

"I couldn't stand it that she wouldn't listen to me, that's all. I think I blacked out then because I don't remember anything more."

"But where was Del?"

"He left, I think. He was angry, and I remember hearing the garage door slam shut." She was quiet for a few seconds, looking out at the palms bending in the breeze. "I told Crystal she needed to leave. She picked up the cat and some of her stuff and headed out to the pool house to get the rest of her belongings. I followed her and she wouldn't listen to me when I explained why she should leave. I was shaking her and yelling at her and I blacked out and killed her."

"What?"

"I passed out."

"You mean you passed out after you killed her."

"No. I was shaking her hard and I was so mad."

"I need for you to explain. Tell me who put Crystal in the trunk. You or Del?"

"I don't know."

"Who set the car on fire?"

"I don't know. I swear," Lane said.

"How convenient. Christ! None of this makes sense. You passed out and yet you killed Crystal. And you don't know who torched her body."

"I don't even remember half of it. I keep telling you that.

"When did Del come back?" I asked.

"I don't know. I heard glass breaking and I looked

out the bedroom window and saw the car. It frightened me and I yelled out, and Del came into my room," Lane said.

She put her head down. She wasn't making noise and she was still except for her shoulders. They rocked and shuddered as she silently cried.

"Look, I'm going to call the police. They'll help you get this all sorted out in your mind and you won't have to let it continue to eat at you. You're going to have to trust me," I said.

"Why should I trust you?"

"Because I believe you, Lane. I know you're a good girl, down deep." It really hurt me to lie.

"Do you really think someone can help me?" Lane asked.

"Yes, I really do. I promise." I crossed my fingers behind my back. Another lie.

She covered her face and moaned.

"You'll be okay, Lane." Holding the gun on her, I walked to the end of the lanai toward the desk. "You tell them your story. Tell them everything you remember, okay?" I put the gun on the desk. I slowly reached my hand into the back of the large front drawer, pushed aside my gun, and pulled out the container of pepper spray I'd kept there since moving in.

"No. No. *No*. I'm afraid." Her voice was shrill and I felt it reverberate down my spine.

I watched her for a few seconds and when she made her move toward me, I sprayed her full in the face. She gasped and fell to her knees, rubbing her eyes and breathing hard. I grabbed my gun from the drawer.

I bent down next to her and said into her ear, "I could have just as easily shot you."

"Oh god, it hurts." She began making a whining noise and hit at the floor with her hands.

"Don't you move a muscle or I'll shoot you," I told her as I punched 911 into the phone. "I'm holding a gun on someone who broke into my house. Hurry, please," I said when the person on the other end asked me what my emergency was.

I knelt down in front of her again. "Look, if everything happened the way you said, there wasn't premeditation. You probably won't get the death penalty. You should be happy, right?" I put my hand under her chin and lifted her face up. "Stop this nonsense. Do you hear me? Stop whining."

She couldn't open her eyes, she scrunched them up tight and tears were falling unattended. Clear snot dripped from her nose, and she was breathing through her mouth. She didn't say anything, but she nodded. I sat in the chair near Lane to wait for the police.

She curled up in a fetal position on the tile floor. After a while, I heard soft snoring and glanced over at a sleeping, scary-looking, Lane. A Lane that wouldn't win any beauty contests. A Lane with swollen, red-rimmed eyes, and draining sinuses. A Lane no one alive would recognize. The real Lane.

CHAPTER 18

Janice missed her plane. I would've taken her to the airport but she didn't want to go alone. She said she was afraid of the idea of traveling by herself. It seemed out of character, but I let it go. Anyway, her sisters were not on her mind.

She wanted the story again. She'd been at me since early this morning.

"But what did you tell the police?" she asked.

I was tired and tried to think of a way that I wouldn't have to talk about it anymore.

"Cassie?"

"I told them what I just told you," I said.

"Well, what are they going to do with her? Is it First Degree Murder Homicide stuff? Or Second Degree 'I'm Crazy and My Step-Daddy Molested Me' Defense? Is she going to get the chair?"

"Did you make up your own version of criminal charges recently or is it something you've always gone by?" I asked.

"She was going to shoot you, wasn't she? Whoopee! Did you give her a Karate chop or something?"

"I guess you had to be there."

"I woulda kicked her Barbie-doll butt. Right on the

spot! Damn, Cassie. You are a real live Miss Magnum PI, aren't you?"

"Hardly."

"You caught a murderer. You should be excited," Janice said.

"Well first of all, your own client shouldn't be the murderer. But what's bothering me is, I had it backward all along. I thought Crystal was the problem. I mean I knew Lane was off her rocker, but I didn't think she would kill anyone."

"Did she?" Janice asked, her forehead crinkled and her eyes narrowed.

"Very funny," I said.

"She killed her sister and came right out and told you she killed her own mother," Janice said. She had an excited look, as if she'd just now discovered this information.

"I know. I was there, remember?"

"She was going to shoot you, wasn't she?" Janice said.

"Come on, Janice. I'm tired."

"What? You should be looking at the bright side of it all. You knew there was something going on, you handled it like a pro, calling in the police and all, and she was arrested. Judge and Jury get to do the rest. The end. Right?"

"Right."

"Jeez, think about this: You could write a book. *How I Put Barbie Behind Bars*." She hooted then smiled and nodded.

"Anyway, Crystal's parents will be devastated. I don't like to think about that. It makes me feel very homicidal," I said.

"Calm down. Look, let's change the subject." Janice said.

"I'd like that."

"Tell me again about how Lane stole into the house and had that gun on you. She pulled your hair too." Janice shook her head back and forth. "Mmmm, mmm, mmm, ain't nobody going to get away with that on me."

I looked at her and let my eyes move upward to her hair. "Don't see how that could happen either," I said.

۵ﻭﻩ۵

The bed was comfortable and the house was quiet. Janice had agreed to stay with me and was asleep in the guest room, everything was just right. However, I couldn't sleep. When I closed my eyes, I heard, smelled, and saw Lane Somers.

Eventually, I realized my thoughts should have been on Crystal. She was the one who was murdered.

What a waste.

Del could have stopped Lane. He was a physically strong man. I had felt the strength in his hand when he ushered me out of his office. He was as responsible as Lane for Crystal's murder, maybe more so given Lane's problems. And he must have helped cover up the murder. Didn't he? Lane didn't remember putting Crystal in the trunk and setting the car on fire. My bet was she wasn't strong enough to do it by herself.

Then again, there was money involved in all of this. Money was a big motivator in many areas of life and it could push many people over the edge toward murder.

A crash shattered the quiet of the house.

Heart pounding, I walked toward the bedroom door and listened. I thought I heard voices. I opened the door and walked down the hall as quietly as possible on shaking legs. The light was on in the dining area and I felt sure I'd turned it off before going to bed. I felt relieved when I heard Janice's voice. Through the entryway, I saw Janice in the middle of the room. A glass ashtray in pieces around her feet. She was looking at the pieces and then she looked up and saw me.

"I don't know what to do," she said and the look of panic on her face gave me a start.

"Don't move," I said and went around her to the closet in the kitchen. I grabbed the broom, dustpan, and wastebasket. When I returned to the living room Janice was in the exact same spot, but now tears were running down her cheeks.

"What's wrong? We'll clean it up. It's okay." I hurriedly began picking up the larger pieces of the glass and tossing them into the basket. I swept up the remaining glass and took everything back to the kitchen. I grabbed another ashtray and returned to Janice. "Come on. It's just an old ashtray."

I put my arm around her shoulders and we walked to the lanai. We sat and I put the ashtray between us.

I turned to her. "Tell me about it, Janice. What's going on?" I had a sick feeling in the middle of my stomach and I could hear the thrumming of my heart.

"I can't sleep," she said.

"Are you crying because you can't sleep?"

"What?" Janice's eyes were moving from me to the ashtray and back.

"What made you cry? Please tell me," I practically begged.

She reached up and touched her face where it was still wet with her tears. "Oh," she said. Then she looked at the table between us and picked up her cigarettes and lighter. After she lit up, she said, "I guess we should talk about my illness now."

I felt my heart flutter. My breath caught in my throat and I no longer wanted her to tell me.

"Cassie. You have to be strong," Janice said when she saw the look on my face.

"No," I said and then I began crying.

"You know I'm going to be seventy-eight next year, right? Well, there's the possibility you'll have to remind me about my birthday. You might have to remind me of your name. I might not remember to eat or change my clothes or—" Janice couldn't continue.

"Please, don't," I said.

She put out her hands. I went to her, and she held me while I cried like a baby.

I knew nothing would ever be the same, and not very much would matter anymore.

ഗരെ

In the morning, Janice wanted to go home and I reluctantly walked her to her house.

"I don't want you to be by yourself," I said when we were on her porch.

"Right now it's best. I've lived on my own for years. Soon, I suppose I'll be in a group home or something like it. But now, I'm still able to take care of myself. I work, and I still drive. I don't want to give up anything. It'll soon be taken from me. Don't hurry it, okay?"

"I'm not. It's just, well, never mind. You know I'm right down the street if you need me, don't you?" I said.

"I do today, Cassie." She put her hand on my face, and then turned and unlocked her door. She said good-bye with her back to me, probably believing I wouldn't realize she was crying.

I put my hand where hers had been just seconds before. It was no longer warm, and the feeling of my own hand felt harsh in comparison.

At home, I made a simple breakfast of yogurt and

granola, took it out to the pool deck, and from there I called Vince.

"Can you come over?" I asked.

"I can be there in an hour or so. Is everything okay?" he said.

"Not really. We'll talk when you get here," I told him.

I went back in to make coffee. I worked my way through two cups of coffee before I gathered some courage.

An hour and a half later, Vince came in the house without knocking.

"What happened to your window?" he asked. His hands were in his front pockets and he held his back straight as a board.

I got up from my desk and walked toward him. "So the duct tape didn't hide it?" I got up from my desk and walked toward him.

"I'm not laughing, Cassie."

"I had a little run in with Lane Somers and a gun. She's been hospitalized for now," I said.

"You freaking shot her?" He stuck his head out and raised his eyebrows.

"No. She's under evaluation."

"What does that mean?" he asked.

I heard impatience and something like disgust in his voice. That pissed me off.

"It means she's fucking Looney tunes, just as I told you. She slipped a gear. She's short a can from her six-pack. She doesn't have pepperoni on her damn pizza! You get it now?"

"Why do I think you aren't telling me everything?" Vince took his hands out of his pockets and crossed his arms over his chest.

"Look. She broke into the house and threatened me

with a gun. She said I needed to mind my own business. Anyway, I got the gun from her and called the cops."

"You okay?" he asked.

"I'm fine. Thanks for asking. I wasn't sure you were going to," I said.

"Yeah, I should've asked you that first." He did look apologetic, but I still had the feeling he was holding back on the rest of whatever else he was feeling.

"I have to tell you some things. Can we sit?" I asked.

"Okay," he said, then moved to the couch and sat down.

I sat at the other end of the couch. "First, I wanted to let you know about Janice. She has Alzheimer's."

Vince hung his head and rubbed his hand over his face. "Wow. I don't know what to say." He looked up at the ceiling. "I want to help in whatever way I can," he said after a few seconds.

"Not sure if there is any help, but you could let her know you're there for her. She thinks you're the best of everything." I said.

Vince leaned forward and narrowed his eyes. "What else, Cassie?"

I noticed his jaw muscle jumping. He already seemed angry, and I leapt in before losing my nerve. "I'm going to just blurt out what I have to say."

"What you got cooking in that head of yours?"

"I need to say this, Vince," I told him.

"Go ahead."

"I was with another man. I really can't tell you why. There's no reason, except I think there's something inside of me that won't let me keep something good."

I kept my eyes on Vince and watched as all signs of emotion left him. He leaned his head on the back of the couch and closed his eyes.

"Who is it?" he asked without opening his eyes.

"I don't believe that matters," I said.

He sat straight and looked at me with narrowed eyes. "Really? What does matter?"

I looked down at the floor. "That's something I can't answer right now. I guess I have to work it out somehow."

"Do you think it's all about you? What about me?" Vince shook his head. Then he stood and said, "I'm leaving."

"Shouldn't you stay and talk about this?" I asked.

"I don't want to be here with you. Got it?" he said.

"I got it."

"I can't believe this." Vince stood at the door, waited head down, and hand on the doorknob. "You know you haven't said you're sorry."

"I am truly sorry to have hurt you. I feel incredibly bad for what I've done to you."

"Aren't you going to blame it on something I've done or some fault I have? Or something I didn't do?" he asked, and then he pulled his mouth into a sneer. "Wouldn't that make you feel better?"

"I can't do that," I said.

"Damn right you can't. You've done this to too many others for it to be my fault. What's wrong with you?"

He opened the door.

"I don't know," I said. "I wish I did."

He left and shut the door behind him.

☙❧

At eight the next morning, I walked down the street, wanting to see Janice before I headed to the airport.

RJ answered her door. He stepped outside and shut the door.

"You knew?" I asked him.

"Sort of. I mean I guessed, anyway. She started doing stuff she'd never done before. You know, forgetting stuff," he said.

"So your friend Nunyor doesn't really live down the street? You've been checking on Janice?" I swallowed and blinked away tears.

RJ leaned against the house. His shoulders bunched up around his neck, and he had his hands in his pockets. "You could say that, I guess."

"That makes you an incredibly remarkable person. I want to apologize for some of the things I've thought about you," I said and felt my face redden when he melo-dramatically simulated amazement.

"Aren't you in danger of becoming nice or something?" he asked.

"Shut up, okay?" I walked around RJ and went in the house to say good-bye to Janice.

ပာပာ

I made a call from the airport.

"Sheila. This is Cassie Cruise. Please don't hang up."

"Did you call to tell me they found my little girl and she's okay? Tell me that, say that to me," Sheila said.

"I wish I could tell you that." There was silence. "Please don't hang up. Would it be easier if I spoke to John?"

"What do you want? John's in Florida."

"What college did Crystal go to?" I asked

"Why?"

"I need to find out what happened, Sheila. I want to know the truth."

"Will it change anything?" Her words were clipped and hard, but I heard the grief too.

"No, I don't think it will. I'm sorry," I told her.

"She went to Penn State," she said.

"Why did she choose Penn State?" I asked.

"I don't know. She had all kind of reasons when I asked her that question. Mostly, because of a scholarship."

"Where did she meet her ex-husband?"

"While in college, I think maybe when she went looking to buy a car."

"And his family?"

"We met his mother the one time. They had a quick wedding at city hall. They were only married a few years," she said.

"What does he look like? Do you have pictures?"

"An ass. He looks like an ass," Sheila said.

"Please? Can you help?"

"Do you know how much this hurts? Do you have any idea?" Sheila asked.

"I do, somewhat. My sister was murdered," I told her.

"I want to hold her one more time. Just one more time. I want to make sure she knows I love her. God, what if she didn't know," she said between gulping air and moaning.

"I wished I could change everything, to make it right," I said, knowing nothing I could say would help.

I had just made the decision to hang up when I heard her voice and brought the receiver back to my ear. "Sheila?"

"His name is Darien Evans. I suppose most women would think he's handsome. He has blondish hair, green eyes, and a big smile. He's tall with a nice build and a smooth talker. And I never liked him. It's just a feeling I have about him. He's sneaky, I guess, like the typical car salesperson. Only, I doubt he's doing that anymore, since he got in big trouble at the Cadillac dealership in Las Cruces. I guess he ripped off some retirees," she said.

"He has green eyes?"

"Didn't I just tell you that?"

"Sheila. Let me come to your house and talk to you. Please?"

"Suit yourself."

The tobacco and whiskey timbre in her voice made me think of Elizabeth Taylor as Martha in *Who's Afraid of Virginia Woolf?*

You are, Sheila. We all are.

℞℞℞

Sheila opened the door wearing a purple cotton maxi dress and red high top sneakers. That was the least of it, there were other things going on with her that grabbed my attention. She'd piled her long hair, an unnatural color of black, haphazardly at the back of her head and used glimmery chopstick-like things to keep the pile in place. She'd rimmed her eyes in kohl and used a deep purple shadow that coordinated with her gown. On her, the effect was amazingly and freakishly natural. Right away I knew this was the real her and not the by-product of her booze.

I stood on the porch and in the heat of the overhead sun while she gave my khaki shorts and peach tank top the once over.

"Humph," she said and finally flung the door all the way open. She then turned to walk into what appeared to be the family room. I followed.

"Have a seat." She waved her hand at a couple of recliners. "Want something to drink?"

"Coffee would be great, if you have it made. Otherwise, I'm fine."

"You want coffee or not?" She stood with her hands on her hips waiting for an answer.

"Sure."

When she left the room, I stood and looked at the photographs on the mantle. A high school graduation picture of a blonde-haired girl held the place of honor in the middle. A gold inscription on the bottom left read, *Crystal 1994.* She and Lane weren't identical, as I had imagined them to be. They were close though. From a distance, you would think them twins, but up close, Lane was beautiful. While Crystal, going by the picture in front of me, was not classically beautiful. Although, she had more vibrancy in her face and eyes than Lane and she, in direct contrast to Lane, came off as earthy and real. I wondered again what Crystal had been trying to do? Save Lane from Del? Or save Del from Lane?

"I hope the killer dies a tortuous death," I blurted out, not realizing Sheila had come within hearing distance.

"Well so do I." Sheila handed me a mug of coffee, sat down on the couch, and curled her legs underneath her. Shoes and all.

I had guessed that Del and Darien were the same on the drive from the El Paso airport. I knew Crystal had some type of connection with Del first, and then when Sheila said Darien had green eyes; it seemed too much of a coincidence.

"How much do you know about Del, I mean Darien? You mentioned that he'd been in trouble over something at a car dealership. Was he always in trouble?"

"Not that I know of. Crystal left him soon after she learned of that incident. I didn't have a reason to keep track of him after that," Sheila said.

"I meant before that. While Crystal was in college. While they lived in the Scranton area."

"Crystal never said. The main problem they had seemed to be his crazy mother. They continually helped her out of one scrape or another."

"What kind of scrapes?"

"Way I understand it; she's what's called a paper hanger." She must have noticed the blank expression on my face. "Know what that means?"

"She decorates using wallpaper?" I guessed.

"Where you from again?" Sheila asked.

"What does it mean, Sheila?"

"A paper hanger is someone who passes bad checks or fake paper money."

"Oh."

"What do you do for a living? You work in a monastery or something?" she asked.

"I'm an ex-court stenographer and an investigator and I own a tattoo parlor."

"Wow. Aren't you the worldly one? How's come you never heard of paper hanging?" Sheila asked.

"I don't know. I could tell you the legal term for it, if you like," I said.

"Go ahead."

"Uttering and Publishing."

She looked at me as if I'd made it up and picked up her glass of amber colored liquid from the coffee table in front of her. She continued to look at me while taking a long drink. "Why are you doing this?"

"I have never been able to stand it when someone gets away with doing something wrong," I said.

"Lane killed Crystal. That's what they told me." Her voice caught on Crystal's name. She jerked her head to the side and looked at the wall for a few minutes before turning back to look at me, composed again but with tears and mascara running down her face. "Last I knew she was in jail for it."

"I don't think she did it."

"Yes, I gathered that. I'm slow, not stupid," Sheila said.

"I don't think you're stupid or slow."

"What do you want from me?" she asked.

"Show me the pictures from the wedding."

Once Sheila showed me the wedding pictures, I had no doubts about what I had figured out.

"Lane is in a relationship with Del, known to you as Darien. Crystal's ex-husband," I explained.

"Bastard," Sheila said

"You got that right," I said.

"Yes, but when I say bastard I mean it literally too. His momma was knocked up young. I'd say she was seventeen or so. Unfortunately, for her, the guy dumped her. But word has it, he paid her off."

"Who told you all that?" I asked.

"Mostly Crystal. Occasionally Darien would talk about it. Evidently, Tillie and Darien had it pretty nice for a time during his childhood."

"So who was Darien's father?"

"I never asked and he never said. Didn't seem like it bothered him much to not have a father around. She spoilt that boy. It wasn't a healthy relationship. She used him to get things from people, and seemed like he was eager to do it. Nearly blew everyone over when Crystal married him. Didn't last too long, though."

"Why do you think Crystal went to Florida?" I asked.

"I believe she wanted to meet Lane. And from what you've just told me, I suppose it's possible she knew Lane was going to be hooking up with Darien. Crystal's the type that would warn Lane about his background," Sheila said.

"What did she look like? I mean his mother?" I asked thinking of Tillie as she looked now.

"She was a pretty in her day. Not so hot these days, I bet. Big fat ass last time I saw her," Sheila said.

"You knew her when she was younger?"

"I knew of her. She was in Maureen's graduating

class. Never liked her then and don't like her now."

"In Scranton?"

"Yes. That's where we're from." Sheila shook her head and crossed her arms over her breasts.

"Sheila?"

"What? I don't see how talking about all this is going to help anything. Especially talking about Loretta Evans," she said.

"She's Loretta Evans?"

Without realizing who she was, I had seen her picture in her high school yearbook. Jennifer had brought it out to show me Maureen and her mother's pictures.

"Yes. That's her name." She waved her hand as if swatting at flies. "There was always something about her though. I can't really explain it other than to say she was overripe."

"Do you mean over the top? Or maybe overblown?"

"No. I guess I do mean overripe. You know when you have a piece of fruit and it looks great, but you bite into it and its soft and mushy inside and you're disappointed because it looked so good. Well, that's what I mean about her. She looked good on the outside, but inside there's something rotten."

"If you're talking about who I think you're talking about, she really does look like an overripe piece of fruit."

"Here's a picture of her from the reception. When it comes to morals and scruples, she has very few. And the same with her son, I believe," she said.

"Did Loretta know Charles? In high school I mean."

"She could've, I guess. He was older and I think he went to a private school," Sheila said.

"How did Maureen meet Charles?"

"Some party she got invited to. She always managed to get invited to those things somehow."

"How did it happen that he married her? Sounds like

he would've had many to choose from," I asked.

"I told you before, that was Maureen. She could do that to people. Convince them that what she wanted was what they wanted."

Sheila pulled her feet out from under her and put them flat on the floor in front of the couch.

She leaned forward and hung her head. "I just want to know why."

"I'm going to make sure they have to pay for whatever part they played in Crystal's death. Please believe me. I'm not here just to waste your time." I stood up, ready to leave.

"Okay." Sheila said, not looking up.

It didn't seem as though she was any longer aware of my presence, but when I left, she followed me out to the driveway and stood near the car.

I waved and started the car. She knocked on the window. I put it down and left the car in park.

"I should thank you for doing this, Cassie."

I nodded. "See you, Sheila." I didn't want any thanks. I didn't deserve anyone's thanks.

As I backed out of the driveway, I saw Sheila from the car window. She smiled, but it was obvious she was trying to hide her next looming episode of breaking apart.

I stopped and put the window down again.

"Hey, Sheila? Where's John?"

"Florida. Bringing Crystal's remains home."

"When's he due back?"

"Tonight. Why?"

"You okay?" I didn't want to leave her alone.

"Go away, Cassie," Sheila said and then turned around and walked back toward the house.

It wasn't until I pulled into the parking lot of the Las Cruces Public Library that I noticed how uneasy and anxious I was feeling. My hands were wet with sweat and I was shaking. I wanted to get this finished. I stepped into the hellish ninety-nine degree weather and took a deep, calming breath.

The bright red modern adobe library building didn't look inviting, but it looked as if it had air conditioning. The library assistant was helpful. She showed me how to use the microfiche machine to find the archived newspaper article I was looking for and helped me make a copy.

Next, using the library computer, I dug into Loretta Evan's past. I knew many things about Del now, and they were all bad, but they didn't add up to murder until you threw in the money. Lane's money.

I also knew Tillie—formerly known as Loretta—wasn't just Del's "fat-ass" mother and a paperhanger with a record. I was betting she was Charles Somers black-mailer.

CHAPTER 19

The manager of the car dealership was not helpful. He was new, he said, and he didn't know much about the incident. He found a reason for me to leave. He had a busy schedule and he seemed certain there was a need for him elsewhere.

I hung out in the used car lot until a craggy-faced man in pointed boots, blue jeans, and a plaid cowboy shirt asked if I needed help.

"I think you can help." I showed him the copy of the newspaper article.

As he read, the lines in his face deepened. I imagined he was wondering why he had to be the one to come out of the air conditioning and offer to assist someone who didn't intend to buy a car.

"I'm not trying to burn anyone here," I said, meaning specifically, anyone currently employed at the dealership.

"What are you doing?" he asked.

"I'm not interested in the fraud in that article. I don't want to know who else here could be involved. I'm a selective tattletale," I told him, and I explained about Rachel's Mercedes and its untimely demise.

He listened without interrupting and then he said, "The man knew what he was doing and didn't care. He's a selfish bastard." He took my arm and walked me around the lot, stopping every so often in front of a car. "What he did was get people to buy a car. Nothing illegal about that, right?" he asked.

I nodded my head and waited for him to explain. We walked to a silver blue 1999 Cadillac. Leather seats and automatic everything, he said while pointing at it. He smiled at the Cadillac, then looked over at me, winked, and nodded his head. He laid his hand on the hood and gave it a pat. "This here's a beauty. Just like you."

I felt my face heat up. "Just when I thought you were every woman's dream of the perfect used car salesman, you try selling me something I don't need."

"You can't get no better than this," he said and opened his arms wide.

"Cute," I told him and winked.

He smiled and then he was cute. "Back to Mr. Evans. Now, these gentlemen, they weren't really buying the cars. He got them to sign contracts for a lease and padded the amount needed to start the deal. Say he needed a couple thousand down, okay? He'd get them to put down four. He'd smooth talk them and wear them down and pretty soon, they'd be fine with that, you know. Had them thinking they'd just owe less on the total price of the car. Meantime, he'd pocket the major part of the money down."

"Didn't anyone here question the contracts?" I asked.

"Look, he knew what he was doing. He made it appear legit. You know, most people don't think the way he thinks. It wouldn't enter their minds to do something like that. To them he was just a damned good salesman." He glanced at the new car sales building and shook his head. The plastic row of flags above our heads flapped and rattled in a hot breeze.

"Well, he got caught eventually. I heard some retiree

wanted to trade in his car. He was thinking he had the car near paid off. That's when the dust hit the paint job, if you know what I mean. As soon as he gets wind of it, the boy scrams. Packs up his momma and leaves town. Meanwhile, we got people, mostly seniors, trickling in wondering what kind of deal we can make them with their trade in, that ain't no trade in."

"What do you know about his momma? Anything?"

"Nothing, really. She seemed very interested in her boy's life. More than the usual. I did hear she left owing a lot of people and businesses for things and services rendered." He took my arm again and we walked over to a Lincoln Towncar. "Now this here's the one will replace the Benz."

Pointing at the Lincoln, I laughed. "That's not the kind of statement my sister would want me to make."

He shrugged. "You know, if you want, I can give my buddy a call. He just happens to be the police chief and he's right down the road. He may be able to give you some information. No guarantee, but it might be worthwhile."

"I'd appreciate it," I told him.

"I'll go do that. Take care, ma'am." He scribbled something on the back of his business card, handed it to me, and headed to the used car sales office, a trailer with air conditioning.

Once on the steps, he raised his arm and tapped on a sign above the door that said, *Candy Cadillac – We Have $ome $weet Deals for You!*

ℯ∼ℯ∼

The Las Cruces police department was easy to find, but not so easy to enter. The fear of being patronized or worse, laughed at, overcame me. I sat in the car and thought of lighting up a cigarette. But I knew I wouldn't want it if I gave in and lit it. I tried on reasons for leaving. Nothing fit.

Then I thought of shit-head Del getting away with all that he had done. I thought of the woman that Crystal would never become. Knowing in my gut Del had something if not everything to do with her death, and more importantly, trusting in my gut, I stiffened my spine and shoved open the car door.

"Here I go."

I stopped at the edge of the sidewalk leading up to the building. *Why am I getting involved in this?*

The thought of Rachel pushed me along. I remembered her saying, "I only know one reason for living quiet. That's if you're too old to live any other way."

I'd walked through the doors of the police station, when suddenly I realized Rachel's saying was from a movie, and I muttered, "That's a line from *Long, Hot Summer.*"

"It's always hot here," said a woman in uniform standing behind the counter in front of me. "What can I help you with?"

I put the card from the salesman on the counter in front of her. We both looked at it and I realized, Johnny Johnson, Certified Used Cars, Candy Cadillac, was not information she needed or understood. I flipped it over. The scribbling on the back spelled out, Ronald Hernandez, Chief of Police, City of Las Cruces.

"Uh-huh," the police officer said. She waited patiently with her hands folded together on the countertop. Her crisp, beige uniform shirt, neatly tucked into a thick black leather belt, and beige uniform trousers, emphasized her female shape. Her natural curls accentuated the effect.

"I thought maybe if he was free, I could talk to him for a few minutes," I said.

She raised her eyebrows and looked at me for a few seconds. "What's this about?"

"I have some information about a person with a warrant from Las Cruces and I would like to get more information about some people," I told her.

"That's not really telling me anything," she said. "Do these people have names?"

"A couple of names," I said, not wanting to tell her the whole damned story. *Just get me the chief.*

She pulled a stool over, sat down, placed an elbow on the counter, put her hand to her chin, and waited.

I reached over and flipped the card to Johnny Johnson's information. I pointed at the card. "He's a friend of the chief," I said and flipped the card over to the other side. "He said he would call the chief and let him know I would be here to speak with him."

"Uh-huh," she said, not moving from her position on the stool.

"Okay, well, I'll just wait over here." I walked five feet across the room to a plastic chair lined up with two others against the wall near the door. Once I had sat down, I called out to the police officer. "What time does your shift end?" I asked. I wanted to let her know I'd wait all day if necessary.

"We got about three more hours." I knew she was implying that three hours was a piece of cake to her. She hadn't moved from the stool.

Stubbornness could take over a person if they let it. There didn't have to be a real reason. Neither of us wanted-ed to swallow our pride and do what we knew we should do to end our little showdown. I didn't know why we provoked each other. We were two people who decided not to cooperate.

I looked down at my flip-flops with a beaded design and attempted to count the beads. Failed and tried again. I reached up, fluffed my shaggy layered hair, and tried to remember when I last had a trim. I went through the crap in my handbag and sorted it by date.

Finally, Rachel and I had a mental tête-à-tête. "Just go up to the counter and tell her Del's name and why you came here. Get this over with and stop being so hateful. You don't have to fight with everyone do you? Not everyone in authority is your enemy."

I crossed my arms over my breasts and sat in the chair for a few minutes longer. Then, drawing in a big breath, I walked over to the counter and stuck my hand out. "I'm Cassie Cruise."

She hesitated, but then took my hand. "Sergeant Lilly Reese," she said.

"I need to talk to the chief about Delbert Welling, also known here in New Mexico as Darien Evans. I believe he has a warrant for fraud or something along that line."

"Uh-huh," she said.

"Would you please see if the chief will talk to me?"

"I'll be right back," she said and turned to walk away. She stopped after a few steps and said over her shoulder, "Have a seat."

Right then I had a sudden itch on my nose and chose to scratch it with my middle finger. She narrowed her eyes, but continued walking.

Twenty minutes later, Sargent Reese called my name.

"Follow me," she said and pushed a button somewhere under the counter that made the door next to it click. I turned the handle on the door, walked through the threshold, and followed her down a hallway. She stopped at the end of the hallway and knocked on the frosted glass door. Without waiting for a response, she opened the door and stepped aside to allow me to enter.

"Come on in," a deep voice with a light Hispanic accent said.

I looked toward the window on the right side of the office, the street side, and found the man with the voice sitting at a large glass topped desk. Blinds covered the window and the overhead lighting seemed dim compared to the bright lobby and hallway, but I could see the chief of police clearly, once my eyes adjusted to the darker setting. His dark blue uniform and arm patches supported his position as chief, but it was the hat that held all the insignias that really shined. It was no wonder he had placed it on his desk rather than his head.

A dimple on each cheek deepened as I held out my hand and introduced myself. He stood to take my hand and took the opportunity to adjust his belt, which had fallen far below his ample belly. His handshake was firm and welcoming.

"Why don't you just get right down to why you're here?" he said.

"I wanted to talk to you about Darien Evans and his mother Loretta Evans. I believe they may have warrants here. And I'm going to do everything I can to make them pay for their involvement in Crystal Evans' death," I said.

"Okay, well let's talk," the chief said.

I told him about Lane Somers and her story of killing Crystal Evans, formerly Crystal Lane. I explained my reasons for believing that Lane Somers story wasn't the complete story. After a half hour or so Chief Hernandez wrapped up our conversation. "Okay, Ms. Cruise. I'll talk to Detective Winslow and we'll share information. I can't guarantee anything else."

"Are you going to call him today?" I looked at the clock on his desk and noted it was 4:40 p.m., which would make it 6:40 p.m. in Florida.

"First thing in the morning," he said.

"Thanks for your time." I left his office.

It sure was great to tattle.

Sergeant Margaret Reese was at the end of the hallway to let me through the door leading to the lobby.

As I left, I said, "Thanks for your help, Sergeant Reese," and turned around in time to notice her scratching her temple with her middle finger.

She casually dropped her hand and, with a big smile said, "My pleasure."

I laughed. "I think this is the beginning of a beautiful friendship."

"That's from *Casablanca,*" Sergeant Reese said as I opened the door to leave.

ﾍﾟﾍﾟﾍﾟ

I couldn't get a non-stop flight out of El Paso until six the next morning. I found a cheap motel near the airport and ordered pizza. In between stuffing pizza in my mouth and flipping stations on the television, I made a call to Winslow.

"You need to carry a phone," he said.

"I've been thinking about it," I said.

"Lane says Del was not involved," he said.

"So she dragged Crystal from the pool house, picked her up, and put her lanky body in the Benz's small trunk by herself? I don't think she was capable of that. She struggled with a bag of rock I handed her."

"Well, that's what she says."

"I don't believe it," I told him.

"Don't have any reason to believe otherwise," he said.

"Listen to me, please. I'm betting whoever killed Crystal was strong. I'm betting the person that killed her could put her in the trunk on his or her own. That doesn't describe Lane."

"There were items belonging to Crystal in Lane's pool house. This corroborates her story."

"Just think it through. It doesn't work," I said.

"It does for me." I heard frustration in his voice, and he wouldn't answer my questions about cause and time of death.

"I need to find out the whole truth. I'm not ready to just let Lane take all the blame," I said.

"Why not? What's it to you?" Winslow asked.

"Don't be upset."

"You're really starting to worry me," he said.

"Please. You shouldn't monitor my behavior. It's not your place to do that."

I was going to hang up, but heard him say, "Hey, Cassie."

"Yes?"

"Are we okay? You okay with what happened with us?" he asked.

"I'm okay with what happened. I enjoyed being with you. I'm struggling with why it happened," I said.

"Something to think about," he said before disconnecting the call.

Next, I punched in the number to Scranton police and asked to speak to Detective Tucker. Once they put me through, I apologized for my previous behavior and we had a nice long talk about Loretta Evans.

"I'm probably wasting my breath—"

"I know. Let you do your job," I finished for her.

Now, I needed to get back home. Time was running out, and people were going to start running.

CHAPTER 20

Back in North Harbor, I stopped by my house long enough to grab the mail and read the one piece that I was waiting for. It was the detailed information from the State of Florida Department of Health. The problem was that there was no detail, just the same bit of information as found on the web. It didn't matter so much now that I had figured out some other things. Whatever Del had done to bring about the disciplinary action from the Department of Health was not murder. I was concentrating on the murder.

To clear my head, I took a quick shower and then decided to drive to The Big Prick.

Janice wriggled away from me when I hugged her. "Why are you acting strange?" she asked.

"No reason," I said, noting her healthy appearance but still worried about her being on her own. What if she forgot to turn off her coffee pot, dropped a cigarette on her carpeting, or got lost coming home from the golf course?

"Knock it off," she said when she caught my gaze.

Not knowing what to do about my worries, I shrugged and went to my office. I sat at my desk, ordered supplies, and paid the bills necessary to keep the shop open for another month. I waved a good bye to Janice and blew off RJ when he tried to get my attention. I left through the back door into the alley, but stopped immediately after shutting the door behind me.

Sitting on the ground, leaning her shoulder against the back tire of my rental, a red Ford Mustang convertible, was a slim woman with honey colored hair. Her tan legs were folded to the side and her fuchsia and white running shorts and white tank were dusted with sand and crushed shells. One of her arms hung loosely by her side with her hand in a clenched fist, and the other was awkwardly tucked behind her back, elbow out at an angle.

"Hey!" I picked up my pace, thinking the woman had heatstroke or some other health issue. I had parked on an angle near the back of the building and in front of a group of shabby bottle-brush trees. One half of the woman's face was shade dappled by leaves moving with the breeze and the other partially covered by her highlighted, wavy hair. Crouching in front of her, I moved her hair aside. I gasped and pulled my hand away.

Nothing was normal with her face. The skin paper white, lips blue edged, and brown eyes—the right eye halfway opened—bulging with red speckled sclera. Still, I recognized her.

No. It doesn't make sense. How could it be Tiffany?

"What the hell? Tiffany?" Confusion paralyzed me and I remained squatting until I noticed the white twine embedded into her neck. Standing, I took a step back and bumped into RJ.

"Oh, shit. Tell me she ain't dead," he said.

"Why is she here? What the hell?" I looked at RJ and knew my face and expression most likely mirrored his. Widened eyes, cheeks splotched with color, opened mouth.

"Call 911," I said.

He pulled his phone from his pocket and punched in the numbers, his eyes veering from Tiffany and back to me. Neither of us moved, remaining in our respective spots a few feet from Tiffany's body, until the sirens stopped and police cars covered the alley.

eৎৡeৎৡ

They questioned RJ and me separately. I was offered a seat in an unmarked car, while RJ walked with Winslow to his car. I answered the questions put to me in as few words as I could get away with and then left the car to stand in the alley and wait for RJ.

When I tired of what I imagined to be accusatory and angry looks thrown my way, I left the alley and returned to my office. Shutting the door blocked out the activity surrounding the crime scene, but it didn't block out the scene flashing through my mind. I sat in the desk chair and stared into space.

Janice poked her head into the office. "Are you okay?" Janice poked her head into the office.

"I'm not the one who died by throttling. So I'd say the answer is yes," I said, still standing in the center of the room.

"You look like crap," she said as she walked to the chair against the wall.

"I suppose I do, but again, I'm not dead. I, at the very least, can hope to look better another day."

Janice winced and got up from the chair, shaking her head and wiggling her fingers at me as she left the office.

Apparently, I needed to figure out appropriate answers regarding my feelings before anyone else asked. Truthfulness, in these situations, is rarely appreciated or expected. People seem to want the usual fluffy platitudes. They want tears and wringing hands. They wouldn't want to know I felt numb and disconnected from Tiffany's death. Every supposedly normal feeling or reaction to her death was not in me. I knew I didn't wish her dead and I couldn't wish her alive. I had nothing but a desire to hunt down the person responsible. Who would I say this to? Who would understand?

As if he'd heard my thoughts, Detective Brick Winslow opened the door and stepped into my office.

"Where's RJ?" I asked, surprised he hadn't followed Winslow inside.

"I sent him home," he said.

"Why? He has clients scheduled," I said and then sank into my chair at the desk. "Sorry. That was cold," I said.

"You know what those two were up to?" he asked.

"Probably. They were working together to produce some sort of comeback for *Cruising*. But what's that have to do with Tiffany getting a rope necklace?" I nodded at the chair across from my desk.

Winslow shook his head and remained standing in front of my desk. He was such a man. And that wasn't totally a compliment. His tough detective persona or whatever theatrical role he was playing was beginning to irritate me.

"That's what I wanted to ask you," he said.

"Me? How would I know?" My head filled with a nervous and clammy energy. "You don't think I could do that to someone, do you?"

"Don't get stupid on me. If I thought that, you wouldn't be sitting in that chair. You'd be on your way to—"

"You know what? I don't need this waste of time. You should leave and go figure out who killed Tiffany." I leaned forward with my hands on the desk in front of me and my breathing increased with every word I spoke.

"Yeah?" He had a smirk on his craggy Marlboro Man face, and damn it all if he wasn't sexy as hell.

I closed my eyes, took in a deep breath, and sat back in the chair.

"I'll call you, okay?" he said in his deep and gravelly voice.

"You do that, Winslow," I said without opening my eyes.

"Brick," he said.

"Whatever," I said just as the door clicked shut.

CHAPTER 21

I decided it was up to me to get to the bottom of Crystal's murder, especially when it seemed everyone else believed Lane had killed Crystal. I made a phone call and then readied for a little surveillance.

An hour later, I parked my car at the rear of a shopping plaza in Venice. To the left, a row of green garbage dumpsters backed up to a chain link fence. Along the edge of the fence, a sporadic weed garden grew, graced with a dirty ruffle of papers, fast food containers, and soft drink cups with gas station logos.

Behind the fence, there was an alley. Just beyond the alley, a row of houses, all white, of the same dimension, and all have a screened enclosure off the back. Very boring. To amuse myself, I tried to think of ways one would individualize a home in that neighborhood and make it stand out from the others. The amusement didn't last long. I began thinking of Tiffany and the cord wrapped around her neck.

Shaking off my thoughts, I realized I had to trust that others would be focusing on Tiffany's murder.

Mulling over the information I'd discovered about Del and Tillie, I bumped up the air conditioning. The car had a dark interior, and it was sucking up the sun. I felt like I was baking. Just when I thought I couldn't take it anymore and decided to find an ice cream parlor, I saw Tillie drag herself out of her car and work her way to the back door leading to the therapy office. The effort it took her to walk those few short steps made me determined to lose the extra five pounds I'd been trying to ignore.

Ten minutes later, she waddled back to her car. Disappointment was all over her face. I saw the shimmer of tears on her cheeks and watched as she pulled a tissue out of her bag and used it to blow her nose. I waited until she settled and pulled out of the parking lot before I followed her.

Since this was Sunday, I guessed she was returning home, where she probably would have still been if I hadn't lured her into going to the office. I had called the answering service and told them I wanted to leave a message for her or Delbert Welling. I said to tell them I was making a big payment on some overdue office visits. "Tell them it's cash and I'm sliding an envelope through the mail slot on the door," I said. I had them read the message back to me and I told them that they must relay the message as soon as possible.

I didn't lie. To some people twenty dollars was a big payment. I didn't think Tillie would agree with them. I had the feeling she was expecting a bit more. Her reaction to the twenty dollars, and the speed in which she ran to the office for it, confirmed that they were in a financially tight spot now due to Lane's incarceration. She was their main source, I was betting.

I followed until Tillie parked her car in the center of a circular drive, directly across from the entrance to a grand house in Boca Key.

Boca Key was a small town with homes and communities along the shoreline of Gasparilla Island. The homes were exclusive, and the small downtown was up market. For me, it had the same feel as walking in off the street to enter the lobby of a big city four-star hotel just to use the restroom. You knew you weren't registered, but you were hoping no one else would notice. Within a few seconds you realized the clothes you were wearing weren't right, your hairstyle wasn't really a style after all, and, no, you didn't belong there nor would you ever. You could choose to leave and run for the nearest Holiday Inn or dredge up some confidence and stroll across the lobby, smile haughtily at the concierge and take care of business. I'll usually chose the latter.

"Tillie," I yelled after parking on the side of the road near the end of the driveway.

She turned to look and stumbled on the short step up to the double entrance door. In seconds, she was in a heap on top of an Oleander bush. Before I could get to her to give her a hand, the auto timed landscape sprinklers turned on. She screamed and rolled off the bush into the landscaping. The Chinese Wisteria didn't have a chance.

She landed face down and attempted to get up by digging in with her toes. Her legs were oddly spread. The knees were apart and pointing outward, while her feet were close together, sole to sole. When she dug in, she raised her arms above her head and grabbed at the vine covering the ground. It looked like a sort of ballet movement. Plié and rise, I thought it was called.

"Here, Tillie, grab my hand." I bent down to give her a lift and pulled her up to her knees. She ended up on her widely spread knees facing the house. She began to topple forward, so I wrapped my arms as far around her chest as I was able and lifted with all my might. She came up through no effort of her own, but with a great deal of creaking and popping of my knees and back. When she turned to face me, her mouth was wide open in a Lucille Ball cry. I waited for the words, "Ohhh, Rickeeeeee!" They never came. There was only a big gasp and a snuffle.

She seemed dazed and embarrassed. She glanced at me for a quick second, but wouldn't meet my eyes as she smoothed down her dripping wet knee length muumuu. "What are you doing here?" she asked.

Wiping the water from my face, I said, "We're on the same committee for the North Harbor Care and Share Club and I'm—"

"I know who you are," she said in a dismissive manner. As my eyes left her mascara streaked face to follow down to her feet with the ground-in mud and vegetation embedded into her gold sandals and maroon colored toenails, I reminded myself I was here for a reason. I needed to pretend, I needed to be an actor.

It was hard. She disgusted me. I didn't like women who played weak and convinced others to "help" them. They were the ones who took up everyone's time. They got all the special attention and assistance. It was a sure thing, the extras in life would go to Sally Simper and not Susie Strong.

Tillie's snuffling began again as she bent over to brush off her knees. I noticed the knotting of muscle and sinew that made up her tan calves. Her forearms were similarly strong looking.

I quickly leaned over and grabbed her gold handbag from beneath the Oleander, making sure she didn't notice my thievery.

Her house keys were near her feet. She picked them up after brushing off her legs and turned to go toward the entrance.

"Let's get you inside and check you out. Your ankle looks a bit swollen," I said and grasped her elbow to lead her inside. She faltered and then I realized that she expected more compassion so I tucked the handbag in my right armpit and wrapped my left arm around her shoulders.

"Just lean on me," I told her.

Once we'd managed to work our combined bulk through the double doors, a small, yipping, and beribboned ball of fur greeted us.

"Oh, Honey. Stop," Tillie said.

Honey continued running a yipping, panting, circle around Tillie's feet.

I led Tillie to the faux leopard skin couch in the center of the sparse formal living room and Honey leapt up to sit on the mound of flesh where Tillie's lap should have been.

"Here, this should help," I said while reaching for the bronze colored velvet pillows on the couch. I placed the pillows on the floor, raised her feet to rest on them, and slid her gold sandals from her muddy toes.

"I'll get some ice and a cloth."

I returned from the kitchen with a freezer bag of ice and a large plastic bowl. I placed the ice bag on her ankle and asked her to point me in the direction of the bathroom. She switched the bag to the opposite ankle and pointed to a hallway to her left. Her face was in a grimace and she sighed heavily when she leaned back into the couch.

In the hallway, I opened a set of white doors and grabbed a couple of towels. The bathroom was four feet down and on the same side as the linen closet. Its size was close to the dimensions of my guest bedroom and was equipped with all the newest luxuries.

I quickly went through the contents of the medicine cabinet and drawers of the vanity. There didn't seem to be anything of interest other than the large number of drugs prescribed for someone named Loretta Evans. These days she went by Tillie.

"What are you doing in there?" Tillie yelled.

I grabbed a pill bottle and stuffed it in my waistband. Then I turned the water on and yelled out, "I'll be right there."

I took the wallet out of her purse, looked at her driver's license, and found it had her new name. There were a few credit cards with a mixture of names. The rest of the items in the purse were not of interest, although I noticed the Priceless Peach lipstick would not be her color at all. Too bright, too young looking. Someone should tell her to stick with the red shades.

I tossed the purse onto the counter of the vanity and heard a metallic clunk when it fell against the marble countertop. I found keys in a zippered side pocket. The keys had a little dot of fluorescent orange paint on the top of each of them. All of Rachel's keys were color coded with florescent dots of paint. Orange for the vehicles. The keys were Rachel's. So why did she have Rachel's car keys?

Looking up into the mirror, I saw a vein pulsing in my neck. My bones ached from holding myself rigid. "Only one reason she would have these keys," I said to my reflection.

Taking a deep breath, I filled the bowl halfway with warm, soapy water, and snatched a heavily embroidered washcloth from the set arranged on the ledge of the octagon shaped whirlpool tub.

"Where are you? What's taking you so long?"

"Coming, Tillie. This is going to help you feel better."

In the living room, I knelt down, put Tillie's handbag on the carpet next to the couch, and picked up her uninjured foot. I handed her a towel, placed her foot in warm water, and begin washing off the dirt.

"Ooooh. That's so nice." She leaned her head back and closed her eyes. Honey nestled on Tillie's ample bosom and looked at me with a miniature snarl. I checked to see if Tillie still had her eyes closed before returning a silent snarl. Honey picked up her ears and tilted her head.

"Tillie, you're having a pretty bad day, aren't you?" I crooned in what I hoped was a soothing manner. I wanted her to concentrate on herself and her situation. I didn't want her to remember that I was a stranger and have her begin to question my presence.

"Oh, you don't know the half of it," she said and opened her mouth wide for a spit-spraying yawn.

"Once your ankle starts feeling better, things will look different," I told her, ducking away from the spray.

"I have such rotten luck. Nothing ever seems to go right for me," Tillie said.

"So you don't believe that people make their own luck? That the choices you make with the options you're given is your luck?"

"No. As I said, I think I have rotten luck. Any break I've gotten in my life has been because I begged and pleaded for someone else to help me. Other people have good luck, not me," she said with tears running down her cheeks.

I expected to see self-pity on her face. Instead, I saw bitterness and envy, and that's when I knew she was shedding real tears. These were tears of frustration and anger.

She had relied on other people to do the work and make the decisions in her life and they had let her down. She used them to coerce, bribe, and twist her "luck." She would always be unhappy, but she would always have someone other than herself to blame.

"You've got this lovely home with a beautiful view and it seems like you're doing pretty well."

"This isn't my home. We're house sitting for the summer."

"Oh, it belongs to snowbirds? What did you plan on doing this fall?"

"Why do you ask so many questions? Can't you see I'm in pain?" Tillie said.

"Sorry. Didn't mean to be rude."

I finished rinsing her foot and set it on a pillow next to the bowl of warm, sudsy water. A knot of revulsion began in my stomach and maneuvered its way up my throat. What was I doing? She wasn't worthy of this treatment. I stifled the urge to stand and leave, reached under my shirt, and brought out the pill container from my waistband.

"Do you think you should take one of these pills? I found them in the medicine cabinet when I looked for aspirin." I held up the pill bottle and read the label aloud. "This says, Vicodin, take one or two tablets every four hours for pain. Oh, wait. This prescription is for Loretta Evans. Who is that?"

When she didn't answer, I studied her face. Her skin was unlined and creamy smooth. Her bottle green eyes were clear and, if you looked at her eyes alone, you would think she was a twenty-year-old. She had full, well-shaped lips and an equally well-shaped nose. Tillie didn't exhibit outward signs of badness or evil toward others, she just had a supreme case of self-concern. Over-all, her face was attractive; yet, Sheila was correct, there was something not right, an emotional slackness or emptiness.

She was leaning forward now, her eyes narrowed and nostrils flared. "Tell me again why you're here."

"There's a new project. I'm with the North Harbor Share and Care group, remember? We, um…" I said, my voice lowering with each word. That's when something that had never before happened to me, happened. I couldn't think of a lie.

Panic started to set in and I froze. No advice came from Rachel, not one helpful line from a movie entered my head.

"Tillie? Who is Loretta Evans?" I blurted.

She grabbed the container from my hand. "I don't know. I'll have to ask Del. Just give them to me." Her voice suddenly sounded strong and threatening.

"Here, let me clean your other foot." I picked up her injured foot, raising it higher than I needed to, forcing her to lean back into the couch.

"Ohhhh. What are you doing?" she yelled.

Honey hopped around in circles on the couch, yelping in a high-pitched fever.

"Oh, dear." I comforted Tillie with a look of sympathy and began to wash off the mud and grass. Pointing out that her ankle did look swollen, I raised her leg higher still as if to show her the bruised area. She screamed and I calmly looked at her. "I'll try to be more careful." I lowered her leg slightly while keeping my eyes on her. *I'm in charge here, Tillie.*

She tried to raise herself from the couch and when she found she wasn't able to, gave me a look that sent a shock down my spine as if I'd stuck a wet finger into a socket. Tightening my grip on her ankle with my right hand, I looked around for a phone. Not finding one, I resolved to start carrying one at all times.

"Should I call an ambulance? Where's your phone?" I asked.

"No!" She attempted to sit forward again, pushing her hands into the couch cushions for use as leverage. I nonchalantly tipped the foot higher to wash the back of the ankle. "You bitch!" she screamed while grasping at the fabric of the cushions in an effort to raise her body off the couch.

Honey jumped in place and then became quiet.

"Guess I'm not cut out to be a nurse," I said.

"Let me up," Tillie said, still struggling to gain some leverage on the couch.

"I also found these keys that look suspiciously like my sister's keys to her car. You know the one that was torched. Any reason you would have them?" I continued holding the foot.

"Where did you find them?" She spit the words through her clenched teeth.

"In your bag. Want to tell me how they got there?"

"You'd better leave," she said.

She was right. I knew I should try to leave and find the police. One thing stopped me. I wanted the story. The whole story. Right now, I had the upper hand and I decided to use it.

"Tell me what happened that night at Lane's house. The night you torched my car," I told her.

Her face crumbled.

"Don't start that business. It doesn't work with me. Let me help you out a little."

She tried to move forward, reaching for my hands on her ankle. Again, I picked up her foot, lifting it as high as necessary to let her know she wasn't going anywhere yet.

"I already know how you blackmailed Charles Somers way back when. You told him he fathered Del or Darien or whatever his real name is, and you knew he wanted to marry Maureen. It worked pretty well, didn't it? At least for a time. That is, until he realized he couldn't father any child."

"I really thought he could be the father," she said between sobs.

"Okay. I'll give you that. You were young, afraid, and alone. You had slept with more than one person and thought Charles could help. Then you went down the wrong path and never looked back."

"I did what I had to," she said.

"You had to steal, write bad checks, and lie? How could that be?"

"We had nothing." Her crying became louder.

I snapped my fingers in her face. She snuffled a bit more and then began to look around the room in desperation. I adjusted the height of her leg to bring her attention back to me.

Honey began yapping and alternately jumping onto the couch and down onto the floor.

"Tillie. After all that, after all the people you've stepped on and hurt, don't you realize you still have nothing?"

Her jaw clenched and she pursed her lips.

Honey jumped to the back of the couch and continued barking.

Suddenly, Tillie's expression changed into a smirk. She looked beyond, at something behind my right shoulder. I knew I no longer had the upper hand. Someone else was now directing this production.

When I turned my head, I saw Del standing behind me.

"I didn't know you were having company." His voice was calm and his words were precise. He was smiling, yet his eyes appeared as hard and intense as his mother's eyes.

"Ohhh, baby," Tillie began and ended with a long drawn out wail.

I cringed and waited for more wailing to start up.

"You seem to be in capable hands, but let me take a look," Del said.

I moved out of his way and he bent down to check his mother's ankle.

"Cassie, what are you doing here?" he asked in a voice that rode over his mother's sniffling.

"Tillie and I belong to the same woman's group and I needed to talk to her about a function," I told him.

I knew he didn't believe my lie. He had to notice my ragged breathing and jittery hands. To make matters worse, Honey made a lunge and sank her teeth into the heel of my leather sandals. I did my best to brush her away nicely.

"Don't you believe her," Tillie said, and when I looked, her eyes were like glass and had darkened a shade.

"Actually, I'm glad to see you. I wanted to tell you how sorry I am that you became mixed up in Lane's problems. I'm glad you weren't harmed," Del said.

I wanted to believe he meant it, but I didn't. "Have you seen Lane?" I asked.

"I went to see her but she didn't want me there. I'm not sure if she is embarrassed, or if she is blaming me, or what," Del said.

"Should she blame you?"

"Perhaps," he told me while he looked at Tillie with a harsh face.

"Baby, don't," Tillie whined.

"You don't, Momma," Del said and held Tillie's ankle while drying her foot with the embroidered towel. "I think you'll be fine. You should go lie down and elevate the foot for a while. Don't leave," he said and cut his eyes toward me.

He helped Tillie to stand and led her toward the hall. She moaned, wrapped her arm tight around his waist, and leaned her head against his shoulder. Once they were out of earshot, I growled at Honey and watched as she jumped in place and then turned to run down the hall and follow Tillie.

I grabbed my purse from the floor beside the couch and headed for the door, shivering at the thought of what

would happen if anyone tried to get in between Tillie and
Lane's money. What would she do? And what would Del
do?

"There. I gave her some pain medication," Del said
from behind me.

"Jesus!" I yelped. "Don't sneak up on people."

"Sorry. She should rest for a while. She can be difficult at times, but your mother is your mother, no getting
around that, right?"

"That's true. Well, I'd better be leaving," I told him,
side stepping away from him.

Del asked as he took a step toward me. "Really?
Don't you think we should talk?" he asked as he took a
step toward me.

I took a step back. "No. I'm not thinking that's a
good idea."

"I do. I think it's a good idea," he said.

"That makes one of us," I said and laughed a faux little laugh. Again, I tried to step around him to get to the
door.

"What are you afraid of, Cassie? Do you think you
have it all figured out now?" Del asked as he backed up
to the door.

"I definitely am not thinking that."

Now his hand was on the door handle and he was
facing me. I watched him as he looked down at the floor.
I heard him sigh. He raised his head and met my eyes. "I
know you figured out who I am, who I was. Now, you are
jumping from finding out how I've screwed up in the past
to thinking I killed Crystal. Right?"

"I do know that you cheated people and that you ran
from the consequences. I know that you more than likely
haven't changed your ways, and the odds are against you
ever changing. I know you played a part in killing Crystal." As I spoke, I pulled my gun from my handbag.

Pointing the gun at him, I felt my heart bumping double time. I felt it was going to be him, or me. I chose me, and although I really didn't want to use the gun, I prepared myself to do whatever it took to get away.

"I have people waiting for me," I said.

"I don't believe that." He looked at the gun, showing no signs of fear. He continued blocking the door.

"I'm leaving now. Move out of the way," I told him.

Del took a step toward me. I backed up.

"I don't know how to shoot to wound, Del. I'm only skilled enough for one thing. I aim for the big target, if you know what I mean." I gulped in a lungful of air and tightened my grip on the Colt.

"You shouldn't have sicced your partner on me," Del said.

I felt blood rush to my face and heard a roar coming from inside my ears. "So you killed Tiffany."

He shook his head.

My hands began shaking. "Let me guess, she was on to you, too. Didn't know she had it in her."

"She was lurking around, poking into places she didn't belong," he said.

"You fucking choked the life out of her, you piece of shit," I said, my voice cracking as I took a step closer.

He raised his hands and backed up. "Okay. Okay. Just calm down. I didn't kill her. It's not my MO to choke. I have better uses for my hands."

"So someone else is going to take the blame for that, too? Lane believes she killed Crystal, but we both know she didn't. Want to tell me who did?" I asked.

Del swallowed and his gaze remained on the gun. "Lane did fight with Crystal. I pulled her away, brought her into the house and gave her some meds to calm her down."

"What, then you went back outside and killed Crystal?"

"Actually, Momma killed her," Del said.

"What the fuck?"

"She wanted Crystal out of the way, didn't want her running off at the mouth to Lane," Del said.

"Because of her money, right?"

"Of course. That's what Momma's all about," Del said.

"And what about you? You're just an innocent bystander?" I asked.

Del shrugged. "Believe it or not, I loved Crystal. I didn't know what Momma was up to until it was too late. By the time I went back outside, she'd already killed her."

"You know, I'm not as stupid as you'd like to think," I said.

"You have no idea what it is like to have that cow for a mother."

"I think I have an idea. Just makes me wonder why you didn't kill yourself rather than Crystal," I said.

Del ran a hand through his hair. "I'm telling you she killed Crystal when she tried to leave Lane's house. Momma didn't want to take the chance of me choosing Crystal over Lane and her money, so she choked her and put her in the trunk of your car. That's Momma's MO, by the way." He smirked. "I want to thank you for so conveniently leaving your car on the street. It was like an invitation, especially with the keys dangling at the ready."

My head felt like a ball of blistering heat. I clenched my jaw. "It was you who arranged her body. You torched her body. How could anyone do that to someone they claimed to love?"

"Many countries have funeral rites that involve pyres and cremation," Del said, keeping his eyes locked on me.

"Think of it as an act of respect or a way of sanctifying her body."

"Jesus. You're really sick." Swallowing down nausea, I tried to maintain my focus on him through the tears blurring my vision. The roar in my head increased, and breathing became an effort.

He took a step toward me.

I shot him.

He twisted to the side, leaning upright against the wall. He put his hand over the right side of his chest and looked at me with his eyes bulging in fear and shock. Then he doubled over and landed on the floor where he remained motionless. I heard him breathe in and out with uneven and quick puffs of air. Then there was one long exhalation followed by silence.

I felt my knees relax and fell to the carpet while attempting to keep the gun aimed in Del's direction, not sure he'd truly died.

Honey sat in front of me and whimpered. I picked her up and held her in the crook of my arm as if I was holding a lifeline. She quieted.

Suddenly, I felt her body tense. Then I heard movement coming from the hallway and remembered Tillie. After putting Honey down, I scooted backward to Del and pulled his phone out of the holder attached to his belt. I scrambled away from him and punched in 911.

"Oh, what did you do?" Tillie screamed, and fell to her knees next to her son.

Honey ran to the nearest corner and made herself into a shivering ball of fur.

"Nine-one-one. What is your emergency?"

Holding the phone to my face with an upraised shoulder, I made a few attempts at speaking before finding my voice. I heard the operator's voice, but couldn't understand what she was saying.

I had to yell over Tillie's bawling.

"Someone's been shot," I told the operator and then gave her directions. Tillie sat next to Del and ran her hands over his face and through his hair, all the while shrieking. "Baby! Get up, Baby!"

"Shut up," I begged her.

She continued to shriek as I moved away from the both of them. I thought of the line in Psycho—a boy's best friend is his mother.

From somewhere in the direction of the kitchen, I heard the sound of a clock ticking. The sound matched the thud of my heartbeat and I began to worry that one or the other would stop.

As soon as I glanced toward the clock, Tillie scrambled toward the door.

"Stop! I swear I'll shoot your fat ass."

She sat and began wailing. I wondered if she would make a move toward me, and then I wondered if she did, would I shoot her too. I decided I would, but the truth was I didn't want it to be that easy for her. While I wished that water boarding was a practice employed by the sheriff's office, I decided the humiliation of jail, the court process, cell mates, and prison food would be enough torture for Tillie. I believed Del when he said choking was Tillie's method of operation, but I wasn't so sure the body count only included Crystal and Tiffany. She had to be alive for anyone to find out. As far as Del's part in all of it, no one would ever get to the truth, thanks to me shooting him.

Just when I heard the 911 operator saying, "Miss. Are you there? Talk to me," the door banged open and RJ ran into the room. He looked at Tillie on the carpet, her eyes and nose red rimmed. He looked at Del lying nearby in a circle of blood. "Shit. They ain't gonna believe this shit," he said.

"Go get the lamp over there on the end table," I told him.

"Huh?" RJ looked at the lamp and then looked at me, not moving. "Huh?"

"For pity's sake. Just go get it," I said.

He ripped the cord away from the wall plug and brought the lamp to me.

I shook my head and pointed at Tillie. "Tie her hands behind her back with the cord."

"What?" he asked.

"This is the last time I'm going to ask without using this," I waved the gun in his direction with shaking hands.

RJ looked at me and nodded. Then he grabbed Tillie's right arm and wrapped the plug end of the cord around her wrist. When she resisted, he lifted the lamp and clunked her on the head. She screamed and fell forward. Bending over her, he grabbed her left arm and wrapped the remaining cord around both of her wrists, leaving the lamp attached.

He stepped back and I finally felt I could breathe in a normal way.

RJ was smiling at me. "Look at that," he said pointing at Tillie and his handiwork.

"Seriously? I don't have the patience for your nonsense." Tears were running down my cheeks, but I couldn't think of a way to stop them without putting down my gun.

He turned toward the front door, a smile on his face. I followed his glance and saw a man whose face was partially covered by a Canon 7D.

Speaking to the 911 operator, I said, "Please hurry. Someone else is going to get hurt."

CHAPTER 22

That night, out of habit, I called Vince. "I've told you the whole story and you haven't said anything," I said, and rested my head on the back of the couch waiting for his response.

Honey jumped on the couch, tilted her head, and stared.

"I don't know what to say. It doesn't seem real, I guess," Vince said.

"It is." I wished I hadn't called him. I wished thinking of us as a couple didn't feel so awkward.

"Cassie?"

"Yes."

"I'm glad you're okay," he said.

My throat closed up and I couldn't say anything.

"We'll talk again some other time," he said.

"When?" I managed just as he disconnected.

After pacing the lanai for a good part of an hour, I made a pot of coffee and called Janice.

"Please come stay with me," I said.

RJ walked down with Janice. "Did you call your agent?" he asked before he was fully inside the door.

"No. Next subject," I said and scooped up Honey to prevent her biting his ankles.

"You will," he said as he left.

Taking a long look at RJ as he walked away, I realized there are people who'd bend and flow with whatever
script changes were thrown at them. They took the cuts
and edits in stride and remained strong yet flexible during
the production we called life. It was my belief that RJ fit
into this category of people.

And there was a different sort of person. No bit part
was going to cut it for them. They wanted the starring
role, they wanted their close up, and they wanted no
questions from the fan club. They had their idea of how
to run the show. In other words, they didn't see the big
picture. They only saw their picture.

I didn't want to belong to that group, but I was sin-
cerely afraid I did.

"What is that?" Janice said and pointed at Honey.

"She's a Norfolk Terrier. Her name is Honey."

"Why did you end up with that ornery little dog?
And what happened to that cat?" Janice said as she went
to the coffee pot.

I followed. "Scooter is with Sheila, where she belongs. Honey's with me until I can find someone who
likes animals enough to give her a good home, which we
both know isn't me."

We sat in our usual spots in the lanai. Honey sat on
the floor between the two of us.

Janice lit a cigarette. "It about makes me sick to see
that dog looking at me like I'm an intruder."

"She likes you," I said.

"Well? Aren't you going to tell me about it?" Janice
asked.

I spent the next forty-five minutes going over the
case and its result.

"Really? You shot Dr. Hayward?" Janice asked. Her
brow was furrowed and she leaned forward in her chair.

"Doctor who?" I stared and thought, oh, no, she's becoming very confused. My heart felt heavy and skipped a beat. It's happening too soon, I thought and reached over to put my hand on hers. "You mean Del, don't you?'

Janice hooted and slapped her hands together. Honey jumped and began yapping until Janice shushed her.

"Oh, Cassie, I'm just messing with you!" She hooted out another laugh, stopping when she noticed Honey shaking like a fan waiting for Humphrey Bogart's autograph. Turning to me, she said, "I ain't that far gone yet."

"That was so not funny," I said.

Janice picked up Honey and held her in her arms. "Was too funny, wasn't it?" she cooed in the dog's ear.

After she finished her coffee, she held out her cup. "Tell me again. Did you have any idea that Loretta Tillie did it?"

I went into the kitchen and poured her a refill before answering "No. I mean, her name was Loretta Evans. She called herself Tillie while she was here in Florida."

"Anyway…"

"Anyway, I knew she was involved, but I thought Del killed Crystal. When I found Rachel's keys in Tillie's purse, I knew she had played a bigger part in killing Crystal. I hadn't yet connected Tiffany's death to this mess."

"And you say Del thought it was okay to set Crystal on fire." She shook her head. "That's crazy stuff."

The vision of Crystal's body flashed into my mind again. "I'm so tired of talking about it. Enough okay?" I said, flipped on the player, and turned my attention to the movie on the screen.

Scarlett O'Hara and Rhett Butler were on the staircase and he was getting ready to leave her.

"Oh, Rhett, where will I go? What will I do?"

"I need to ask you one more thing," Janice said.

I paused the movie. "Now what?"

"Why don't you start learning to golf?" she asked.

Honey hopped off Janice's lap and stood in front of my chair. I patted my thigh and she jumped up and made herself comfortable.

"Golf sucks," I told her.

"You know what I think? I think you need to get busy over at The Big Prick before you end up like the rest of this neighborhood and live your life around some damn animal. And would you take that stupid ribbon out of that dog's hair. It just ain't like you," Janice said.

"Honey really does like you, you know."

Janice waved her hand in irritation. "Do you have any idea when we're going to start on the next case?"

I smiled and turned the movie back on.

"Frankly, Scarlett, I don't give a damn."

THE END

About the Author

S. L. Ellis came from a small-town in Michigan, where life consisted of family and work and too much winter. After a few decades of shoveling and scraping snow, Ellis was ready for a fresh start. A move to Florida and time on the beach improved her disposition a hundred-fold. It was there that writing became more than a thought. Classes were taken, workshops worked, and a few books written.

Ellis's short story *A Brush with Death* was published in *Vol. 12, DARK TALES*, a UK magazine and reviewed by: Vince A. Liaguno, *Dark Scribe Magazine Anthology Reviews:* "*A Brush with Death* is a solid, at times poignant, chiller in which a dying woman—who knows death well after a lifetime of obsession—makes a deal with the Grim Reaper. Ellis's keen observations on aging and death are spot-on."

Also, Ellis's short story *If the Shoe Fits* was accepted for publication in *HARDLUCK STORIES* for its final issue.

More information can be found at www.cassiecruise.com